ROYALLY INDECENT

KELLY JAMIESON

CHAPTER
ONE

Chelsea

"You'd look good knocked up."

My mouth drops open as I stare across the small table in the restaurant. Considering this is my first date with Berk, in fact the first time we've ever met, that seems...inappropriate. I shift on my chair, not even sure what to say to him.

He smiles. "Getting ahead of myself, right?"

"Uh, yeah." I blink a few times and look down at the table. I'm not very experienced at dating but this doesn't feel like a good start. Am I being prudish? Maybe he was making a joke. Should I laugh? God, I feel like an idiot.

Luckily our server arrives with our dinners, so I sit back in my chair while she sets the plate of pasta in front of me. I've never been to this restaurant, Berk suggested it, but it seems nice, although the tables are close together. The place is full, which should be a good sign.

"So you said you're a work from home consultant," I remark in an effort to get things back on track and have a conversation. "What kind of consulting do you do?"

"My background is in finance."

"Have you been doing consulting work for a long time?"

"No, this is pretty new. I decided that whole climbing the corporate ladder and waiting in line for the C-suite isn't for me. I don't want to wait to start working on corporate-wide strategic problems. As a consultant I can do that right now."

"Awesome. Who are some of your clients?"

"Well, I don't actually have any yet."

"Oh. So this is really new."

"Yeah." He shifts his gaze away from me. "They did some redundancy elimination at my last employer about a month ago. Time to move on to new opportunities."

He got fired and he's unemployed. Great.

This is what I get for going on my first date from a dating app.

I rarely go out on dates, and when I do it's usually someone my dad has introduced me to, someone he thinks is suitable. And safe.

But I'm tired of my dad picking my dates. It's ridiculous. I'm tired of my whole sheltered, safe life. The dating app seemed daring and exciting and, well, normal.

Berk has an attractive face, clean shaven with a bit of a cocky smirk. I went for the superficial, I admit it, but so far he's not living up to his profile pic.

"Well, I'm sure you're working hard at it, and will soon have all kinds of clients." I smile as I pick up a pumpkin ravioli on my fork.

"Oh yeah, it's gonna be great. And how about you? You said you work for a non-profit."

"That's right. I work for the Morgan Institute for Democracy."

"Wow, that sounds exciting."

That was totally sarcasm in his tone. I suck briefly on my bottom lip, repressing my *fuck you*.

Okay, I just want this over with. I try to keep the conversation going as we eat and I'm eating way too fast because I want out of here.

"Wow, you're really shoveling the food in." Berk smirks. "But at least I know you can swallow, right?"

Again, I stare at him blankly. He can't mean what I think he means. What is happening to me? My temples throb. "That's totally not appropriate." Oh my god, I sound like an old lady.

"Bah." He dismisses me with a wave of his hand, then pulls something out of his pocket and holds the small square packet up between his fingers. "So is this getting used tonight or what?"

I focus on what he's holding. It takes a few painful seconds for me to clue in that he's holding a condom. "Oh, for god's sake." My patience gone, my cheeks hot, I glance around the restaurant. Keeping my voice low, I lean forward. "*No, that is not getting used tonight.* In fact, I'm done. Now."

"You can't leave."

"Oh yes, I can."

"I brought you here."

"I can take a taxi home, thanks."

He scowls, and there's an ugly gleam in his eye that takes me aback. "Babe, I know where you live. I picked you up, remember?"

My eyes go wide.

Suddenly, there's someone else at our table. A very large man with a forceful presence has grabbed a chair and pulled it up. He sits and gives Berk a stern look. "I thought I just heard you threaten this young woman. Is that right?"

Berk's mouth drops open. "I, uh, no, I—"

"I'm an Assistant U.S. Attorney in the Special Litigation Bureau. Under Illinois assault law, you can be found guilty of committing assault without ever touching another person. The state defines assault as the threat of causing immediate physical harm, which means you don't actually have to cause physical harm to be charged with assault. You hear what I'm saying?"

"I'm not assaulting her!"

The entire restaurant is watching this play out. My face is flaming. I want to slide under the table and disappear from view. Forever.

Who the hell is this dude? He's gorgeous—well over six feet of thick muscle, short dark hair, beard stubble, and eyebrows drawn down low over unusual eyes, the color of Gyokuro green tea, clear and calm.

"We could definitely call the cops and get them down here to charge you with assault." He's speaking in a low, compelling tone. "But I'm in the middle of dinner and I'd rather not. So how about you give me your ID while you go settle up the bill for your dinners."

Berk gives the guy an angry stare and doesn't move. "I'm not giving you my ID!"

"Yeah, you are."

Their eye contact is uncomfortable for a tense moment.

"Cops?" The stranger holds up a cell phone.

Berk stands, throwing down his napkin. The guy stands too, and he's inches taller, pounds heavier, and about a million times tougher than Berk.

"For fuck's sake." Berk pulls out his wallet and hands the guy his driver's license, then stomps away.

The guy sets the license on the white tablecloth and holds out a hand to me. "Your phone."

I hand it over and he calmly takes a picture of the driver's license. My hands are now shaking, so I curl them into the napkin on my lap. He glances up at me as he gives my phone back, his eyebrows sloping down with concern. "You okay?"

"Um. Yeah. Just embarrassed." I grimace.

"If you want to press charges, I can still call the cops. I know some of them."

"Who are you?"

His green eyes glint. "Ford Sullivan." He extends a hand.

"I'm Chelsea Alderidge." I shake his hand in a polite gesture, although this is a bizarre meeting.

"Nice to meet you, Chelsea, although not under the nicest circumstances."

"Are you really an Assistant U.S. Attorney?"

"Yeah."

"Um. I feel so stupid."

"You shouldn't feel stupid. He's the dumbass." He jerks his head.

Berk returns. Ford hands him his license. "Just remember...this lady has all your info."

Berk snatches his license from Ford's hand and disappears.

"Thank you," I say in a near whisper, humiliated even though he assured me I shouldn't be. I feel like an ass for being brainless enough to end up on a date with someone like Berk.

"Happy to help. You, uh, probably don't want to finish your dinner alone."

Now I'm wondering if he's trying to pick me up. He just rescued me, but I don't know him either. Yet, he definitely feels safer than Berk. There's a quality in his eyes that's kind and honest, despite his stern manner. I may not be experienced at dating in the Tinder age, but I'm usually a pretty good judge of character when I meet someone in person, and although I've never had a lot of respect for lawyers, he seems honorable. Protective. Not to mention, insanely attractive.

"I'm here on a date, too," he says. "But you could join us."

Damn. Disappointment clogs my throat for a moment, but my mouth twists up into a wry smile. Of course he's on a date. "Oh no, I don't want to interfere with your date. I'll just go."

"You have a way to get home?"

I'll call Dad's driver to come pick me up, but I don't say that. "Yes. No worries."

I don't know if Berk added a tip to the check, but I pull out some bills from my purse and leave then on the table as I stand. "Thank you again."

"Sure you don't want to join us?"

I shake my head. "I'm fine."

I watch him return to his own table, near mine, and resume his seat. His date is another man. I huff out a small laugh as I make my way out of the restaurant. Not only already on a date with someone else, he's gay. Ah well.

In the vestibule of the restaurant, I call Lawrence. He answers right away. "Hello, Chelsea."

"Hi, Lawrence. Are you busy? I kind of need a ride."

"Not busy. Your dad's at the Langham, at a charity function. I'm waiting for him to be done."

"I'm not far away." I give him the name and address of the restaurant.

"I'll be right there."

"Thanks." I hold onto my phone and lean my head against the wall. I probably shouldn't rely on Lawrence. I've been whining to myself because I feel so trapped and suffocated living in my dad's house, my dad's world. If I want to escape and be my own woman, I should take a taxi or an Uber like other women my age would. But I'm a little rattled by what's just happened, so once again—as always—I'm playing it safe.

Three days later, I'm at Starbucks on State, getting a mid-morning coffee to take back to the office. The lady in front of me orders a "trenta iced coffee", which is huge, but the day is warm already, so I consider having an iced coffee too.

She continues. "With four added shots, sixteen pumps of white mocha and six pumps of vanilla. With whipped cream on top."

"We don't have trenta lids," the barista says. "Is a flat lid okay?"

"Okay."

When the barista tells the woman how much that will be, she freaks out. "It's just a trenta coffee refill! It should be like, fifty-five cents!"

"I have to charge you for all the modifiers," the barista says with admirable patience. "Four added shots, sixteen pumps of white mocha and six pumps of vanilla."

I bite my bottom lip and glance to my side at the line up to see how people are reacting. I meet the eyes of a man to exchange a "some people" look and...it's Ford Sullivan.

He smiles. "Chelsea."

My god, he has a beautiful smile.

"Mr. Sullivan."

"Ford."

I tip my head in acknowledgment.

"I'm glad I ran into you."

The woman in front of me steps aside, clearly still miffed, and it's my turn to order. Never mind anything fancy. I request my usual flat white.

Ford holds up a finger to me as I step aside and also orders a flat white. My eyebrows fly up. I watch him pay, taking in the suit he's wearing—charcoal gray that fits his wide shoulders admirably, with a pristine white shirt and a tie in a shade of green that almost matches his eyes. He's well-dressed but that doesn't hide the hint of rough edges that say he's someone you don't mess with.

When he joins me, he says, "Did that asshole ever give you any trouble?"

I shake my head. "No. I never heard from him again."

"Good." He gives a firm nod of satisfaction. "Can I give you my number in case you need to contact me?"

I hesitate and he notices.

"Good girl," he murmurs. Those words should piss me off, because it sounds like something my father would say, but Ford's tone and his look are not parental. In fact, they're warm and sort of proud, and make me feel a flutter low in my belly. Except I know he's gay so I shouldn't be getting all turned on by one little comment. "You do need to be careful."

"I know." I roll my eyes. "I learned my lesson."

"Use it only if you want to."

I take his number and enter it into my phone.

"How'd you meet that douchehole, anyway?"

My lips twitch at his name for Berk.

"Chelsea!" the person behind the counter calls out.

I take my coffee and step away, reluctant to tell Ford I met Berk on-line.

"Ford!"

He also grabs his cup and moves closer to me. "Let's grab a table for a few minutes."

I guess I have time, since my only meetings are later this afternoon.

Ford gestures toward a small empty table. I slide onto the wooden bench and he takes the chair across from me.

"We're drinking the same coffees," I point out to him. "Flat white."

"Huh. How about that." He lifts the lid of his cup and gives me a quizzical look. "So? How'd you meet him?"

"I met him on a dating app," I admit. "I swiped right."

He squints at me doubtfully. "A dating app?"

"Yeah." I sigh and set my lid on a paper napkin. "I was trying something...different."

"Ah. And that was the first time you met him?"

"Yeah."

"Well, you know, I'm actually glad to hear that, because I would have been disappointed in your judgment if you'd seen him before."

"I'm not sure how to take that." I frown at him.

"I mean, I'm sure if you'd met him before you would have realized what a huge asshole he is."

I huff a little laugh. "True. It didn't take me long to figure that out."

"You shouldn't let men you've never met pick you up at home." He frowns.

"I didn't. I'm not *that* stupid. He picked me up at a friend's place."

"Ah. Okay. But still. He knows where your friend lives."

"True."

He nods. "Don't do it again."

I sigh with annoyance because I get this all the time at home. "Hey. I'm a grown woman. I screwed up and I know it. I don't need lectures from strange men."

He tilts his head, seeming taken aback. "You're right. I'm sorry." He nods. Then adds, "And I'm not strange."

A smile tugs my lips. "You know what I mean."

His lips quirk. "I do."

"I know you're a big hot shot attorney, but I don't really know you. You could be as much of a creep as Berk."

He chuckles. "I'm not a hot shot attorney. It's the Attorney General's office. We don't bill by the hour like hot shot attorneys do."

"Ah. Okay."

"And you're totally right. I *could* be a creep."

"You did rescue me that night. So I don't actually think you're a creep."

"Thank you."

"How did *your* date go that night?"

His eyes crinkle up. "Great. We've been seeing each other for a while."

"What's his name?"

His eyes flicker. "Jeff. He's a great guy."

I smile, maybe a bit wistfully. "That's nice."

"Do you work near here?"

"I do. Just around the corner, on North Wells."

"And what is it you do?"

"I work at the Morgan Institute for Democracy."

His eyebrows lift.

I continue. "I'm assistant to the executive director of the Chicago office."

"Interesting."

I study him. Berk was unimpressed with my job. Is Ford being sarcastic too? "Really?"

"Yeah. Really."

He seems sincere. "We want to get people involved in democracy, so we focus on voter registration, voter education, and voter activation."

"Democracy works better when people participate."

"Exactly!" I beam at him. "I haven't worked there long. I'm still figuring things out."

"How old are you?"

"Twenty-five."

One corner of his mouth hitches up. "Well, I'm thirty-four and I'm still figuring it out too."

"You seem like you have everything figured out." He comes across as confident, in control of his life, rock solid.

"It's an illusion," he says lightly, picking up his cup.

I shake my head slowly. "I don't think so." I think he knows exactly what he wants in life. I lean closer to the table. "Do you come here often?"

"That sounds like a pickup line."

"Ha. Yes, it does, but I ask in all seriousness. Don't ever use the milk from the thermos." I wave a hand. "There's a homeless lady who comes in here all the time and drinks from them."

"That's Ramona."

"You know here?"

"Sure. Like you say, she's around here a lot."

I give him a suspicious look. He rescued me. He's an attorney. He knows the homeless people in the neighborhood. He seems too good to be true. I'd marry him right now...except he's gay.

I repress a sigh. "I'd better get back to the office."

"Yeah, me too. What time do you take your coffee breaks in the morning?" He glances at his watch, a sleek, all-black stainless-steel number. "Ten?"

"I don't always take a coffee break."

"Ha. Me either. But if you come back at ten tomorrow, maybe we can have coffee together again."

I gaze at him for a few seconds. "Why?" Then I close my eyes and shake my head. "That sounded rude."

"I'm not hitting on you."

"Well, I figured that, since you're dating a man."

His mouth curves into that so-attractive smile again. "No reason we can't be friends."

I could use more friends. And there's something so...likeable about him. He's easy to talk to, and I feel safe with him. "That would be nice."

"You have my number. Text me when you're going for coffee."

"Really?"

"Yeah. Really." He escorts me out of the coffee shop, holding the door for me to leave. "So maybe I'll see you tomorrow. Or...the next day."

I nod, smiling, then we head in opposite directions.

CHAPTER
TWO

Ford

My morning so far has been rough. I met with two FBI special agents who presented their evidence to me, explaining their case against a state senator involved in a bribery scheme along with another senator and one of his lobbying clients. I think we can indict him for federal wire fraud, but we don't have enough evidence. We talked about what more we need, and I sensed their frustration. I know I'm demanding. I made it clear to them that I don't want to decline this case, but I have to do it right—especially when it's a state senator. We talked about how to get the additional evidence and they left to continue their investigation.

I actually get a lot of satisfaction from this part of a case—planning our strategy and tactics with the special agents, how to use our investigative resources to go after the bad guys, to finally put the screws to them. I fucking love punishing evil.

Then I had to deal with a bunch of bureaucratic delays on another case, which is the least favorite part of my job. Jesus. I'm not the most patient guy, but I've mastered it over the years. When I go into court, I have to be in control of myself. I have to argue to the finish but control my emotions, control my temper, sometimes accept criticism or defeat (although rarely) and stay calm.

But delays frustrate the hell out of me, especially when I busted my ass to get the work done and now I have to sit and wait.

Then I have an exasperating phone call with a defense counsel about disclosure of evidence. I've dealt with this guy before and he's an idiot, another test of my patience.

When I'm done, I blow out a breath, pick up my phone and send Chelsea a meme that says, "The chill pill I took this morning appears to have been a placebo."

She messages me right back. *Rough day?*

Hell yeah. How about lunch?

We've never had lunch together. I usually eat a sandwich at my desk while working and I know she often does that, too.

Coffee together a few times a week has turned into frequent text messages and Snapchats, sending each other funny memes we know the other will enjoy, and snippets of our day whether amusing or frustrating.

We've gotten to be friends.

Something about her appeals to my protective instincts. She's trusting and optimistic, with a gentle, kind manner. Maybe too trusting. Maybe a little unsure of herself. And yet...there's something about her that belies that fragility and hints at resilience and strength.

She messages back. *Sure. Where and what time?*

We arrange to meet at a restaurant a couple of blocks away, right across from Millennium Park. I wait outside for her, checking emails, and when I look up and see her walking toward me, my tension shifts and fades.

Her long brown hair shines in the sunlight, bouncing as she walks, and her smile on seeing me lights up my insides and lifts my mood.

Her eyes remind me of warm, sweet maple syrup, and they crinkle up as she smiles. Today, she's wearing a knee-length floral dress in shades of pink, white sandals on her feet, her bare legs long and smooth.

I shove my phone into my pocket. "Hey, beautiful. How's your day going?"

"Mine is going great. Unlike yours."

I open the door for her, and we step inside the upscale pub. Since it's a nice day, we ask to be seated on the patio, and settle in our chairs beneath a big umbrella, surrounded by tall pots of flowers and greenery.

She looks around. "This is nice."

"Nice to get out of the office for a change."

"True. I think you're even worse than I am for working through lunches. And dinner." She lifts an eyebrow at me.

My smile undoubtedly appears guilty as I pick up the menu. "I know." My hours are officially done at five, but I'm often at the office until six or seven, unless I'm in a trial and then who the hell knows how late I'll work.

I order fish and chips and Chelsea asks for a salad, both of us sticking to water in the middle of the day.

"So what's up?" she asks once the waiter departs.

I sigh.

"I know, I know." She eyes me sympathetically.

I can't say much about the cases I work on. "New fraud case. Not enough evidence. Yet. And a hurry up and wait on another case that we need to move on *now*. Plus the usual dealing with an uncooperative defense counsel."

"Ah." She sips her water. "You hate it when people break the law, don't you?"

One corner of my mouth hooks up. "Doesn't everyone?"

"No." She shakes her head. "I may be a little naïve, but even I know some people don't care. Like, criminals, for example."

I chuckle. "Yeah."

"You believe in right versus wrong," she continues. "I admire that about you."

It's amazing how much that means to me. I haven't known her long, but we're friends, and she reminds me why I do this job, which sometimes I forget. "Er, thanks."

"But I hate that it makes you so cynical. And pissed off."

I huff a laugh. "Sorry. I guess I'm not being a good lunch companion."

"That's okay! We all have bad days. Do you want to talk about it? Or be distracted from it?"

"I can't say much."

"I know." She gives a firm nod. "At least you're doing something about it, which is more than most people."

My smile turns wry. "I try. Sometimes it's frustrating."

"You're very successful."

Again, my chest warms at her praise. I tilt my head and pick up my glass of ice water. "Thanks. Is this the distracting part?"

"Maybe?"

"You can keep flattering me. It helps."

She laughs. "It's not just flattery. It's true." She pauses. "In my job I'm just trying to make sure people vote."

"That's important."

"I really want to believe that if people vote for the right candidate, there won't be as much corruption."

"That *is* naïve." Hell. I'm too blunt. I smile to soften my words.

She purses her lips. "I know. That's what happens when you live a sheltered life."

She knows that about herself, at least. "I don't want to harden your heart," I say. "Believing in the good in people is important."

And I really mean that. More than once she's balanced my pessimism. My jaded belief that every person is crooked as hell.

"You're not hardening me. You're giving me a reality check. And you're showing me that justice still exists."

"Sometimes." I rub my mouth.

"You only see the bad guys. So you think everyone is bad. Remember...there are millions of people out there who aren't."

I have to smile. "Yeah. You're right. It's easy to lose perspective and forget that."

She beams at me. "Exactly."

"Tell me how your day's going."

She grins. "Well, today we had an epic 'reply all' disaster."

"Ha! Tell me more. I love these."

"Right? One of our interns thought he was replying to a friend, but he was replying to a company email and told us all he was 'busy doing jack-shit' and spent his morning 'bullshitting with people.'"

I laugh. "I guess he's not getting hired at the end of his internship."

"Probably not."

Our lunch arrives and we dig in, chatting as we eat. When I mention seeing Jeff later, she says, "I need to meet him."

"Yeah." I want them to meet. They're both important to me. "Why don't we all have dinner one night? Friday?"

"Let me check my busy social calendar. Okay, sure."

I smile. "No more dating apps?" I hope the fuck not.

"Nah." She waves a hand. "I'll let you fix me up with some handsome lawyer."

I snort. As if.

She frowns. "Why not? That's what friends are for!"

"I'll keep it in mind." No, I won't.

Chelsea arrives at my Streeterville condo with a bottle of wine and expensive chocolates that both Jeff and I will devour. "Come on in."

She walks in and checks the place out. "This is so nice."

"Thanks."

I take the wine and chocolate and lead the way to the kitchen that's open to the living and dining room, where Jeff is finishing his dinner creation. "Chelsea, this is Jeff. Jeff, Chelsea."

They smile at each other and shake hands across the counter.

"So great to meet you, Chelsea," Jeff says.

"You, too."

"Glass of wine, Chelsea?" I open the fridge.

"Yes, that would be great. I walked along the river and I was very envious of all those people sitting there drinking wine."

I pour her white wine without asking. I already know what she likes.

Taking the glass, she swirls, sniffs, then sips.

"You look like a wine connoisseur," I say.

She lowers her chin and gives me a look. "I had to take wine tasting classes."

"You *had* to?" Jeff asks.

She rolls her eyes. "Since my mom passed away, I've acted as a hostess for my dad when he entertains. He wanted to make sure I know what I'm doing when it comes to the wines we serve."

Jeff's eyes widen slightly, and he glances at me. "Oh."

I've never mentioned who Chelsea's dad is. Or how much money he has. "How is it?" I ask.

"Wonderful. Zesty, with hints of green apple."

Jeff and I stare at her.

"What?" She laughs. "Do I sound pretentious?"

"No." I shake my head. "You sound like you know what you're talking about. I don't even know what I'm drinking, except that it's red."

Jeff shakes up a container of salad dressing, a big bowl of greens sitting on the counter in front of him. I grab the charcuterie platter I prepared earlier and set it in front of Chelsea.

"Oooh, yum." She nabs a gherkin and crunches it.

"We were just talking about baseball before you got here," I tell her. "Your favorite sport."

She wrinkles her nose. "Riiiiight. It's as exciting as watching a turkey thaw."

Jeff barks out a laugh. "Hey now!"

She grins at him. "I'm exaggerating. I'd rather go to a hockey game though."

"No hockey at this time of year," I say.

"Duh." She rolls her eyes. "Thanks for the news flash."

I meet her eyes, dancing with amusement at our teasing.

"Baseball can be exciting. Hey, you should take Chelsea to the game on Sunday." Jeff turns to me. "We have tickets, but I have to go to that work function."

Huh. Great idea. "Yeah, come with me," I tell Chelsea. "I'll make you a baseball fan."

"You're going to have to buy me beer and hot dogs to tempt me."

I chuckle. "Well, if I have to."

"Okay, then." She swivels on the stool to survey my condo, taking in the view out the window. "This is a great place."

"Thanks. It's basic, but I like it. Good location. Close to work."

"And to Whole Foods," Jeff says. "Which is what you usually eat."

"Who's cooking dinner tonight?" Chelsea asks.

Jeff raises his hand and smirks at me. "Ford's learning." He nods at the charcuterie board, which we're all digging into. "He made that."

Chelsea grins. "Not much cooking involved in this."

"Come on, you have to put together the right things," I object.

"I'm kidding. You did a great job. I love these crackers."

We move over to the living room with our drinks and Jeff brings the charcuterie platter as well. Chelsea pauses at the big windows to gaze out at the lake, blindingly blue in the evening sun, and sighs. "I love this view."

"Want to step outside?" I ask her.

"Sure."

I unlock the door and we walk out onto the balcony. It's not huge, but I like having outdoor space.

The fresh breeze blows Chelsea's hair back. "Sweet. You should have some chairs out here."

"Yeah. I'm going to get to that eventually."

Back inside we chat, and Chelsea and Jeff get to know each other better, then we eat dinner. Jeff made an amazing Greek strudel with chicken and rice, and for dessert there are tiny donuts that I knew Chelsea would love.

"I didn't make these," Jeff says with a smile. "They're from Sweet Glitz."

"I've heard of that place, but I've never been there. Now I have to go!"

Later, I drive Chelsea home, although she tries to tell me she can take the train, but that's not happening.

"That was a lovely evening," she says as we cruise along I-94. "Thanks for inviting me. It was nice to meet Jeff."

"Yeah, it was good."

She directs me to her home in Lake Forest and even though I know her family is wealthy, I'm thrown by the mansion we pull up to. I park on the curved driveway and survey the brick house illuminated with spotlights, vines climbing up the brick, over windows and the arched front door. "Nice place."

She rolls her eyes. "Yeah, yeah, I know, it's huge. I've told Dad he should sell and move into the city, but he likes it here."

"Don't blame him."

We make arrangements for the ball game Sunday and I wait in the driveway until she's safely inside the house before I drive out of the property. Chelsea may be a little sheltered and innocent, but she's remarkably unspoiled for having grown up in this kind of environment. I fight back my cynical view that a wealthy businessman like Gary Alderidge is probably doing shady shit. I have to remember what Chelsea said—I only see the bad guys. Not everyone is a bad guy.

And actually, I kind of like being reminded of that.

Sunday afternoon, Chelsea and I settle into club seats at venerated Wrigley Field to watch the game. I've provided Chelsea with her promised hot dog and beer, the weather is warm and sunny, and we're sitting in the shade so it's perfect. She may not be a baseball fan but she's happy and interested.

As we watch the game we talk. "So you went to college after you got out of the army?" she asks me.

"Yeah. I'd done some courses when I was in the army, so I had a start. Got my JD and a job right out of college." I tell her about interning with a local congressman during summers and the student action group I was involved with in college.

"I was involved with an action group in college, too!" she says. "That's so cool." She pauses. "Do you see politics in your future?"

I don't hesitate. "Yeah." Then I smile. "Why do you look so surprised?"

"I don't know." She purses her lips. "I grew up around politicians. My dad never got into politics, but he's friends with a lot of them—Congressman McQuade is a good friend of his. Dad helped a lot with his election campaign. Also the mayor and a bunch of aldermen. He likes having influence in high places."

I nod. I already knew that about her father. He's well known in the city.

"I guess I like that feeling of having influence too," Chelsea says thoughtfully. "It bugged me when I thought politicians weren't doing enough about things I cared about. That's why I got to be so passionate about voting." She pauses. "Do you have a plan? For politics?"

"Yeah." I've thought about it. Talked to some people.

"Will you tell me about it?"

I smile. "Some day."

She gives me a twisted smile, then turns her attention back to the game. We watch and cheer as a Cubs player hits a home run.

Then she says, "Tell me about being in the Army."

Ugh. Not something I want to talk a lot about.

"Why did you enlist?" she asks.

"I had nowhere else to go."

Her head whips around. "What?"

"Yeah."

"Your family…?"

I shrug, not looking at her. "Not around."

At that moment, a big cup of soda hits the steps beside us, spraying liquid over Chelsea's feet in sandals. She lets out a little shriek.

I jump up. "What the…"

We both turn to see a small boy on his knees staring at his spilled drink. His face crumples as he bursts into tears.

"Oh hey." Chelsea jumps up and crouches down beside him. "Are you okay, little guy?"

His mom arrives behind him, breathless. "I'm sorry, I'm so sorry."

"That's okay." Chelsea smiles and shakes her head at the mom. "No harm done."

Except her feet are all wet and sticky. She's way nicer about this than I would be.

"Corey, look what you did!" The mom takes hold of her son's arm and pulls him up.

He cries harder. "I spiwwed my dwink!"

"You spilled it on this nice lady! Say you're sorry!"

"It's okay," Chelsea says again gently. "Hey, Corey."

He looks at her, his bottom lip quivering, his face red.

"It's okay," she repeats. "It was an accident."

"You shouldn't have been running!" his mom says.

His face scrunches up again.

"He's little," Chelsea says to the mom.

"I'm sowwy," he says, then hiccups.

Chelsea smiles. "Okay."

"I'm sorry," the mom says again, taking Corey's hand and leading him to their seat.

Chelsea sits and extend her legs to inspect her feet. "I may need to hit the ladies' room."

A member of the stadium cleaning crew has arrived to mop up the spilled drink, and Chelsea slips out. When she comes back, she jogs a few steps past our row, carrying a drink. I crane my neck to see what she's doing and watch her hand the drink to Corey. "Here, buddy. No hard feelings."

He looks at her with amazed blue eyes. "Thank you!"

I watch her return to her seat next to me and settle in, something soft unfurling in my chest.

She turns to me as if feeling my gaze on her. "What?"

"You're a sweetheart."

She blinks. "Um. Okay." Her sweet smile pokes at my heart.

"Seriously. Lots of people would have been pissed off at that kid."

"He's a *kid*."

"Yeah. And you're a sweetheart."

The game is close, which holds our attention, and the Cubs end up winning four-three. I turn to Chelsea for a high five as we prepare to exit the stadium, both of us with big smiles on our faces. I always enjoy a ball game, but her enthusiasm and enjoyment have added to my own.

THREE

Chelsea

Ford works long hours during the week and even weekends sometimes. I love his commitment to his job and dedication to righting wrongs. He's also a cycling nut, going for miles-long bike rides at least four times a week, and of course seeing Jeff. But we have coffee together nearly every day and some weekends.

Sometimes, I think it's weird that this man wants to be friends with me. But it doesn't feel weird. It feels natural and easy and right. Also, I need all the friends I can get. And yes, there may be times where I feel a tug of attraction toward him, but I quickly subdue those inconvenient urges.

"I can't stand it anymore," I complain to him one sunny Sunday afternoon as we walk along Lake Michigan eating ice cream. "My dad's making me crazy. He wants to know where I am every minute, who I'm with, what time I'll be home."

Ford nods. He's heard this before, but he's amazingly patient. "He's your father. It's normal."

"No, it's not." I swallow a growl of frustration. "Women my age live on their own! If I did, he wouldn't know where I am every minute." I sigh. "I know why he's this way, but..."

He glances at me. "Why *is* he like this?"

For some reason I want him to know. I want him to understand I'm not just whining. "When I was fourteen, my mom and my sister were killed in a drive-by shooting."

"Jesus Christ." He stops walking and turns to face me, his face drawn into lines of dread. "Were you with them?"

"No." I shake my head. "My sister had volunteered to clean up trash at a park. That's what they were doing. It was totally random. Wrong place, wrong time."

With his free arm, Ford pulls me in for a hug. I lean into his warmth and his strength, maybe longer than I should. It feels so good. It kindles heat down low inside me, which I know is not just friendship. I wish I could wrap my arms around him and press my body against his...but no. I have to stop that kind of thinking. He is not available, in any way.

"I'm so sorry," he says. "I knew they died, but..."

I nod and draw back to meet his eyes. "Thanks." I resume our walk.

"Was it gang-related?"

"The police called it that. But...I've learned a lot about gang violence since then."

"What do you mean?"

"I mean..." I hesitate. "They're people, right? I think it's easy to blame "gangs," but violence comes from frustration and anger, from not having the money for rent, or not having food. Not having a good job. Those are the issues we need to fix."

He stares at me.

"What?"

With a small shake of his head, he says, "You're fucking amazing."

I laugh, then frown. "Why?"

"Someone killed your mom and your sister. And instead of talking about justice or revenge, you're...sympathetic to them."

My stomach tightens and I swallow, his praise affecting me. "Well. I don't know who did it. They never caught them."

"Fuck."

"And it took a while for me to get to that point, believe me. Honestly, the year or two after it happened is a blur to me." I take another lick of ice cream, aware of Ford listening intently. "I was angry. My dad's never forgiven himself for what happened, causing his obsession with keeping me safe. Then I was pissed that they'd done that to *him*. And pissed that I was being so confined. I tried to rebel a little, but I suck at rebellion."

Ford chuckles.

"I had someone escort me everywhere, which really messed up my teenage years. While other girls were dating and having fun, I was sequestered at home or being accompanied to social events my dad deemed suitable."

"Ah." The one word contains a world of understanding. Now he knows.

I pause to lick around my ice cream cone, then continue. "At first, I didn't mind it because I was scared, too. But then, I wanted to know why it happened. I started reading and researching, learning about gangs and poverty and how kids get involved in stuff like that. It really opened my eyes."

"That's amazing, Chels," he says quietly.

My heart expands in my chest. "I started dreaming of the day I'd go away to college and escape, but in the end I gave in and went to the University of Chicago, and lived at home with Dad." I sigh. "Anyway, I don't hate Dad; in fact, I kind of feel sorry for him. I know he loves me, and I feel like he needs me too, which is part of the reason he's trying to hold on to me."

"You're all he has."

I wince. "I know. And he's all I have, too. But I'm twenty-five years old, a grown woman. I want to live like a grown woman, in my own place, responsible for myself."

"So do it."

"Ugh. My dad's rich, but I don't have much money of my own. I'd end up renting some crappy little apartment. I've looked at what I can afford on my meager salary and it's not pretty."

"You're spoiled."

I sigh. "I know."

"I'm kidding. You're not spoiled. But if you really wanted to be on your own, you'd do it, even if it was in a crappy little apartment."

I wrinkle my nose and frown at him. He's usually supportive, but maybe he's getting tired of my bitching. Hell, *I'm* getting tired of my bitching. Then I realize...he's right. Also, knowing his background of being homeless, I'm ashamed of myself. What's more important... freedom and independence? Or the easy life at home with my dad?

"I'm sorry," I say. "I need to put on my big girl panties and just do it."

"What's stopping you?"

The easy answer is money. But that's not the real answer. "Damn you, Ford. Why do ask the hard questions all the time?"

He smiles.

I swallow. "I'm afraid."

There aren't many people I confess my fears and insecurities to. It's scary, making myself vulnerable—admitting I'm afraid I'll screw up is admitting I'm weak and stupid. I'm afraid I'm not equipped to live on my own. I'm afraid of failing, of having my dad say *I told you so*, afraid of stepping outside my comfort zone.

But now in my mid-twenties, I'm getting desperate. I can't live like this forever. But my rebellious dating app date turned out to be a disaster, which made me doubt my ability to survive on my own if I did leave.

"I know," Ford says quietly.

I bite my bottom lip. "And I think my dad needs me."

"That's not healthy. He can't expect that from you."

"I know." I *do* know it.

"Move in with me."

I don't respond because I'm not sure I heard those words. Did he really just say that?

I give him a squinty-eyed look.

He stops walking and faces me. "Move in with me. I have two bedrooms and bathrooms. My place isn't huge, but it's big enough. It's a decent neighborhood. You won't be alone."

"That's crazy."

"Not so much."

"What about Jeff?" I search his face. "Why aren't you asking him to move in with you?"

His gaze flickers. "I don't want to live with Jeff."

"Oh." I don't know what that means. I thought things were great with them. Does this mean he's not that serious about Jeff? Ugh.

"It'll be fine," he says. "Jeff will be cool with it. You and I are friends, right?"

"Of course, but I still think he might be...hurt."

Ford's face tightens ever so slightly. "I'll talk to him."

"My father would freak out. Me living with a man."

"It's platonic. And maybe he'd feel more at ease knowing you're not alone."

"Uhhh...I don't know about that. Also, I don't know how much your mortgage payment is, but I'm pretty sure I can't afford to pay half of it."

"We'll work out what you can afford."

"Are you really serious?"

He meets my eyes, lips quirked. "Yeah. It can be a...a stepping-stone. You're just starting your career. It's your first time living on your own. It'll prepare you."

This idea is so tempting. I'm eager to be out on my own, but not necessarily alone.

"Okay. I'll talk to my dad about it." I start walking again.

Ford stops me with a hand on my arm. "Chelsea."

"What?"

"Don't talk to your dad about it. Make a decision. Then tell him what your decision is and do it."

I let that sink in. Once again, he's right. I nod. "Okay. I'll move in with you."

His eyes crinkle up. "Great."

~

My dad freaks out. As predicted.

"Absolutely not. You are not moving in with a strange man."

My dad is imposing. When he started losing his hair, he shaved his head bald, and it suits him. He has a short dark gray beard and moustache, and although he's not very tall, he's a solid man. His compelling eyes can freeze you in place, and he knows how to negotiate.

"He's a friend, Dad. Not a strange man." I already told him that Ford is gay and in a relationship with another man when he wasn't happy I was having dinner with them. I know his protectiveness is because he cares, but it annoys me. It makes me feel pressured. It makes me feel like I'm a teenager. "You don't have to worry about me."

"Of course I have to worry about you. Why would you move out? You have a beautiful home here. There's no need for you to do that. You're safer here than living in some crime infested neighborhood."

I sigh. "That's ridiculous, Dad."

He's adamant and refuses to discuss it. His curt aloofness and unwillingness to even talk about it hurts. My dad annoys me, but we're each other's only family and I hate this barrier between us. After that discussion, I sit in my room, thinking about what to do.

I consider calling Ford, but after reflection, I realize he's already given me his advice. *Make a decision. Then tell him what your decision is and do it.*

I remember the fights Dad and I had when I insisted on taking the train to and from college every day, rather than having Lawrence drive me. I remember the arguments over the same thing when I started working. I hated it. I don't like conflict and I don't like it when things are tense between us.

But my aversion to conflict is one of the things about myself I recognize as a weakness. It's something I need to work on. I took college courses about it. Conflict is supposed to be healthy, and I need to deal with it rather than avoid it.

So I continue with my packing, gathering things from around the house. I *will* talk to Dad about it again, but I've made my decision.

When he sees me placing a couple of plants into a box, he sighs heavily. "Chelsea. You can't go through with this."

It's hard standing up to him. He's so forceful and convincing. But I have to do this, or maybe I never will. "I'm moving out, Dad. This weekend. Ford and Jeff are coming to help."

He doesn't respond and I sense a minute softening of his attitude. A tiny kernel of hope expands inside me.

I sit on the couch. "Dad. I understand you're not happy about this. And I understand why." I meet his eyes steadily. "I feel like you're not trying to understand how *I* feel. And that hurts me."

His mouth tightens. "You don't know how I feel."

"Then tell me."

I wait. And wait.

"I'll worry about you," he finally says.

I nod. "Because you love me."

"Yes."

"I love you too, Dad. And, being real here...I'll worry about you, too."

He frowns. "What the hell for?"

I hold the eye contact. "Because you'll be alone."

"I'll be fine alone."

"Okay. Good." I pause. "When you try to control me, I feel like I'm being treated like a child."

He sighs. "You're not a child."

"Thank you for acknowledging that. What can I do to make this easier for you?"

He gives me a blank stare.

"I'll introduce you to Ford," I offer. "You'll like him."

"Are you sure he's gay?"

"He has a boyfriend."

His lips thin. "I don't like this."

"I know, Dad. But I'm twenty-five. I have to leave some time."

He turns away. I suck briefly on my bottom lip. I study his tense shoulders. He walks over to the window and stares out, then turns back to me. "You're too soft-hearted," he says roughly. "Too easily influenced. Too trusting. You don't know this man."

"I do know him. We've been friends for months now."

His assessment of my character stings. I've made mistakes yes, like that stupid date, like the time in college when a friend told me she had ovarian cancer and over a few months conned me out of a bunch of money to help pay for her "treatment." I felt so bad for her and wanted to help. I know, I was foolish, believe me; I've beaten myself up over that way too much.

"I do want to meet him."

"Of course."

~

I open the door of our Lake Forest home to Ford two days later.

He's dropped me off here a few times, so he knows where I live, and he's teased me about the mansion. He surveys the enormous foyer. "Nice. No wonder you don't want to leave."

"I *do* want to leave. Come this way. Dad's in the TV room." I lead him there. It's a smallish room in this huge house. Dad's sitting on the big beige sectional and he stands when we walk in.

"Dad, this is Ford Sullivan. Ford, my dad Gary Alderidge."

They shake hands, eyeing each other.

"Pleased to meet you, Mr. Alderidge," Ford says.

"Have a seat." Dad gestures to a chair.

Ford sits there.

"Would you like a drink, Ford?" I ask. Dad has his usual scotch.

"No thanks." Ford meets my eyes.

"I'll get you some water." I whisk into the kitchen to get water for him and for me.

They're already talking when I returned, Dad interrogating Ford about his service. He moves on to his education and then his job. "Special litigation," he says. "What kind of cases do you work on?"

"Government fraud. We investigate and pursue civil enforcement actions against public officials who commit fraud against the state or violate state ethics law."

I shift on the couch, remembering a friend of Dad's who went to prison for fraud and income tax evasion. I shoot Dad an uneasy glance.

His eyes are narrowed.

"We also participate in legislative reviews and initiatives."

"Hmmm." Dad glances at me, knowing my job is working with voting legislation and policy. "You want to be Attorney General some day?"

"Possibly." Ford nods, looking more relaxed than he had when he arrived. "I've only been with the bureau a few years though."

"What's your take on public spending on education, health care, and welfare?"

Ford lifts a thick eyebrow.

"Dad!"

"Chelsea here has a bleeding heart," Dad says.

I close my eyes and drop my head back. "Oh my god."

"Chelsea has a lot of empathy," Ford says. "I think that's a strength."

I open my eyes to see a strange look of satisfaction on Dad's face.

Ford continues. "As for social programs, I'm happy to pay my taxes if the money is being used to improve the quality of life of others."

I smile. He's enjoying this.

He and Dad keep talking. Ford and I have talked politics. We've argued about a few things, but see eye to eye on a lot, including things I have passionate feelings about, like reducing crime. I can't believe my dad is getting into these topics with a near stranger. Crap, he might as well ask Ford's opinions about abortion and religion, and really get things going.

But it turns out Dad and Ford have a similar world view. Considering their differing backgrounds, it's amazing.

"Chelsea says you're gay."

"Oh my god," I say again.

"Yes, sir." Ford nods.

I see my dad eyeing him doubtfully, no doubt skeptical of Ford's deep voice, muscular build, and beard stubble. I resist the urge to roll my eyes at Dad's stereotyping.

"So where is this apartment you're moving to?" Dad finally asks me.

Has he actually accepted this? "Oh yay, I get to talk."

Ford chokes on a laugh.

"Streeterville," I answer. "Near the river. It's close to work, actually."

Dad grunts.

"And it's a condo. Ford owns it."

As if reluctantly appeased, Dad nods. "I'll need to visit."

"Happy to have you come by, sir," Ford says. "It's nothing fancy, but it's decent."

"I'll definitely do that."

We chat a little longer, then Ford gets up to leave. I walk him to the door. My legs are weak with relief, and I lean on the wall in the foyer. "Wow," I say. "That went...okay."

Ford rubs his face. "For you, maybe. I felt like a parasite under a microscope."

"Eeep. I'm sorry."

He smiles. "It's okay. Why do I have a feeling, though, that your dad is going to hire an investigator to do a background check on me?"

I bite my lip. "That's not as crazy as it sounds."

"Then there's something we need to talk about."

My eyes slide open wide and my lips part. "What?"

"Not now. Tomorrow. Let's have a drink after work. Okay?"

"Okay." I'm curious and worried. I can't imagine what he's going to tell me.

CHAPTER

FOUR

Ford

The next day after work, Chelsea and I walk to a wine bar on the Riverwalk and sit outside on a patio with grapevines climbing up concrete walls, big pots of colorful flowers, and bright red umbrellas over most tables.

A waitress approaches and sets coasters on the table in front of us. Chelsea asks for a glass of sauvignon blanc then listens carefully to the options the waitress lists. Her earnestness about wine is cute. I order a beer.

"So." She beams me a smile. "What did you want to talk to me about?" Then her smile fades taking in my expression.

"I want to tell you about my background."

She nods slowly.

"I didn't grow up in the greatest environment. My parents liked to smoke dope. They both had good jobs when I was little, but as they got more money, more stress, they moved from weed to cocaine. Cocaine is an expensive habit. My mom started stealing from the company she worked for."

"Oh no." She gazes back at me.

I fucking hate telling her this. It could change the way she sees me, the way she feels about me. My stomach knots as I continue. "She got fired, but she was supposed to pay them back. To make money, she started dealing. My dad got involved, too. Life got crazy. Weird people coming to the house at all times, some of them high as hell, some of them messed up. Not to mention my own parents out of it most of the time. Everything felt out of control. Every day, I went to school terrified about what I'd come home to." I close my eyes on a wave of painful memories. I've tried so hard to forget that shit. "My dad got violent when he was high. He smacked my mom around, blamed her for all their problems because she'd been stupid enough to steal. When I tried to step in to help my mom, he hit me, too."

"Oh no." She covers her mouth with her hand, eyes wide.

"I was a kid. Scared. No idea what to do. They were my parents. They were supposed to look after me, keep me safe. I didn't feel safe. One time..." I swallow. "They owed this guy some money. I think they snorted the blow themselves and didn't have money to pay for it. He came to the house and beat up both my parents."

"Oh god. Were you there? How old were you?"

"Fourteen."

"That's the same age I was..."

I nod. I already picked up on that. I know exactly how a fourteen-year-old feels when something tragic happens to a parent. "Yeah, I was there. I saw it all. The guy knocked out my dad and was going to rape my mom." My voice thickens and deepens.

She presses a hand to her stomach.

"I grabbed a baseball bat and went at him," I continue roughly. "I...hit him. My mom told me to run. So I did." He rubs his face. "When I got home hours later, my mom and dad were there, but the guy was gone." He takes a breath and lets it out. "I don't know what happened to him."

"Oh, Ford." She reaches across the table and grabs my hand. Her eyes shine with sympathy. At least she's not recoiling in horror.

"After that, we moved into a crappy apartment on the other side of town. But those guys...they found us again. We started moving all the time, basically running. I was never sure if it was from drug dealers or because the police were going arrest me for killing someone. I was terrified all the fucking time. Then my mom overdosed and died."

"Did she...do it on purpose?"

I shrug. "I'll never know. She may have. She might have been scared, feeling hopeless...or it could've been a complete accident. Anyway, my dad kind of lost it. Without her, he didn't care about anything, including me. He barely talked to me, just kept snorting and dealing. I couldn't see any way out, and then when I was seventeen, he got arrested. I didn't have enough money to pay rent on the apartment, so at the end of that month I was out on the street. It was only a couple of months until graduation, so I found places to sleep, sometimes shelters. I had a part-time job at Burger King, so I had a little money to buy food. I survived."

"What about your dad?"

"He ended up in prison. He died in there a few years ago."

"Oh, Ford. That's heartbreaking." She squeezes my hand and I curl my fingers around hers. "What a tragedy."

"Yeah." I swallow.

"I hate it that you went through that." She drags her fingertips beneath one eye. "I don't even care what you did to that man, you were a child. Let down by the people who were supposed to protect you."

My throat tightens at her defense of me.

"You were trying to defend your mom."

I clear my throat, remembering the only other person I've ever told about this, remembering the same defense. And how much it meant to me.

"I lived such a privileged, sheltered life," Chelsea says, shaking her head. "I complain about my dad being overprotective, but at least he was there and I knew he loved me. And I mostly felt safe despite what happened to my mom and sister. I can't even image being alone and on the streets at that age." Her gaze moves over my face. "Is...is that what motivates you to want to fight criminals?"

I give a terse nod. "Yeah. I guess. I've tried to..." I pause. This sounds so corny. "I've tried to do something good to try to make up for what I did."

She swallows and swipes at her eyes again.

"Fuck, don't cry." I grip her hand. "I don't want to make you sad. I'm sorry."

She scrunches up her face, attempting a smile. "Don't apologize."

"I needed you to know that before your father finds out. Because if he goes looking, he will find out." I meet her eyes. "If I want to have any kind of future in politics, I have to own that. I can't have any secrets."

"It's made you the man you are."

I feel like she reached out and grabbed me by the throat. It's a few seconds before I can say, "Thank you. I've only ever told one other person about this."

Her eyes widen. "Who?"

"Someone I cared about. A long time ago."

"Oh." She pulls her bottom lip between my teeth. "I'm sorry you felt you had to tell me. But...I'm glad I know. I already admired you. Now I admire you even more."

Relief flows through me like warm sand. "Some people might look down on that. Some people being your father, for one."

She tilts her head. "It's possible, yes. But he's met you. He seemed impressed by you."

I lift an eyebrow. "He did?"

"Yes." Her lips curve into a smile. "He said you have...the 'it' factor."

My lips twitch. "For what?"

"Politics. You know my dad's political. He says you've got 'it,' whatever that is. The presence. The genuine interest in people. The confidence. The calmness."

I smile. "I practice all that in court."

"Well, you dealt with him perfectly, and he was ready to knife you."

I laugh. "Okay, then."

"So I think he might also see your background as something that makes you more relatable. Stronger. Something you've worked hard to overcome."

"Well." I clear my throat. I like the sound of that. I like that it comes from Chelsea. Fuck, I like *her*. "I guess we'll see."

We get Chelsea moved in, which involved an astonishing amount of clothes and shoes, and not much else. I show her around the condo, where things are in the kitchen, and how the security system works.

"I get up at seven," I tell her. "I shower and walk to work, usually around seven-thirty. You can walk with me if you want."

"Seven-thirty?" Her eyebrows shoot up. "Um, no thanks. I'm more of a late starter. I get to the office around eight-thirty."

I grin. "Okay. You already know I work late, so just go ahead and do whatever you want for dinner and I'll eat when I get home."

Somehow she took that to mean I'd eat what she made, which is *not* what I'd meant, but I have to say it's nice to come home and find a plate ready to heat up. She's not the best cook, but I can't complain because neither am I. She's trying. She leaves a mess in the kitchen, but I don't mind cleaning up. I'm great at cleaning.

It takes a bit to get used to having someone around all the time after living on my own for years. But it's not that much of a hardship. She smells really nice and that scent of flowers and warm spice wafts out of the bathroom after she takes a shower. She's a little messy and I have to stop myself from complaining about dishes in the dishwasher the wrong way and leftovers in the fridge way too long. Those are minor things. In the big, important things, we're good. She's thoughtful and considerate, she respects my long hours, and is always there to listen when I've had a bad day or to cheer me on when something goes right.

And I'm trying to respect her need for independence. That's why she's here, right? So it's hard but I try not to watch over her too much or interrogate her when she goes out. For some reason, the idea of her out on a date with another twatwaffle really grills my cheese. I can't help it; I want to keep her safe.

One night, about six weeks after she moved in, I get home early enough to eat dinner with her. We watch the news while we eat.

"If world leaders were all women, there'd be no wars," she says.

"Oh, come on. Women fight, too."

She gives me a long look. Uh oh.

"Remember Margaret Thatcher?" I say. "And the Faulklands War?"

"That was before I was born."

"Well, yeah, me too, but I learned about it."

"There haven't been enough women leaders to say that women would fight as many wars as men."

"Well, then, there haven't been enough to say they wouldn't."

She frowns. "Okay, fair point. But women are better mediators and negotiators."

"What? That's bullshit."

"That's not bullshit! Women are better at communicating. Way better at fostering dialogue and engaging people."

"Oh baby. You are getting into a debate with me, and I'm a master debater."

After a beat, she collapses into laughter. I grin, too.

"You can't be sexist," she says, still giggling.

"I'm not sexist." Truthfully, I just like pushing her buttons. "But women do tend to be more emotional."

Her gasp of outrage is so huge I'm surprised she doesn't suck all the air out of the room. "You did not just say that!"

Okay, I can't keep that one going. "Kidding."

Her eyes narrow. "Really?"

"Really."

"There are all these gendered assumptions," she says. "Women are nurturing and gentle. Men are strong and aggressive. And when women are in leadership roles if they're strong, they're too aggressive. Women have to fight against assumptions that they're weak or passive."

"Which means they could over-compensate."

She gives out a loud huff. "What did I just say?"

I want to laugh. She's fucking smart and adorable. "Point taken."

"You have to admit the world isn't in great shape right now with men running it."

"Okay, I'll admit that."

She eyes me askance. "Really?"

I grin. "Really. I actually agree with you."

"Then why were you arguing?"

"I wanted to see what you'd say next. Also, I enjoy arguing. It's like being in court."

"Remind me not to argue with you ever again," she mutters.

"Oh, come on. You can handle it."

She rolls her eyes, but smiles.

I push myself up and off the couch. "I have work to do."

"What are you working on?"

"Writing a prosecution memo."

"What does that involve?"

She's always curious about my work and I never feel like I'm boring her when I talk about it.

"Basically, I'm summarizing all the facts of the case, describing the evidence, outlining the charges I want to pursue and why."

"And who sees that?"

"My supervisor. I have to get his approval before I can indict. So this has to convince him."

She nods. "Hmmm. Interesting."

I don't mind writing memos like this, but right now I'd rather sit and argue with Chelsea about feminism or whether the person in the middle seat on an airplane gets to use both armrests or whether pineapple belongs on pizza (I'm anti-pineapple to her pro-pineapple).

But I have work to do.

I'm sitting in my bedroom working on my laptop when Jeff texts me. *Hey, boo. Haven't seen you all week.*

Crap. He's right. I rub my forehead then text him back. *Super busy. Working on a prosecution memo right now. How about pizza here Friday night?*

Sounds great!

The dots jump around and I wait for his next message.

Miss you! Keep thinking about your body up against mine

Wanna play with your nipples...

Oh boy.

Kiss your abs...then your big cock...can't wait to suck your balls while I finger you...

Jeff likes to send hot texts. Usually I enjoy them. Tonight I'm not into it.

I tap my reply into my phone. *Fuuuuck. Can't wait too...*

Then I set my phone down and lean my head into my hand.

CHAPTER

FIVE

Chelsea

I've learned a lot about Ford since I moved in with him.

He doesn't cook much, but he's happy to help, and loves to clean up after. I mean, *loves*. I've learned that he likes his condo immaculate, which means I've also learned not to leave five pairs of shoes at the door, or my sweater tossed over the back of a chair, or empty M&M packages on the coffee table.

I'm not a slob, but I'm lax with tidiness compared to him.

I've also learned he has a sweet tooth and he'll steal my M&Ms if I leave them lying around.

He works late a lot, but the evenings when he's home we both like kicking back and watching TV, and weirdly, we both read books while we watch. Baseball games are great for this! Ford reads books about politics and government, and with my degree in public policy, he'll read me passages and we have fun discussions, especially about voter suppression and corporate accountability.

We both like rainy days and thunderstorms and city lights, but we also both love that we live next to a huge body of water and enjoy Lake Michigan when it's calm and reflective but also when it's wild and stormy.

He teases me about how many pairs of shoes I have and the scented candles I like to burn, and we had an intense conversation about the differences between leggings, tights, and pantyhose. He's baffled when I watch multiple episodes of "Say Yes to the Dress" and sob over animal rescue commercials. He now quickly changes the channel when one comes on.

I've also learned that his cycling and workouts have sculpted his body into strong planes and hard muscles. We each have our own bathroom, but I've seen him in his boxers and holy hell, he's magnificent. Although he shaves every morning, he has a heavy five o'clock shadow by evening, which I find incredibly attractive. I'm not supposed to; we're friends and roommates, and that's it. The morning after my first sex dream about Ford, I'm sure he felt the awkwardness radiating off me as I avoided looking at him in the kitchen, each of us grabbing yogurts and power bars to start our day.

The sex dream was so good, I want to go back there, and I find myself fantasizing about Ford. I know I shouldn't; it'll make things incredibly uncomfortable. But damn...I have needs!

I need to try dating again.

Yes. Yes, this is the solution. This time I'll be smarter about it.

My first date isn't really a "date." I agree to meet Ethan for a drink one evening.

When I emerge from my bedroom wearing skinny jeans, a loose silk shell, and pointy-toed flats, Ford looks at me as if I'm wearing a snow suit in August. "What are you doing?"

"I'm meeting someone for a drink." I tuck my phone into my purse.

"Who?"

I shoot him an amused glance. "You sound like my father."

He frowns. "No, I don't."

"His name is Ethan, okay? It's just a drink."

"This is a date?"

I level him with a stern look. "Yes, Dad."

"Ugh. Do not call me that."

I laugh. "Fine with me. I was trying to get away from an overprotective parent."

He shuts up, but his face is rigid, waves of unhappiness coming off him.

"Come on," I say, exasperation clear in my tone. "What's wrong?"

He shakes his head. "Sorry," he mutters. "Nothing's wrong. Go. Have fun."

I arch one eyebrow. "Thanks."

Annoyance from his reaction rubs at me as I walk to the wine bar on Michigan where Ethan and I agreed to meet. I didn't expect Ford to be as ridiculous as Dad. I guess it's nice that he cares enough to be worried about me, but I'm not exactly doing something crazy dangerous here. Women go on dates all the time. Sheesh.

Ethan turns out to be a much better match than Berk was. We spend an enjoyable couple of hours chatting over glasses of cabernet sauvignon and as we leave the bar, Ethan tells me he'd like to see me again.

"That would be nice." I smile at him.

"This weekend? The Taco and Tequila Fair is Saturday in Lincoln Park."

"That sounds fun."

"Great. I'll get tickets."

He kisses my cheek, very sweet, and heads down Michigan. I skip home, happy with my braveness and how things turned out.

Ford's in his room with the door closed when I get home, so I don't see him until the next morning. At least he wasn't waiting up for me!

"How was the date?" he asks casually, opening a yogurt container. He appears to be in a better mood.

"It was really nice. He seems like a good guy. We're going to the Taco and Tequila Fair this weekend."

He grunts. Not exactly enthusiastic, but whatever.

Jeff comes over Friday night, bringing pizza and beer with him. I don't like to assume I'm included when they get together at home; I figure they need alone time. So I'm stretched out on my bed with a book and a glass of wine when Ford comes to the door. "Are you having pizza with us?"

I roll to look at him. He leans against the doorframe, looking casual in a pair of worn jeans and a soft T-shirt that hugs his wide shoulders and clings to his biceps. "I didn't want to intrude."

He snorts. "You're not intruding. Come on, there's lots."

But when I walk out to the living room, Jeff gives me a look that seems…irked. Then he smiles, and I think I misread his expression. Still, I feel…tense.

"No hot date tonight?" Jeff asks me as I sit down with a plate of pizza.

Why is he saying that? Did Ford tell him about my drink with Ethan the other night? "Um, no. But I'm going out tomorrow night."

"Really?" His eyebrows fly up. "With who?"

I flick a glance toward Ford. I guess he hasn't told him. "A guy I met on a dating site. We had a drink the other night, and we're going out again tomorrow."

"That's amazing!"

Why is that amazing?

"I've always wondered why you're single," he adds. "I mean, you're not bad looking."

I blink. And swallow. "Gee thanks," I say with a forced laugh.

I've never felt ill at ease around Jeff before, but after I finish my pizza I tell the guys I'm going to have a bubble bath with my glass of wine so I can leave them alone.

Saturday, I spend a fun afternoon with Ethan and get home around six o'clock, pleasantly full of carnitas and margaritas, my nose and shoulders pink from the sun. I find Ford sitting on the balcony on one of the chairs he recently purchased for out there, a beer in his hand and his bare feet on the railing.

"Hey," I call from the living room as I lift my cross-body purse over my head. "I'm home."

He glances up. "Hey."

I step out onto the balcony. "I thought you and Jeff were going out tonight."

He doesn't answer, lifting the beer bottle to his lips to take a swig.

I take another step closer. "What's up?"

"Jeff and I broke up."

My heart clenches. "Oh no!" I drop into the chair next to him, staring at him, but he continues to gaze out at the city. "What happened?"

"Eh." He hikes one shoulder up. "Things just didn't feel right anymore."

I suck my bottom lip. "I'm sorry. I thought things were good. You've been together for a while."

"Yeah."

"Was it...*your* decision?"

"I guess. He agreed that it was probably for the best."

I nod slowly. "Well, damn."

I genuinely feel sad. I like Jeff. He and Ford did seem good together. But faced with this news, I have to admit the last few weeks, Jeff hasn't been around as much, and last night...something was off. "Are you okay?"

Ford seems down. But not wrecked. I guess that's good.

"Yeah. I'm fine." He leans his head back. "It's just...the end of something. You know?"

"Yeah." Actually, I don't, since I've never had a real relationship. "Well, I'll join you in a beer." I stand. "If that's okay? Or would you rather be alone?"

"It's fine. Bring me another one, too."

"Okay." I traipse into the kitchen to retrieve drinks from the fridge. The kitchen is spotless. I suspect Ford hasn't made dinner, but you never know because he's such a neat freak.

Back on the balcony, I hand Ford his beer. "Did you eat dinner?"

"Nope."

"You should eat."

"Yeah. I'll grab something in a bit."

"I had the best tacos."

"Oh yeah. How was the date?"

"It was so much fun! I've never been to a fair like that. All kinds of taco trucks, and there was music and dancing. I had several delicious margaritas."

"And Ethan?"

"Oh yeah. He's really nice. Considerate. Funny."

"What does he do for a living?"

I don't take this as another "Dad" inquisition; Ford's tone is mildly interested. He's probably only making conversation because he has to. "He's a dentist."

He makes another rough noise.

I chat more about Ethan and the afternoon, but Ford's quiet. It's understandable.

Then I go inside and make him a grilled cheese sandwich with his favorite mix of cheeses.

He comes inside, shakes his head, and smiles when I point to the sandwich, along with a sliced-up apple, sitting on the counter. "You didn't need to do this."

"I don't want you to starve," I say lightly. Then impulsively, I step toward him and hug him. "I'm sorry."

His arms come around me, too. For a moment we stand together, embracing. He presses his face to my hair. I absorb the heat of his big body, enjoying the feel of him against me, so solid and strong. It's been a long time since I've been held like this and...

my body is doing funny things...liquid heat slowly settling low inside me.

I don't want him to be unhappy. It hurts me that he's hurting. I care about him. I mean, as a friend. But...

I sense tension ripple through him. I lift my head from his chest and tip it back to gaze up at him. His eyes meet mine and for a moment I feel like I'm lifted out of time...like I'm in a bubble, with Ford. My chest fills and I have the crazy thought that Ford wants to kiss me. My lips part, my eyes locked on his.

His arms tighten around me, then release me, and he steps back. His eyes shutter, his face drawing into tight contours. "Thank you," he says gruffly.

"You'll find someone else." I grimace. "Sorry. That's a stupid thing to say."

He takes another step away from me. "There's something I should tell you."

I blink at him and cock my head. "What?"

"I'm bisexual."

I blink again. "Oh. Okay." I turn over what that means. "So you're saying...if you find someone else, it might be a woman?"

He gazes at me, his face inscrutable. "Yeah. Yeah, that's what I'm saying."

"Okay. Thanks for letting me know that." I pause. "Why didn't you tell me that before?"

He lifts a shoulder. "I was with Jeff. It didn't come up."

"Right." There's a faint twisting feeling in my stomach. I don't really know what to think about this. But I guess it doesn't change anything. "Okay. Thanks for telling me."

Sunday, my friend Kallista and I go out for brunch. I met her when I started working at Morgan. We're about the same age and were both

single, although she has a new boyfriend now. A few weeks ago, she left Morgan and started a new job at Change, another non-profit.

"Ohhhh I love your hair!" I greet her as we meet on the sidewalk outside Windy City Nosh House, a little hidden-away place on East Chicago. "It really suits you!"

"Thanks! After all those years of long hair, it's a change. I'm getting used to it."

Her formerly long, straight hair has been chopped into a long bob, the brown highlighted with caramel.

"It's sexy," I say. "What does Aaron think of it?"

She grins. "He was totally against me cutting it, but he likes it."

We're shown to a table on the tiny patio, surrounded by tubs of shrubs and flowers.

"So tell me all about Ethan," she says over mimosas and French toast. "I'm so happy you're seeing someone."

I smile and tell her about our date yesterday to the taco festival. "It was really fun. He's a nice guy."

"Did you go home with him?"

"No." I frown a little.

"So you haven't slept with him yet?"

"No." I sigh.

"Why not?"

"I don't know." I drop my gaze to my mimosa. "I feel like I should want to, after..."

"After what?"

I tell her about my dreams about Ford.

Her eyes widen. "Oh my god. Well, I can't say I blame you. He is definitely hot." She tilts her head. "You definitely need to get laid."

I'm not a girl who sleeps around a lot. I've barely dated. The idea of falling in love has always scared me, because of how much it hurt to lose my mom and my sister. "That was why I started dating again. But...I don't really feel that with Ethan."

"Hmm. Just go for it. Scratch the itch."

I bite my bottom lip.

"It's okay for women to sleep with someone who's not your forever guy," she says.

"I know that. Maybe I will. We'll see how things go."

Then I tell her about Ford informing me he's bisexual.

"Whoa." Her eyes widen. "You could sleep with *him*! Obviously you're attracted to him, if you're having hot dreams about him."

"No!" I jerk back in consternation, uncomfortably remembering that last night I thought he wanted to kiss me. I want to smack myself for thinking that. "Absolutely not! He's my roommate! That's all."

"True." She nods and picks up a slice of orange from her plate. "You wouldn't want to wreck things there."

"Definitely not." I shake my head emphatically. "He is still as off limits as ever."

"Just the kind of guy you like."

I frown. "What does that mean?"

"You like guys who are unavailable. Like, whatshisname, that guy you had a crush on in college. The basketball player. Who had a girlfriend."

I wrinkle my nose.

"Then Lucas. He was such a dick. Emotionally unavailable."

"Okay, I get your point."

"Now it's a guy who's gay."

"It's not like that! We're friends."

"Okay then, it has to be Ethan. Or a new vibrator."

I laugh. "I don't have a vibrator."

"What? Okay, now I know what we're doing after brunch."

I end up breaking up with Ethan a couple of weeks later. He's a great guy and good company, but I'm not feeling any real attraction to

him. I debated sleeping with him so I could "scratch the itch" as Kallista said, but I wasn't enthusiastic about it, and he deserves better than that.

I go out with a few other men. They're all nice, but I don't feel much excitement. To be honest, staying home with Ford is more exciting than going out with them. Now that Ford's not with Jeff, we do more things together—another baseball game, happy hour drinks with a few people from his office, a movie. Ford doesn't seem brokenhearted. In fact, after a couple of days, he's back to his normal self. Maybe even happier?

Am I playing it safe? Avoiding the possibility of getting involved with someone by staying home with my roommate?

No. I'll date more men. I will.

The one thing Ford won't do with me is accompany me to the fundraising gala that my employer hosts every year at the Ritz Carlton. Black tie affairs are not his thing, so I'm here alone. My dad is coming though, since he sponsored a table, and I'm going to sit with him and other people from Alderidge Industries for dinner. He'll know everyone here, no doubt.

The committee in charge of planning the gala has done a wonderful job. After years of doing this, they have it down to a science, although there are always last-minute crises that no amount of preparation can prevent.

I arrive early and I'm studying the raffle table where various luxury baskets are arranged for a silent auction, when the CEO of Morgan stops next to me. "Hello, Chelsea. You look lovely."

"Thank you! You as well. I love your dress."

My own dress is new, something different for me. The silvery mermaid-style dress is a layer of beaded chiffon over satin. Thin straps hold up the cups of the bodice, and lace together in the low-cut back. It shows off a lot of skin and hugs my body more than I'm used to, but I think it looks nice. I'm trying to *be* different— braver. More daring. More confident, even though that's more of an act. So this dress is an act of boldness, insignificant as it might be.

We chat a bit and she moves on. Other guests are arriving now, exclaiming over the décor. The room is beautiful, with a celestial theme this year, the ceiling resembling a starry sky. Tall white flower arrangements and glowing candles adorn each round table, along with gleaming glass and silverware, and silver Chiavari chairs. I spot my dad and make my way toward him so we can find our table.

"Hi, Dad."

He turns to me with a smile. "Chelsea."

I move to hug him, but he looks at my dress as if I'm wearing toilet paper. "The dress is fine, Dad," I say as I lean in.

He sighs. "You look beautiful."

We sit. Dad knows everyone at our table and introduces me. I get into a conversation about the new crime report just released by the police department with the man sitting on the other side of me. As dinner is about to start, there's a small commotion across the ball room. We all look over there but can't really see what's happening. It dies down as the host for the evening walks out onto the dais to welcome everyone.

Moments later, one of our tablemates, a woman, slips into her chair after returning from the ladies' room. She whispers something to her husband, and he turns to the woman next to him. They all seem excited and soon we've all been made aware that there's a special guest here tonight—Prince Griffin of Eria.

I've heard of the prince, of course; he's young, gorgeous, a rebel royal who caused some scandals in his youth with his drinking and partying, then went against the protocol of his country by serving in combat. I've seen his pictures on various social media sites from time to time, although I don't go looking for them, which apparently a lot of women do. He's considered one of the most eligible bachelors in the world. So this is pretty cool.

We listen to speeches, eat a delicious dinner of braised veal, and finish with a hazelnut and toffee pavlova, all accompanied with various wines. Then it's time to mingle and make bids on the silent auction items before dancing begins.

I'm elbow-to-elbow with other women admiring one of the expensive designer bags that's been donated. Everyone else is eagerly entering to win it, but I hold back my tickets.

"You don't like the bag?" a voice says next to me.

I turn at the male voice. He's tall, looking down at me with quirked lips and an arched brow. His eyes are the color of expensive whiskey and glint with playful humor.

Oh my god. It's Prince Griffin. For a moment I can only blink at him in stupefaction. Am I supposed to bow or curtsy or something? "Um…" Not knowing what else to say, I cast my glance around, when whisper, "It's ugly."

He laughs. "Everyone else seems to be in love with it."

His accent is elegant and glamorous, his voice low and husky.

"They're in love with the designer label."

His eyebrows rise at my honesty.

"But that's okay, because the whole idea is to raise money for promoting voting rights." I hold up my tickets. "I'll use these else-where. I had my eye on a spa package."

"What would be involved in a spa package?" His gaze is fastened on my face and it's utterly captivating.

I laugh. "I forget, actually. Probably a massage, a facial…"

"Let's go look."

He touches my elbow, politely. What is happening? I let him guide me out of the crowd and into an open space.

I cast him a nervous glance. "Your highness…"

He shakes his head. "Griff."

"I don't know royal protocol."

"There aren't any formal rules. And you are…?"

"Chelsea. Chelsea Alderidge."

"Lovely to meet you, Chelsea."

We've been slowly walking, and I gesture to the table where the spa package is displayed. We move there. It's not as crowded, but people keep looking at Griff and I sense the buzz that surrounds him.

The display includes a plush robe and slippers, some luxury products including moisturizers, shampoo and conditioner, and body polish.

"Body polish," the prince comments. "That sounds interesting." His gaze moves over my bare shoulders and chest in a way that borders on inappropriate but coming from him feels sexy…and flattering.

My skin tingles and my belly heats. "One of the services is a body scrub, cocoon and massage combination."

"Cocoon?"

I wave a hand around myself awkwardly. "They wrap you up."

"I see."

Has this playboy really never been to a spa? It seems doubtful. He's probably teasing me.

I drop a few tickets into the box and look around.

"What else are you interested in?" he asks.

I see one table that's conspicuously empty of people and I point. "Let's go check that one out."

The prize is a collection of items "as seen on TV"—a foot massager, a posture belt, a tactical flashlight, among other things.

Griff and I exchange what-the-fuck looks.

"Is that…" He hesitates and gestures. "What are those lights?"

I inspect the item. "They are color changing LED lights to put in your toilet."

He chokes. "With a motion sensor. Good lord. You put on a light show when you take a crap."

I can't stop the laughter that bursts out of me. "Oh my god."

"And it comes with aromatherapy! Brilliant!"

We're both laughing harder, leaning into each other.

"This is amazing," he wheezes. "We must enter this."

"I'm putting all my tickets in. I feel bad that nobody's interested in this incredible prize."

He gives me a look. "I mean...the prize doesn't have feelings."

I laugh. "I know! But somebody put it together and donated it."

His face softens and his eyes warm. "True. Well, your odds of winning are greater."

"I'm not going to win. I never win anything."

"That's too bad."

"I figure it's because I'm lucky enough in other ways."

He tilts his head and his eyes warm even more. "I like that attitude."

Heat builds between my breasts and flows up into my face. "Um. Thank you."

"Now we've used all our tickets, would you like to dance?"

I look at the dance floor. The music has started, and people are dancing. Then I turn back to the prince. He's asking *me* to dance?

I'm standing here beneath twinkling lights with a handsome prince, like I'm in a fairy tale or something, and I have no idea what to say.

CHAPTER
SIX

Chelsea

I nod.

Griff takes the empty wine glass from my hand and sets it on the tray of a passing waiter, then touches his fingertips to the small of my back—my bare back, where my dress dips low—to direct me to the dance floor. That small gesture is knee-weakeningly sexy.

As we face each other, I'm aware of the beauty of his face—high cheekbones and elegantly sculpted square jaw, lips full but firm. I take in his light brown hair, burnished with gold that matches his eyes, the wide set of his shoulders, and the strong planes of his chest beneath the perfectly fitted tuxedo. He's lean and fit, and I feel his strength in the firm clasp of his fingers on mine, and the solidity of his shoulder beneath my hand as we move to the music. Michael Bublé sings "I Only Have Eyes for You" in a jazzy rendition. As Griff and I gaze at each other, it feels like I'm living the song.

I've never been so instantly mesmerized by a man. The curve of his mouth as he watches me is so engaging, I can't help but smile back. I let the music fill me, guiding my movements. I've always loved dancing and Griff is a good dancer, too.

"Are you here with a date?" he asks me.

I shake my head. "No. I came alone. I sat with my father for dinner."

"Your father is here?" He arches an eyebrow.

I grin. "Yes."

"I'd better watch my step, then." His eyes gleam.

"Yes, you'd better. He's very overprotective." It's true, but I'm teasing him.

"Message received. So no date…is there a boyfriend?"

"No." I don't have to ask about his relationship status—everyone knows Prince Griffin is a most eligible bachelor. "Are you here in the States visiting?"

"I'm here for a while. On business. I've started an organization to help veterans and we're expanding into the U.S."

"Yes…I've read about that. Life Forces, right?"

"That's right. We try to ensure that service members, veterans, and their families have the tools they need to succeed throughout their lives. That includes getting them the supports they need after their service, which sometimes is lacking, and connecting them with career opportunities."

I nod. "That's wonderful. Are you personally involved?"

"Of course." He lifts his chin fractionally. "You thought I was merely a figurehead?"

"You *are* royalty. I'm sure you're busy with, uh…royal duties."

"Yes," he admits. "But this is my project. It's something that's important to me. And you? What do you do with your time, Chelsea?"

"I'm assistant to the executive director at the Morgan Institute. This is our fundraiser."

His eyebrows lift. "Ah."

"I'm only an assistant," I say. "But it's interesting work."

"Nothing wrong with being an assistant."

"I'm very passionate about voting rights. My father has always been very political, and I grew up listening to all kinds of talk about government and democracy. I got interested in reducing crime when I was younger. I read a lot about it and learned that it starts with poverty and education. And I learned how important voting is. In college, I was shocked to find a lot of people my age weren't interested or couldn't be bothered, so I got involved with a student activism group. And worked at polling stations on campus registering voters."

"I admire that."

Again, our eyes lock together and heat swirls around us.

The music changes, now Jason Mraz's "I'm Yours," a more up-tempo tune. We easily fall into the new rhythm together and he swings me out from him then back close to his body. I laugh with delight at the unexpected move and how smooth it is. "You're a good dancer."

"Of course I am. It's all the lessons I was forced to take."

"Ah. I suppose a prince has to be able to dance."

"Among many other things." He smiles, a hint of acidity edges his tone.

"I'm not royalty, but I had to do stuff too. Etiquette lessons. Wine tasting lessons. It never bothered me that much, though."

"This was due to the overprotective father?"

"I suppose it was mostly him. Charm school was when I was younger, and my mom was around. She...died when I was fourteen. After that, I was sort of a hostess for my dad when he entertained."

"Hmm. I'm sorry about your mother."

"Thanks. It was hard losing her at that age." I don't mention my sister or how it happened. That's a lot to lay on someone.

"Is that why your father is overprotective?" He picks up on this even though I haven't told him the whole story.

"Yes. So I get it." I smile. "I recently moved out on my own. Well, not exactly on my own. I have a roommate. My dad's still having a hard time with it."

We dance one more song, then Griff offers to find us another glass of champagne. We wander through the crowd, and he spots a waiter. In an instant the waiter is in front of us with a tray of glasses. Griff picks up two and hands me one. Then he lifts his in a toast. "I enjoyed dancing with you, Chelsea."

I touch the rim of my glass to his gently. "I did too." I take a sip of the bubbly wine. "Very nice."

"Could be colder."

I grin. "You're an oenophile too?"

He shakes his head. "No. I just like my wine chilled."

"At a party like this, it's never going to be the right temperature." I lean closer. "I'll still drink it though."

He laughs softly. "Cheers." He too takes a drink of his champagne.

Betsy and Emma from work appear in front of us, all wide-eyed and smiley. "Hi, Chelsea!"

"Hi!" We greet each other with tiny hugs. They're looking at Griff, so I make introductions.

Griff smiles that slightly wicked smile, his eyes crinkling up at the corners as he greets my co-workers. We make small talk, and then a couple of other people join us. I sense Griff's vexation, and honestly, I feel it myself. I was having fun talking to him and now it's impossible with all these other people. I'm about to slip away when his fingers curve around my elbow. My head jerks to peer up at him. Our eyes meet and he shakes his head almost imperceptibly, but I get the message—*don't go*.

I finish off my champagne and show him the empty glass. His eyes warm, the corners of his mouth tipping up.

"Excuse us," he says to the people around us. "Chelsea needs a refill." He tosses back the last of his drink. "As do I." With a charming smile, he eases me away from the group.

"Smooth," I say as we walk.

"Thank you."

"Um...where are we going?" He's leading us to one of the ballroom exits.

"For a drink."

I blink. "Uh..."

We walk into the hall and toward the bank of elevators. "There's a lovely rooftop bar here." He presses the button to go up.

"Oh." My eyes widen.

The doors glide open and we step into the empty car. It whooshes us up to the roof of the building.

"I hope you don't mind that I stole you away from those people," Griff says, straight-faced.

I burst out laughing. His eyes twinkle.

We emerge on to the rooftop terrace, surrounded by the glittering lights of Chicago. It's a lovely late summer evening, stars faintly dotting the sky above us. There aren't many people up here, and it's quite dark. Griff leads me to a sofa in a back corner near a fireplace that casts heat and a flickering golden light. Sitting next to each other, I take off my small wristlet purse and set it on a low table in front of us.

A waitress appears almost immediately with a smile, setting coasters in front of us. "What can I get you?"

I'm too befuddled to think, so I ask for a glass of sauvignon blanc and Griff requests a Goose Island lager.

My eye is caught by two men who've walked onto the terrace. I sense them looking at us as they take seats.

"I think those guys know who you are," I tell Griff, nodding my head at the men.

He smiles. "They should. They're my security team."

I blink. "Oh."

"Ignore them. They're very discreet."

"Okay." I guess I should have realized a prince would have security. I cross my legs, hitching the beaded skirt of my dress up a bit. Griff's gaze drops to my feet and ankles.

"Sexy shoes," he murmurs.

"Thank you." I point one toe, admiring my strapped stiletto. "I love these shoes."

"That dress is very becoming also."

Heat blooms behind my breastbone. "Thank you again."

"In all seriousness, thank you for coming up here with me for a few moments of respite."

"I guess it gets tiring...always being the center of attention."

"Christ, yes. All those people insisting on introducing themselves and shaking hands." He shakes his head. "Why do they have to tell me their names? I don't need to know their names."

I laugh. "That's what Americans do."

"I know, I know. Hell. I sound ungrateful. I'm not. But...yeah. I like it when I can be my other self."

"Your other self?" I'm amused at his antisocial rant and try to stifle a smile. "You have multiple personalities?"

"I do, actually." He gives me a crooked smile. "It's how I cope."

"Well. I suppose we all do that. I..." I halt. "I'm a different person at work than I am with my father. Sometimes... I worry that I'll never get to be my true self."

Damn, what have I said? I barely even confess this fear to myself, never mind to a total stranger. Who's a freakin' prince.

The times I feel most like my true self are when I'm with Ford.

"Who is your true self, Chelsea?" he asks gently.

I suck in a long breath. "I don't even know," I admit. "I know I don't want to be cautious and fearful. I don't want people to see me as weak and foolish."

He frowns.

"Yes, I've made dumb mistakes."

"Haven't we all," he murmurs.

"I want to be brave enough to take risks. Strong enough to deal with the consequences. Independent. Capable. I want to do something that makes a difference in the world."

He's watching my face with such rapt attention I'm almost embarrassed. I drop my gaze.

He reaches for my hand and squeezes it. "We don't become what we want by remaining where we are."

My eyes widen. I nod slowly.

He continues. "If that's who you want to be...do it. You already have what it takes."

I feel like all the air has left my lungs and I can hardly breath. His words light a flame of inspiration and determination inside me. I meet his eyes. "Thank you."

"Just to be clear about the multiple personalities...I never pretend to be something I'm not." He pauses. "Except sober. I've pretended to be sober."

I burst out laughing, grateful for the lightening of the conversation. He smiles too and I feel a connection flutter between us.

I shift my gaze toward the city. "This view is amazing."

"It is, isn't it? Have you always lived in Chicago?"

"I have. Born and raised here. Went to college here."

"What did you study at college?"

"Public policy."

He nods. "Impressive. Beauty and brains, obviously."

I shake my head slowly, smiling. "You're just full of compliments."

He lays his hand on his chest. "Are you implying they're not genuine?"

I tilt my head. "No. I don't know."

"I assure you, they're quite honest. And deserved."

"Hmm. I suspect the term 'silver tongued' was invented for you."

He laughs, a low rumble of sound that makes my belly flip over. "I see I have work to do to convince you I'm genuine."

The waitress arrives with our drinks, setting them on the table in front of us. "Can I get you anything else?"

Griff looks at me with an arched eyebrow, and I shake my head. "I'm fine."

I take a fast gulp of the wine. I don't know what's happening here. But I'm not nervous. Just a little freaked out that I'm sitting here talking to a prince. What the hell do we have to say to each other?

"I like Chicago." He settles back against the thick cushion of the outdoor couch. The light of the fire shimmers over him. His tuxedo jacket is undone revealing the flat planes of his torso beneath his crisp white shirt. "Magnificent architecture. Beautiful lake. Great food."

"I love all those things too. But you must have seen a lot of beautiful cities."

"I've traveled quite a bit. I enjoy seeing the world and meeting new people. Have you traveled much?"

"Not as much as I'd like. When I was younger, my parents took us on trips, so we did see things like Disneyland and the Grand Canyon and Washington, DC. After my mother died, though, my father wasn't much for traveling other than on business. He and I went to Paris for my eighteenth birthday." I smile wistfully. "It was amazing. I love Paris. But it felt..." I pause. "I don't even know how to describe it. Restricted? Limited? All I wanted to do was escape and wander the city by myself. Every time I saw a group of girls my age, I felt so left out. I kept imagining myself there with girlfriends and how much fun we could have. I wanted to go to dance clubs and cool brasseries, and shop for clothes. I kept imagining meeting a charming French boy and flirting." I wrinkle my nose. "Of course none of that could happen when I was with my dad."

"I understand."

"I sound so...spoiled." I sigh. "I know I was lucky to have that trip at all."

"You don't sound spoiled. And who am I to judge?" He lifts one shoulder. "It's completely understandable. You should go back, now you're on your own." He pauses. "I would love to show you Paris."

A small shiver runs through me. "That would be wonderful." I smile, adding, "I will go back there one day. And other places. What is your country like?"

"Eria is beautiful. We're a small country, of course, but with a great deal of history. The countryside is splendid, from the rocky coast to the rolling green hills, and of course our capital city Wingate is quite cosmopolitan and becoming more and more diverse."

"I'd love to see that, too." I pause. "If you could live anywhere in the world, where would it be?"

His lips thin. "I'll never have that choice. I have to live in Eria."

"Why don't you seem happy about that?"

He drops his gaze, then lifts his head and meets my eyes. "I shouldn't talk like this."

I frown. "What do you mean?"

"Things I say and do get reported to the media. I have to be so goddamn careful." He makes a rough noise in his throat. "But I feel like I can tell you anything."

"Oh. Well, of course you can."

"I'm next in line to the throne. When my father dies, I'll be King of Eria."

"Yes."

He closes his eyes. For all his smooth, cheery banter, the taut lines of his face right now hint at emotions he doesn't like to show. "I hate having my future so predetermined. Sometimes I feel trapped. Like my life's not my own."

"Oh. I see."

He peers at me, studying my face. "I feel like you do understand. We both have so much to be grateful for, and yet there are parts of our lives that restrict us."

"Yes." I draw the word out as I consider that. He's right.

Maybe we do have things in common.

"That's true," I say. "I guess I've never appreciated that my life is my own to make of it what I want. I've always felt controlled by my father, but it's nothing compared to the things that constrain you." I make a face, smiling.

"It might not happen for a long time. My father is healthy and he's only sixty-seven."

"So that means you should make the most of your life right now. Live in the moment. Do all the things you want to do, until you can't."

"Yes." His gaze moves over my face. "You're absolutely right. Of course, I do get myself into a little trouble from time to time doing that."

"I'm aware."

He grins. "I'm doing better. I'm much more mature now." He leans closer to me. "But I still like to have a little fun."

"Who doesn't?" I sip my wine. "I'm just learning how to have fun."

"I would love to show you how to have fun."

My skin tingles as my blood heats at the innuendo in his tone. Does he want to see me again? Or he just flirting? And what kind of fun does he mean? I'm not up for a threesome on a yacht, or wherever he was when he got caught by the paparazzi.

I feel so inexperienced. So unsophisticated, despite my upbringing. This prince is a playboy, a pleasure seeker. Worldly and glamorous.

"Would you show me around Chicago?" he asks.

My heart gallops and my fingers tighten on the stem of my wine glass. "I..." *For real?* I swallow the words. "I'd love to."

"Brilliant." He holds his glass to mine in another toast. "Cheers."

We both take another drink.

"What will you show me first?" he asks. "And when?"

"How long are you here for?"

"It hasn't been determined. At least a month, possibly longer."

"Oh, we have lots of time then! Um...I don't know. Maybe we could take one of the boat cruises on the river. They talk about the architecture of the buildings, and you see the city from a different perspective. It sounds touristy, but it might be fun."

He nods thoughtfully. "Okay, but we need to book the whole boat. I'd rather avoid crowds."

I blink. "Uh... that could be pricey." Then I close my eyes and drop my head back. "What am I saying? You're a prince."

When I look back at him, he's grinning. "I think I can swing it financially. What else?"

"There's so much!"

We spend the next while discussing ideas and things he'd like to see and do, some of which surprise me... the Field Museum. A jazz club. Wrigley Field.

"My friend who I live with loves baseball," I said. "Maybe he could come with us. He knows a lot more about baseball than I do."

"He?" He lifts one eyebrow.

"We're just friends," I assure him quickly.

"Okay, sure. And ice hockey. I'd like to go to an ice hockey match."

A laugh bubbles up my throat. "Just FYI...we don't call it 'ice hockey' here. It's just hockey. And it's not a 'match.'"

His smile makes my heart flutter. "Okay. A hockey game."

"The season hasn't started yet. But if you're still here at the end of September we might be able to go to an exhibition game."

"What do you like to do for fun?"

I wrinkle my nose. "I don't have much of a social life. When I was seeing Ethan, we went to a taco and tequila festival; that was fun. There are always things like that going on. There's a jazz festival at the end of the month. Or we could go to an improv show."

We enter each other's numbers into our phones.

"I'm sure I don't have to say this…but please don't give out my number to anyone."

I gaze at Griff. Should I be insulted? But I can see the regret in his eyes that he has to say this. "Of course I won't."

"I'm here working," he says. "But outside of that I'd like to stay low profile as much as possible. The press is morbidly fascinated with me."

"I understand."

We've finished our drinks.

"I suppose we should get back," Griff says.

"Yes, I suppose we should." Neither of us make a move, though, and then our eyes meet and we burst out laughing.

He sets some bills on the table to cover our drinks. Holding out a hand, he stands. I take his hand and rise too, picking up my purse, and we leave the terrace, passing by his security team. I cast them a curious glance and a hesitant smile, but they ignore me.

In the lobby area, waiting for the elevator, Griff turns to me and touches my face. "Thank you for the breathing space."

Heat shimmers around us as I gaze into his eyes. "I enjoyed talking to you."

"Likewise." And he bends his head and brushes his mouth over mine.

My belly pitches and heat blooms between my legs. Lord, at such a simple, innocent touch! I'm so attracted to him, if he *really* kissed me, I'd probably dissolve into a puddle at his feet.

We share a slow smile that tugs at something deep down inside me.

Back in the ballroom, the first thing Griff does is steer us to the bar. This time I elect to have a glass of water. The wine is going to my head, or maybe that's lust, I'm not sure, but I think it's safer if I stay sober and upright around Griff. Soon, he's surrounded by people again. Once more, he uses me to make an escape, but I don't mind being used because he leads me onto the dance floor for another slow dance. We stare into each other's eyes as we move to "All of Me" by John Legend.

Eventually Dad finds us, and the look on his face when he sees who I'm with is comical. I introduce them and they exchange firm handshakes and make small talk.

Then Dad turns to me. "I'm leaving in about ten minutes. If you'd like a ride, Lawrence and I can drop you off."

I don't want to leave. I could easily walk to Ford's apartment from here, even though it's night, or take a taxi. But it's getting late and the crowd has started to thin. Probably Griff needs to call it a night soon too. So I say, "Okay, thanks, Dad. I'll meet you out front."

He nods. "Good to meet you, Your Highness."

"Please. Call me Griff."

"Griff. Good night."

With a last look, Dad leaves.

I meet Griff's eyes. "Sorry. Another introduction."

His lips curve upward. "Don't worry."

"I guess I'm leaving."

"I'm going to find my mates I came with and get out of here, too." He pauses. "I'll call you."

I'm quivering inside, almost afraid to believe he'll call. Guys always say that. And he's a *prince*. "I'd like that."

He casts a glance around. "I'd kiss you properly, but I'd put money on someone here having a camera on us right now."

I swallow, my heart knocking. "I understand."

He bends closer, so his mouth is near my ear. "Next time, I'll kiss you senseless."

My heart misses a beat, then patters faster. "Promise?"

He grins. "Oh yes. I promise."

As I walk away from him, I resist the urge to turn back for one last look. Well, this may have solved my problem—I don't think I'll be having sex dreams about Ford tonight.

SEVEN

Chelsea

I sleep late Sunday morning, which is unusual, then go for a bike ride with Ford. I don't mention what happened last night. I'm still processing it all.

I've pretty much convinced myself that I'm being a naïve, gullible fool again. Why would a *prince* be interested in *me*? He was just having fun last night, flirting with a girl, making empty promises. He doesn't need me to show him around Chicago. For god's sake, he can rent out an entire tour boat himself!

I'm not going to humiliate myself by talking about him, when chances are I'll never hear from him again. I'm not going to be like Amanda Kennard in eighth grade who told us she met Justin Bieber when she was on vacation, and he was coming to the school dance with her. Needless, to say, Justin never showed, and Amanda never lived that down.

I'll have the memory, though, of last night...dancing to John

Legend beneath the ballroom chandeliers, wearing my beautiful sparkly dress, him so handsome and regal in his tux, talking with his sexy accent about duty to his country…and kissing me. I almost wonder if I was drunk enough to imagine all that.

When I get home from the bike ride, I check my phone and…*yessss*! There's a text from Griff.

Hello beautiful lady. I hope you are having a lovely Sunday. I enjoyed spending time with you last night.

I hold my phone in both hands, smiling at it.

"What?" Ford asks, opening the fridge.

I blink at him. "What, what?"

"Why are you laughing at your phone?"

"I'm not laughing. I'm just…" I stop, heat flooding into my face. "Just a funny meme."

"Show me."

"No!"

Frowning, Ford unscrews the lid of the bottle of water he's holding. "Why not?"

"It's, uh…never mind. I need to, uh…go to the bathroom."

I dart into my bathroom and close the door. I'm still hot and flustered. I sit on the closed toilet and look at the text again. My smile returns. *I enjoyed it too.*

I don't know if he'll answer right away, so I spring up and wash my face and hands and hustle into my bedroom. I sit on my bed and scroll through social media, checking out Instagram until my phone pings with another text.

I've arranged for a river tour on Saturday at 1. Does that work for you?

My heart expands and my blood pulses hot through my veins. *Yes. That sounds great.*

Except too far away. But I don't type that.

Perhaps we could meet for coffee or a drink before then? I have free time Wednesday evening.

I nod vigorously, which is ridiculous. *I think I can fit that in.*

You choose the place. Somewhere I can blend in.

I bite my lip. *I'll think of something.*

Lovely. Enjoy your week.

You too.

I fall back onto my bed, arms outstretched. I haven't had many experiences like this. As a teenager, I was excited when Rick Sokolowski flirted with me and invited me to go to a movie. Then Dad put an end to that idea.

But now...I'm doing this. I'm going on a date. *With a prince!* A handsome, charming, sophisticated prince who effortlessly draws people into his web of glamour. Me!

Okay, wait. I'm not excited because he's a prince. I'm excited because I finally met someone who excites me. Someone who interests me. Someone who gets me...even though we only talked that one night.

Also, I'm getting way ahead of myself here. It took me weeks to figure out that Ethan wasn't my soul mate. I've only met Griff once. After our drink on Wednesday night, maybe I'll see that he's a total jerk. I don't even know him yet. I need to calm the hell down.

Things are busy at work this week, which is good as it keeps my mind off Griff. My boss, Arlene, is meeting with state officials on Wednesday and we're preparing for that, as well as meetings later in the week with community organizations we hope to partner with. I admire Arlene; she has so much experience, from grassroots organizing to lobbying at the highest levels of government. Plus, she's a wonderful person to work for, supportive and encouraging.

"Thank you for all the research you did on this," she says on Wednesday morning as she leaves for her meeting.

I've spent a lot of time working on her presentation and making sure she's prepared. We've been working on a project to develop a legislative tracking curriculum for Chicago schools, which is intended to help kids understand the legislative process and make sure they have input in the policymaking process. This is something I feel strongly about given my own experiences. The program involves learning how a bill moves through the House and Senate, choosing an actual bill to track, creating a campaign plan for it, and reaching out to lawmakers.

"You're welcome," I answer, happy that she recognizes all my work. "I'm really excited about this!"

I've given some thought to where Griff and I should go on Wednesday. I want it to be the perfect place. I'd hate it if we went somewhere he was uncomfortable and I feel very much out of my depth, since I know nothing about royalty and not much more about discreet local bars. I'd love to take him to a bar on the Riverwalk, but along with a lot of Chicagoans there are tons of tourists there, and the chances of him being recognized would be high. I decide a speakeasy would be perfect.

So we meet at Frank's on South Dearborn. I take a taxi there. I'm relieved Ford is working late and I don't have to explain to him where I'm going.

When I walk up to the bar, the door of a black car parked at the curb opens and Griff slides out. He smiles, and my knees go wobbly. "Hello."

"Hi." I beam back at him. Inside I'm a tangled mess of emotions —happiness, relief, disbelief, and nerves.

"My men have already been inside to check out the place." Griff pulls open the door for me.

"Oh." I glance back at the car. "Jesus."

Griff laughs softly as we pause at the hostess stand. "Could we sit at the back?" I ask the hostess.

"Of course." She picks up menus and leads us to the back of the room, past a long bar lit in red—the bottles behind it glow scarlet and the bar itself shines red in the dimly lit space.

We're seated on a red leather loveseat in a dark corner, a low wooden table in front of us. This building is old, with worn wood floors, a beamed ceiling, and crystal chandeliers that add to the 1920's prohibition atmosphere. The hostess sets the menus on the table and disappears.

None of the other patrons pay any attention to us. That's good.

"This is wicked," Griff says. I think he approves. "What shall we drink?"

"They have a lot of martinis. I think I'll try one of those." I pick up a menu and peruse it. "Gin, Cointreau and cranberry. That sounds good."

After a few seconds, Griff decides and when a waiter approaches, he orders the martini made with gin, Flora Hemp Spirit, and lime.

"Flora hemp spirit," I say after we order.

He grins. "I have no idea what that is. Maybe I'll get drunk *and* high."

"I've never been high," I say wistfully.

"What?" He gives me a mock incredulous look.

I roll my eyes. "It's not that weird."

"It's legal here, now, yes?"

"Yes."

"Then we're going to do that."

"We are?"

He nods firmly. "Not tonight. But some time."

"Um..." My dad would die. But...I don't live at home anymore and my dad doesn't need to know every little thing I do. "Okay."

Our drinks arrive, and we settle into the small couch, shifting so we're almost facing each other. I pick up my martini and sip. "Mmm. This is good!"

"Mine's good too. Would you like to taste it?"

Our eyes meet and I may be innocent, but his words make me think dirty thoughts. I can't help it—my eyes widen and I say, "Oh, I'm sure it's good."

After a startled beat, he grins. "Oh, you dirty girl."

"I'm not! I'm not usually like that!" I set down my drink and press my hands to my hot cheeks. "I don't know why I said that."

He laughs softly. "You keep surprising me. I like it."

I glance at him, then away. "I keep surprising myself," I mutter.

He hands me his drink, and I take a sip. "Hmm. That's not bad."

He picks up mine and helps himself to a taste. "Yours is tasty, too." His voice is laden with innuendo.

Oh god. I want to wave a hand in front of my face. But I have to at least try to act worldly. Instead, I beckon him to hand over my drink.

He grins and complies. "Tell me about your work day."

I don't know how it could interest him, but I talk about the research I did to help my boss prepare for her meetings.

"I don't understand this registering to vote," he says. "We don't have to do that in Eria. I would think that might deter people from exercising their right to vote."

I blink at him in surprise. "Yes. Some say that. Which could result in lower turnout." I continue talking about the percentage of people who aren't registered to vote and voter turnout, and when I realize I've gotten a little animated, I shut my mouth. "Sorry. I got carried away."

He's watching my face, smiling, his eyes warm. "I enjoy listening to you. You're very passionate about these things."

I grimace. "I am. Not everyone is, though."

"I think you could make others passionate. You're very persuasive."

"Oh. Thank you." I take another drink of my martini. "What about your day? Week? Have you been busy?"

"Yes. Meetings. Talking about fundraising. Planning. Sounds a lot like your work."

"It does." I eye him over the rim of my glass. "What made you want to do this?"

"Obviously, the fact that I served. Not long enough, though."

"Why was that?"

"The only reason I was allowed to go into combat was that the media agreed to keep silent about it. And then they didn't." His mouth tightens. "I loved what I did. I was pissed when I had to go home."

"Tell me about what you did?"

He talks about Afghanistan and flying Apache helicopters and their role in working with the allied forces there. He tells me about his friend Caden, who now struggles with PTSD and how it's been hard for him to get the help he needs because people still think he should just "get over it."

I'm reminded that Ford fought in Afghanistan too, although he doesn't talk much about it.

I'm blown away by Griff's commitment to his army career and how seriously he took that. He's not just a playboy prince. My heart softens in my chest, listening to him. He doesn't brag, but it's clear he's been in dangerous situations and saved lives.

"I wanted to go back," he says. "I think I might have been able to at some point, but my grandfather died, making my father king, and me next in line to the throne. There's no way they would have allowed that. And I wasn't staying in the army if I had to sit safely at home while my mates were going to war. Fuck that. So I ended up resigning."

"I'm sorry." I reach for his hand and cover it with mine, feeling his disappointment.

He turns his hand and curls his fingers around mine. "Thanks. It was a hard reality, that I'd never have a military career. So I've tried to find a new direction."

"It sounds like you have."

"Yeah."

The waitress stops by to see if we want to order food.

"I'm bloody starving." Griff picks up a menu again. "Let's get some food, yeah?"

"Sure." I grabbed a piece of leftover pizza at home before I came, which wasn't much.

There's not a huge food menu here, so we order wings and sweet potato fries.

"All right." Griff leans back into the couch. "Tell me what your most unusual talent is." He laughs. "What? What is that look on your face?"

I smile, shaking my head. "I don't have any unusual talents."

"You must have something you're good at. Something surprising."

"Okay." I hesitate, then say it. "I have no gag reflex."

He blinks rapidly, his mouth open. Then he swallows. "Well, hell," he mutters. "You're shitting me."

I laugh. "No. It's true."

He still seems dumbfounded. I start giggling and lean into him. "I'm sorry. Are you okay?"

"No. I am not okay."

I'm still laughing, but so is he.

"Jesus, woman. I did not expect that."

Satisfaction has me shimmying my shoulders. "Also, I can play the harmonica."

"Ah. Not quite as...exciting. But interesting."

"What about you?" I meet his eyes challengingly.

"I have many hidden talents."

"Uh huh."

"I'm a superb polo player."

I nod. "Okay."

"I also like to ski."

I tilt my head. "Come on. Those are not that unusual."

"Okay. How about skateboarding?"

I shrug. "Only unusual because you're a prince."

"You're hard to impress. How about this." He pauses, focuses, then sticks his tongue out and folds it into the shape of an M.

I fall back into the couch, laughing. "Oh my god!"

He grins. "Now are you impressed?"

"Oh yeah!" I press a hand to my stomach. "A talented tongue! I can't believe you haven't bragged to the world about that."

"Only to you, pet."

"I'm honored." I set my hand over my heart, then look up at him through my eyelashes. "Also...intrigued."

Oh. My. god. I'm getting flirty. Who am I? I give myself a mental smack across the face.

"How did you learn to fly helicopters?" I ask.

He tells me about his military training, including stints in California and Canada. I'm impressed with his technical knowledge. Again, there's much more to this prince than parties and polo matches.

We talk about college and trying to make a life apart from our families, which are totally different and yet there are similarities. We talk about music and movies. He's so attentive, focused all on me, and it's intoxicating. Captivating.

He drives me home. Or rather, Rhys, his bodyguard, drives. We sit in the back. When we pull up to the curb at my building, Rhys gets out and opens the door for me. I slide out, followed by Griff, who walks me to the condo entrance. "Nice place."

"Thank you. It's not mine; I pay rent to my friend who owns it."

"Ah."

He bends his head close to mine. "So, I'll see you Saturday, yeah?"

"Yes. I'm looking forward to it."

He breathes in. "Christ, you smell good."

My belly flutters. "Oh."

"I still want to kiss you senseless. Taste you properly. But I'll wait."

My eyelids grow heavy and my heart leaps. "I want that too."

"Good." His nose rubs alongside mine, then he brushes his mouth over mine. "Good night, Chelsea."

"Good night. Thanks for the drinks. And snacks."

"You're very welcome."

I enter the building and wave to him through the glass door, and as I stand waiting for the elevator, I watch him get back in the car and shut the door.

Wow.

CHAPTER

EIGHT

Griff

This American girl is fucking up my head.

I can't stop thinking about her.

Chelsea's beautiful, yeah...long, soft brown hair, creamy skin, big brown eyes with amazing, lush lashes. A sweetly curved mouth. And that dress she was wearing that first night...Jesus. Her face is wholesome and pretty, but that dress hugged every sexy-as-fuck curve, showing off cleavage in front and a spectacular ass from the back. Not to mention the sweep of her bare back that my hands itched to touch.

I've been with a lot of women. And men. But something about her grabbed my insides and squeezed. And as I talked to her, I became more and more intrigued.

I'm only here for about a month. I have no intention of getting involved with anyone. Even one-night stands are tricky, with my security lads always keeping an eye on me, not to mention the paparazzi and media. Cameras are everywhere these days. So I don't know why I'm doing this. I just know I want to see her again.

There's something...calming about her. I'm cynical. Jaded. I fight the bitterness inside me that's a battle between duty to my country and my people, and my selfish desire to life my own life. But Chelsea touches something soft and vulnerable inside me. Something I've almost forgotten exists.

I pick her up outside the building where she lives. She's standing on the sidewalk, dressed appropriately for the cool day in a jacket, a big scarf, jeans, and boots. I step out of the back seat of the car to greet her, and she moves toward me with a bright smile. "Hi!"

"Hello." I take her hand and bend to kiss her cheek. "You look lovely."

She glances down at herself. "Hmmm. Thank you."

I help her into the car and slide in next to her. "Ready for our adventure?"

She smiles. "I'm not sure how adventurous a river cruise is, but I *am* excited."

Her brown eyes sparkle, her mouth curves into a smile, and the genuine pleasure on her face softens that hardened part of my soul. "Me too." And weirdly, I am excited.

It's a short drive over the bridge and onto East Wacker. Rhys stops to let us out and we walk down a couple flights of stairs to dockside. Our boat is waiting for us—a forty-eight-foot vintage yacht I've hired for the day.

Before we board, I pull on a Chicago Cubs cap, tugging the brim low, and slide on my aviator sunglasses. Chelsea grins at me. "Nice disguise."

I grin back. "Thanks."

Jac is already here and on board, along with the captain, a bartender, and the docent from the Chicago Architecture Center who'll talk to us about the buildings we see as we cruise the river.

We elect to sit on the padded bench at the bow of the boat, and once Rhys joins us, we embark on our voyage. I've had a picnic lunch catered, and the bartender serves us champagne to start.

Chelsea flashes me a startled glance. "I didn't expect this."

"Cheers."

The docent begins by talking to us about the Great Chicago Fire, which destroyed many buildings, so much of the architecture we see is relatively modern. We learn about the Chicago School and the first skyscrapers. I'm fascinated by the fact that many buildings were designed with their neighboring structures in mind, so as to be complimentary in style.

We pass by what appears to be a wedding on an outdoor deck as we enjoy the bubbly wine and prosciutto, genoa salami, chorizo, stuffed green olives, crackers, cheeses, and fruit. We wave to people on the bridges as we slide along beneath them, and study the unusual appearance of Marina City, which resembles corn cobs.

"I think I'd freak out parking a car there." Chelsea points to the vehicles on the parking floors.

"The movie *The Hunter* with Steve McQueen features a car chase up Marina City towers' parking ramp," the docent tells us, smiling. "It ends with a vehicle losing control on the fifteenth floor, plunging into the river."

Chelsea and I exchange looks. "I have to watch that movie now," she says.

"We should do that."

The docent takes a break and goes back to chat with the captain, leaving Chelsea and I alone up front. She snuggles her chin into her scarf and sips her champagne, the sun highlighting her hair.

"You get such a different view from here," she says. "It's very cool. And even though I've lived here all my life, I'm learning things."

"I'm impressed with the city." And with her. "But it can't be perfect."

"Of course not. There's crime and corruption. Poverty and racism."

I nod slowly. "I guess most cities face those problems."

"True. But we can work on them. I'm naïve enough to think there's hope."

I study her face. "I admire that about you."

"That I'm naïve?" She wrinkles her nose.

"That you're optimistic. Hopeful. That's important."

She dips her head briefly, then our eyes meet. "I suppose it is. If nobody believed there was hope, we'd be lost."

"I guess I've hoped for so many things that haven't happened."

She gazes at me steadily. "Hope shouldn't have a particular outcome. That's...wanting. Expecting. But hope is a belief that there is the potential for something good."

I purse my lips, thinking about her words.

"I mean, we've all been hurt. Disappointed. But hope puts that into perspective and reminds us that things always change. It shows us a path toward something better."

My chest tightens and I force a smile. "How did you get to be such a wise woman at such a young age?"

"I'm not that young."

"How old are you?" I don't even know that.

"Twenty-five."

I nod. "I'm thirty-four. You're young."

She smiles. "It's all relative."

"True."

"I've felt hopeless," she continues. "I've felt like things were out of my control."

"Yeah. You're talking about your mom dying?"

She nods. "It wasn't just my mom. It was my sister, too."

"Oh no. I'm sorry. Was it an accident?"

She shakes her head, her mouth soft. "They were killed in a drive-by shooting."

"Jesus Christ." I reach for her and pull her against me in a hug. "That's atrocious."

"Yes."

"How old were you? Did you say fourteen?"

"Yes."

"I can't imagine. Bloody hell." I tighten my arms around her, then release her and look into her face. "Yeah, I'm sure you *have* felt hopeless."

Her bottom lip pushes out adorably. "Yes. The way it happened —so random. So completely out of control. That was scary. I felt so helpless. But you must have felt hopeless, too, at times."

"Yes." I think about those times. I think about Afghanistan and having to leave, knowing I'd never be able to go back. "And you're right. Hope is what gets us through those times."

"How the heck did we get here?" She shakes her head and sit back. "Oh right, we were talking about the city's problems. Does your country not have similar issues?"

"Oh yes. Definitely."

"You're going to be king one day. Do you have ideas for how to fix things?"

I grimace. "I do. But the king doesn't have any real power. The king is the head of State and has to remain strictly neutral with respect to political matters."

"Oh."

"According to tradition, the king is the ultimate source of power, but in modern practice he wields no real political power to act independently of Parliament or the prime minister."

"I see."

"It's better," I add. "It's better that the voters and elected officials make decisions. Not a monarch."

"Right."

"The king can have *influence*. But members of the royal family find other ways to feel like we have some kind of power."

"Hence your foundation."

"Exactly."

The docent strolls back up to the bow of the boat and asks if we have any questions.

"The tower on the Wrigley Building," I say. "It looks like something I've seen before."

The docent smiles. "The bell tower is styled after the Giralda Tower of the Seville Cathedral in Spain."

"Ah, yes!"

"You've been there?" Chelsea asks.

"I have. Seville is a lovely city."

She sighs.

I recall her wistful description of her trip to Paris. It made me want to take her there and do all the things. Now I want to take her to Seville. I want to take her wherever she wants to go. If a simple boat ride along the river of the city in which she lives delights her so much, I love to imagine how she'd react to seeing other amazing sights.

Soon we're docking back where we started. Jac tips the docent, the bartender, and the captain for me as I help Chelsea disembark. Instead of climbing the stairs, we pause on the Esplanade. I don't want this to be the end of our. "What else can you show me?"

She tips her head and sinks her teeth into her lush bottom lip. "Would you like to walk?" She gestures toward the lake. "We could walk toward the harbor. We could go all the way to Navy Pier if you like, but it's pretty touristy. There's a chance people could recognize you."

"Like this? Bah."

"If you're sure…"

"It'll be fine."

I relay the plan to the guys, who aren't entirely pleased about it, but they're used to my impulsive ventures, and we start walking. They follow not far behind.

Nobody pays any attention to us as we stroll along the river, enjoying the sun and fresh breeze. Chelsea points out various buildings along the way and I admire more of the unique architecture. Soon we arrive at a park with a multi-layered fountain pouring water.

"Stop here?" Chelsea asks. "Or keep going?"

"Let's keep going."

We end up at a little coffee place right on the beach.

"This is fantastic." I sit facing the lake, with Chelsea to my right, so my back is to the other patrons. The beach is surprisingly crowded with people, high rise buildings towering in the distance along the curve of the lake.

"Good." Chelsea smiles.

"Um...your men...?" Chelsea asks hesitantly.

"They're fine."

"Do they need a drink?"

I smile. "They'll get one if they need."

"I'm not used to that. It felt weird with them following us. Although I did forget about them at times."

"You'll get used to it."

She grimaces. "I don't know about that."

I lift one shoulder. "It's necessary. And these lads have been with me for a while. They're friends, too. They know me and I trust them. Obviously."

"With your life." She gives me a solemn look.

"Well, yes."

She searches my face. "Have you ever felt...at risk?"

"There have been a couple of times. There are always haters, as you Americans say, out there. Some people didn't like it when I went to Afghanistan. Some people didn't like it when I came home alive." I shrug. "Some people hate everything I do."

"That's awful." Her forehead creases.

"Those people aren't worth thinking about." I lean closer to her. "Don't worry. You're safe."

"Oh! I'm not worried about me. I just can't imagine that people hate you. You're so…"

I smile and lean my chin on my hand. "What, love? I'm interested."

Her cheeks get pink and she drops her gaze, those long, thick eyelashes fanning on her smooth cheeks. "You're charming. Fun. Thoughtful."

"Ah. Thank you. I also think you are charming and fun and fascinating."

"I'm not fascinating!" Her eyes fly open. "I've led such a sheltered life, I'm boring."

"Not at all. I find you immensely intriguing."

Her smile is tentative. I can see she's not convinced.

The server brings our beers served in plastic cups and I sit back in my chair to survey the beach. "This is relaxing."

"Good. I'm sure you don't get a lot of time to relax."

"Very true. It would be fun to play volleyball down there. Or to be on one of those boats." I gesture at a number of watercraft out on the lake.

"I'm sure you could arrange that. Maybe not the volleyball." She wrinkles her nose. "But you could definitely rent a boat."

"That's a fine idea. I shall look into that."

"Do you like cycling? That's something else that would probably be safe. You can rent bikes and ride all along the lake."

"I do enjoy cycling."

"You seem athletic."

"I enjoyed sports at school, yes. You?"

She rolls her eyes. "I'm not an athlete, but my roommate bikes a lot, so I've taken it up too."

"Good. Then you can keep up with me when we go."

"I should be able to." Her eyes sparkle.

"Shall we plan that for tomorrow? And end with hot dogs for dinner?"

A slow smile spreads across her face. "That would be nice." She pulls out her phone and checks it. "The forecast is warm and sunny tomorrow."

"Excellent."

I'm all for fun and outdoor activity, but I'd also like to have Chelsea to myself for a while. I need to plan an evening where that can happen. Restaurants are risky, but I'll figure something out.

When we finish our beers, we head back outside. It's late afternoon now.

We stop on a sidewalk and I stand close to her, face to face. "Unfortunately, I have dinner plans tonight," I tell her in a low voice. "Otherwise, I'd like this date to continue."

"That's okay."

"Rhys has brought the car round here. He's waiting for us in front of the pier."

"Oh! Wow. Okay."

"We can drop you at home."

"I can walk from here."

"Absolutely not."

She huffs out a little laugh and follows me to the car. Rhys has already figured out the route and makes the short drive to where we picked her up earlier. She's right, it's not far, but I get her alone in the back seat.

I take her hand. "I had fun today, Chelsea."

"Me too." Her smile reaches something deep inside me and tugs.

I lift my other hand to cup her cheek and lean in. I pause as our mouths near, holding her gaze. Her eyelashes flutter down and she closes the distance between us, our mouths joining in a slow, soft kiss.

Heat explodes in my groin and I swallow a groan, opening my mouth on hers to kiss her more deeply. I lick over her plump bottom lip and into her mouth. Her breath hitches and her fingers curl around mine.

I make a low sound of pleasure, tilt my head and go in again for more, tasting her deeply. She tastes like sunshine and warm woman. It goes to my head and my entire body pulses for more.

We kiss like that the few blocks to her building and as we pull up to the sidewalk I draw back and smile. Her eyes open, dark and hazy, and her lips curve into a seductive smile. "Thanks for a lovely afternoon," she whispers.

"Thank *you*." I give her one last peck on the lips. "I'll text you about plans for tomorrow."

"Okay." She slides out as Rhys opens the car door for her. "See you then."

I watch her walk into the building, admiring the fit of her jeans on her ass and the bounce of her long hair as she moves. Something pinches in my chest. She's just left and I already miss her. This is...unexpected.

CHAPTER
NINE

Chelsea

I still can't believe this is happening, but it's feeling more and more real, the more time I spend with Griff. He's wonderful and my heart is definitely in danger here. I love his playful side and how he likes to escape from his guards from time to time. He's showing me how to have fun in ways I never have. But he's also serious and focused when it comes to his country and his charity. He works hard and I admire that.

And the way he treats me, as if I'm a princess—that goes straight to my head. He's always so gallant, holding doors for me, helping me with my jacket, asking my opinion on wine or beer or whether I want sprinkles on my ice cream. He looks at me as if I'm beautiful, he touches me like he can't keep his hands off me, and he listens attentively to everything I say.

I'd be floating around except for the fact that I can't tell anyone about this, and that keeps my feet firmly grounded. Ford knows I'm seeing someone, or a few someones, but I don't say much about our dates. I can't tell people at work who I'm seeing. I don't tell Kallista. I can only imagine what she'd say—I'm dating the most unavailable man in the world! A prince who has to go back to his country at some point!

And I sure don't tell my dad.

I feel guilty about this. Like there's something wrong with what I'm doing, sneaking around. I'm not doing it for me, though, I'm doing it for Griff to keep his name out of the gossip blogs and magazines. And I know that in the end, this is not going to amount to anything more than a dreamlike summer/fall fling with a handsome prince.

He's taken me sailing, one gorgeous sunny day, with Jac and Rhys sailing the boat, he and I relaxing, drinking wine and eating as the lake breeze cooled our skin. We've gone to a new exhibit at the Art Institute, and we've walked on the beach. Tonight, after a few weeks of seeing each other, I'm going to Griff's place for dinner. He's been staying at a friend's home. The friend, a wealthy socialite, is in Europe right now, so Griff and his entourage have the place to themselves. He's going to order dinner in for us and we can have a quiet evening alone, which is difficult when we go out.

I'm hoping that tonight, since we'll be alone, maybe...we'll have sex.

I'm dying for him.

Yes, my heart is tangled up in him, but my body wants him too. I've never lusted for a man like I do for Griff. My sex dreams about Ford were smoking hot, but I could never let myself truly fantasize about Ford, my gay best friend who had a boyfriend. But Griff...I think he wants me as much as I want him.

I'm excited.

The girls at work talk about their sex lives and so I've learned that I should have a clean pair of panties, a toothbrush, and a few cosmetics in my purse just in case. I feel ridiculously optimistic as I drop these things into my bag, but whatever, I'm prepared. I even have condoms. Just in case.

Heat breaks out over my skin like a fever.

I emerge from my bedroom with my purse. Ford's not home yet, probably out for happy hour drinks with people from work since it's Friday. It's getting harder and harder to avoid telling him anything about Griff so I'm relieved I can leave without seeing him.

At first after he and Jeff broke up, Ford was a little distracted, but then he was back to normal which meant paying attention to me and what I was doing. His long hours at work make it a little easier to go out without being noticed, but still, he notices. And a couple of times he's suggested we do something together when I already had plans with Griff, and I had to turn him down. His wry smile and teasing about my new social life didn't quite hide his disappointment, and I felt shitty.

Waiting for the elevator, I pull out my phone to text him that I'm out tonight. I'm about to hit send when the doors slide open. Ford is right there.

"Oh! Hey!" I smile, stepping aside for him to exit the car. "I was just texting you."

"On your way out?" He stands in the opening, holding the door.

"Yep! Out for dinner."

One eyebrow lifts. "Again?"

"I know! Isn't it great?" I give a light laugh. "I feel like a normal woman."

He frowns. "You are normal."

"You know what I mean."

"Yeah." He still doesn't move. "Who's the guy tonight?"

"Why do you assume it's a guy?"

"Oh." He's still frowning. "So it's a girlfriend."

"Just dinner! I'll see you later. Or maybe tomorrow." I brush past him into the elevator. "Not sure how late I'll be." With a big smile, I give him a wave and he reluctantly steps aside so the doors can slide closed. I catch the way his brow lowers in concern.

I lean against the elevator wall as soon as they doors are closed. I *hate* lying to Ford. He's my best friend, really. And I know he's concerned about me.

I lift my chin. It's my life. I can have other friends and go on dates.

The elevator opens onto the lobby, and I cross it to see the familiar black car parked at the curb. Was the car there when Ford came in? Did he notice it? Yikes.

Rhys is leaning against the car in the evening sunshine, his gaze sweeping the area with deceptive casualness. He straightens when he sees me and opens the door. I slide in next to Griff.

The car smells like him—spicy and warm and sophisticated. His smile is a like a light in the dim interior, his eyes affectionate. "Hey you."

"Hi." I lean over for a long, scorching kiss. Breathless, I draw back. "Wow."

"Yeah. Wow." He touches my hair, still smiling. "I'm glad you're here."

"Me too."

I don't pay much attention to where we're going, busy smooching with Griff and talking about our day. We make one stop while Rhys goes in to pick up our food. But when we turn off Highway 41 onto Old Elm Road, I immediately recognize where we are. I shoot a startled glance out the window. "Holy crap," I say. "Where are we going?"

"My friend's house. Remember?"

"Yes, but..." I start laughing. "This is where I grew up. My dad still lives here." I point. "Right up that street."

"Christ." Griff makes a face. "Do you think he knows his neighbor? Knows I'm staying there?"

"No, he would have said something when he met you at the gala."

"Right. And Sophia is very discreet. She knows not to tell anyone."

We drive through a wrought iron gate. This house is even huger than Dad's. Rhys parks on a curved driveway in front of the entrance. In the two-story foyer, my jaw drops. I've been in lots of houses in this area, but this one is crazy—marble floors and columns, a big, curved staircase to the right with a grand piano next to it, and a seating area to the left.

"I feel like I'm in a hotel lobby," I comment, taking it in.

Griff laughs. "Yeah, now that you say it, I agree. Come on back."

I follow him to a big kitchen, which is open to a casual dining area and a large living space.

"I don't even use much of this place," Griff says. He gestures to wine glasses on the granite counter. "Wine?"

"Yes, please. White."

He retrieves a bottle from the fridge, which is hidden behind doors that match the cream cabinets, and pours us each a glass.

Rhys sets the food on the counter. "Would you like me to help with this?" he asks Griff.

"That's okay, man, we got this," Griff says easily. "Thanks."

Rhys smiles at me and disappears.

"There are appetizers in here." Griff opens the bag. "Paté with homemade croutons and cornichons. We can start with this. Do you want to sit at the table or here?"

"Here is fine." There are tall chairs at the enormous island. I hop up onto one while Griff sets out the food.

"Our meal is a family style dinner for two—coq au vin." He reads a pamphlet from the bag. "Reheating instructions...okay, I'll put this in the oven while we have the paté."

"Yum. This is so nice."

"It's not quite the same as being waited on hand and foot while dining in a lovely establishment, but it'll do." He gives me a cheeky grin.

"It's fine."

"*I'll* wait on you hand and foot," he adds.

"And what about you?"

"I'm used to being looked after." He rolls his eyes. "I like taking care of other people sometimes."

My heart gives a little bump. I pick up my wine.

"I'd especially like to take care of *you*," he continues in a low voice, his smile wicked.

I smile back. "Is that so?"

"Yes. There are many things I'd like to do...for you."

"Hmmm. I'm intrigued."

He rounds the island and smooches my mouth, then takes the stool next to me. "Good."

We snack on the delicious paté and drink our wine while dinner heats. Griff tells me about meetings he's had this week and I tell him what happened at work today.

"My boss Arlene called me into her office. That always makes me nervous."

"Oh yeah," he agrees. "I get it."

"But it was good. She's impressed with the work I've been doing on one of our projects and she wants me to take over."

"That's fabulous."

I grimace. "It's great, but I'm terrified! I don't have a lot of experience and I'm afraid I'll screw up."

"You're brilliant, Chelsea." He leans over to kiss my cheek. "You can do anything. What is the campaign?"

"It will help kids understand the legislative process and make sure they have input in the policymaking process. And emphasize the importance of voting."

"Just what you love."

He remembers. Something fizzes in my chest. "Yes. Arlene said

I'm passionate about it and that will make me a great campaign manager."

"I agree." He tilts his head. "Is your organization affiliated with a particular political party?"

"No." I shake my head. "We're nonpartisan. We're all about using organizing and advocacy to change politics. To get people involved and get them voting."

"That's really admirable."

He smiles warmly at me and at this moment I feel like I can take on this campaign. I can take on *anything*. I smile back at him.

"I'm proud of you."

"Thank you."

He asks more questions over dinner. He's very well-informed about democracy and interested in learning more about the American system of government.

When we're finished eating dessert, a piece of apple crème caramel cake that we share, we move into the family room off the kitchen.

"This place is amazing," I sit on a very ornate sofa. "But not exactly my taste."

"Mine either. Check out those." He points at cushions on a chair with a familiar checkerboard pattern.

"Oh my god! Are those Louis Vuitton cushions?"

"I think so, yeah."

I have to go look at them. "Wow."

"You grew up in this neighborhood. You didn't have Louis Vuitton cushions?"

"Nope." I sit again, beside him on the sofa. "Definitely not." I shoot him a glance. "Do you have them at your, uh, castle?"

He grins. "No. The castle is full of dusty old velvet shit."

"Do you really live in a castle?"

"Yes." He sighs. "It's not a big castle, by some standards, but there is a lot of space. I have rooms in a wing with my own kitchen and my own space, or I can dine with my parents."

"How old is it?"

"It was built in the eleventh century."

"Good lord!" I stare at him.

"Indeed. It is ancient. Over the centuries, it has been modified and updated. My grandmother did an extensive renovation when she was queen. The grounds are lovely."

"I'd love to see it."

"Perhaps one day you will."

I truly doubt that, but I smile. "What will you do when you're king? Are there things you want to change?"

"Hmm. Not something I've given a great deal of thought. Spending money on things like that can be troublesome. Some Erians frown on the royals spending money on themselves."

I tip my head. "I can understand that. Somewhat like politicians enriching themselves through their elected office."

"Yes."

"But spending money on the castle—wouldn't that be for the country? The castle belongs to the people, I assume."

"That is correct, but it often isn't seen that way."

"Yes." I nod. "I can see that. People see you living in a castle and enjoying the benefits of that."

"But not enduring the disadvantages." He shrugs. "There is always talk about abolishing the monarchy."

"Really?" I shift on the couch so I can face him more directly. "Could that happen?"

"It could."

"You don't seem worried."

"I think you know by now that I'm a reluctant royal." His mouth twists. "Don't tell anyone."

"I won't. You know that."

He takes my hand and twines our fingers together. "I do. What do you think? In a democracy, should the people elect the head of state?"

"Of course. You've told me the king doesn't have any political power, though."

"True."

"Which means the king's functions could be taken over by a president. Or prime minister."

"Yes. And the monarchy is hereditary, which means I will become king even if I don't want to. Even if I'm not suited for it."

"Do you not think you're suited to be king?" I study his face.

"I've questioned that. And so have others, believe me." He makes a face.

I smile. "I suppose when you become king you can do whatever you want and abolish the monarchy."

"It's probably not that easy." He sighs. "Something to think about."

"There are good things about it, though. Look at the work you're doing."

"Yes. And my parents and my sister are also very active in various charities. The royal image does help to raise money for them."

"Tell me more about your sister." He's mentioned her a few times in passing.

His face softens. "Catrin's okay."

I laugh. "Just okay?"

"I can't get too fulsome." He shrugs. "She's my annoying big sister. She constantly gave me a hard time about becoming king. She was quite convinced that she should be queen instead."

"It doesn't work that way, I guess."

"No. Succession is determined by descent and sex. My first-born male will succeed to the throne before her."

"That doesn't seem right in this day and age."

"I agree."

"Is she married?"

"Yes. She married about two years ago. To Simon. They are the perfect couple. Attractive, intelligent, both with busy careers, and sickeningly in love with each other."

"That's wonderful."

"It really is. She was always the good girl to my bad boy."

"With my sister, it was the opposite. I was the good girl and she was the naughty one. But she was so much fun." I sigh wistfully.

"I'm sorry you lost her so young." His fingers rub over my hand.

"I am too. So, appreciate that you *have* a sister."

"Right."

"What does she do? Her career, I mean."

"She's a financial analyst with Dunn and Phelps. They're a big financial consultancy firm."

"Wow."

"She's very bright."

"I'm sure. Do they have children?"

"No, not yet. Our parents harass her constantly, now she's married. They want grandchildren."

"They don't harass you?"

"They know better." He grins. "Since there's no wife, they know it's futile. Also..." He hesitates. "I don't know if you've heard rumors about me, but I'm bisexual."

Whoa. "I didn't know that."

"I've had relationships with men in the past. Does that bother you?"

"No. But what does that mean for your future. Do you have to marry someone...appropriate?"

One corner of his mouth hooks up. "Define appropriate." He shrugs. "I don't have to marry a virgin. Or a member of the nobility. But someone who takes on that job will have to be prepared for it."

"The job of your wife. Or partner."

"Yes."

"That sounds very...cold."

"It does. But it's reality."

Ugh. I don't want to think about Griff's wife. He'll be going back to Eria soon and I'll be staying here and reading news about his queen in the tabloids. I should never have started down this conversational path.

"So! You said you wanted to go to a baseball game. We should go to one soon before the season is over. Well, I guess there could be playoffs. I'm not sure how the Cubs are doing. Eek. I'm a terrible Cubs fan."

He grins. "Let's do that, yeah. I'll get tickets."

"Okay. That'll be fun."

"And what about hockey?"

I grab my phone. "Let me check the Aces schedule." I bring it up. "Okay, the first regular season game isn't until October fourth." I look up. "How much longer will you be here?"

"I don't know." His gaze moves over my face in a way that heats my insides. "Things aren't moving as quickly as I'd hoped, so I may end up staying longer."

"Oh." I try not to break into a smile and jump up and down. "Maybe we *will* be able to go to a game, then."

"I'll check into that too."

"I guess you'll have 'your people' do it for you."

"Yeah." He leans over to kiss my nose. "Are you impressed?"

"Phhht."

He kisses my cheek and nuzzles my hair. "Damn."

"I don't think you really care about impressing people." My eyes are drifting closed as his mouth brushes over my jaw.

"Live life to express, not to impress." He sucks gently on the side of my neck and my head falls back and to the side, heat flowing through me.

"That's your motto?"

"Unofficial family motto. Work for a cause, not for applause."

I smile slowly. "I like it."

His mouth hovers near mine. "However, I do admit to craving your approval."

"I approve." I meet his gaze with heavy-lidded eyes and curl my hands over his shoulders. "I very much approve."

"Good." And he kisses me.

God, I love his kisses. I love his mouth on mine, so firm and warm, tender and claiming. I love giving myself up to his kisses, opening to him, letting him know how much I want them. How much I want him.

I caress the side of his neck, then the back of his neck with my fingertips while his tongue plays with mine. Heat grows and intensifies, and his hands slide over me. We've kissed and made out a bit in the back of his car, but this is the first time we've been alone like this...

He pulls me onto his lap and slides his hands up under my top, gliding over my bare skin, and every nerve ending stands up and cries for more. Pleasure vibrates through me, my insides fluttering and twisting.

This is my first time to more fully explore his body, too, and I'm eager to feel the planes of his chest and abdomen, the bulge of his biceps, without clothes between us. I mimic his moves, finding bare skin beneath his button-down shirt that isn't tucked into his jeans. My fingertips search out ridges of muscle alongside his spine, the corrugation of his ribs, the rise of one pectoral.

He groans into my mouth and fists his hand in my hair, tugging my head away from him. We stare into each other's eyes. His are dark. His lips are parted and wet, his chest moving with his fast breathing. "God, I want you, Chelsea."

My heart leaps. "I want you, too."

CHAPTER
TEN

Chelsea

"My bedroom is upstairs." Griff kisses my ear. "Shall we...?"

My heart, already racing, contracts sharply, and my stomach tightens. "O-okay."

He draws back and peers at me. "Are you okay, love?"

"I'm..." *Freaking out. I'm freaking out.* "Fine."

He cups my face in both hands. "No. You're not. You've done this before...yes?"

"Yes!" I gulp in air. "I'm just..." I close my eyes. "You're a prince."

He lets out a low laugh, his thumb rubbing over my bottom lip. "I'm just a man, Chelsea. A man who wants you. You're beautiful and sexy and so much fun to be with."

I take another deep breath. "I feel the same. I don't know why I'm suddenly terrified."

"It's okay." He kisses my forehead, letting his lips rest there for a moment. "Breathe. It's okay. We don't have to do anything you don't want to do."

"I do want it. God." I'm so embarrassed. Heat suffuses my chest and my face.

"We'll wait. When you're ready. When it's right."

I packed a damn toothbrush. I wanted this. What is wrong with me? My hands are shaking and now I feel like crying. "I'm sorry."

"It's okay," he repeats. He pulls me into his arms, tucking my head beneath his chin, and slowly rubs up and down my back.

"You're so nice," I mumble.

He snorts. "People don't usually say that about me."

"You are. People don't know you...like this."

"Just you, love." He pauses. "How about we watch a movie?"

"Okay." I'm disappointed and relieved. And guilty. I got him all wound up and then backed off. That's not fair. But he's not angry. Or if he is, he's hiding it well. I think I've just fallen a little in love with him. Or a little *more* in love with him.

I can't fall in love with this man. He's a prince. He's leaving. He's going back to his country to become king one day. This is insane.

I need to focus on my breathing again as Griff plays with the remote to find a movie for us to watch. I smile when he finds *The Hunter* with Steve McQueen.

"Let's watch this, shall we?"

"Yes."

He keeps me close in his arms as we watch the movie, an action flick about a bounty hunter who's being threatened by a criminal he put away. I try to focus on it and not my unsettled feelings—regret and frustration and fear that after this Griff will never want to see me again.

If that's the case, though, I'm better off. I enjoy spending time with him, and I'm physically attracted to him, but I'm not here just for sex. If that's all he wants, he can easily find someone else.

I wouldn't blame him if that's what he wants. He's certainly not looking for anything long term when he's here for such a short time.

And I need to remember that.

~

Griff takes me home after the movie. On the way, he says, "I have to go to a charity function next week."

"Oh?"

"Mmm. It's at the Field Museum. Raising money for AIDS and HIV-related research."

"That sounds nice."

"Would you like to come with me? As my date?"

My entire body seizes with disbelief. I stare at him in the dark. "Really?"

"Really. I'd love to have you with me. But...you need to be aware of what that will mean for you."

I nod slowly. We'd be in public.

"There will be paparazzi there. They'll take pictures. They'll ask a million questions. The whole world will see it."

"You're not *that* famous."

He laughs. "Perhaps not. But you'll likely have to answer questions from friends. Your father." He pauses.

"Yes." I can't say the idea of being the center of attention appeals to me, but...I want to go. I want to go with Griff and be out in the open and have fun without worrying someone will see us. I want to be honest with everyone in my life. "I'd like to go with you."

"Wonderful." He smiles. "It's Saturday night."

"Okay." I smile back at him. He does want to see me again. Not only that, he wants everyone else to see me with him. My heart grows bigger in my chest.

He walks me into the lobby of my building, something he hasn't done before in case we're seen. I guess it doesn't matter as much now. At the elevator we share a long, heated good-night kiss that again makes me regret not letting Griff take me up to his bedroom.

"Good-night, beautiful. We'll talk during the week."

I nod and push the elevator button. The car is waiting so I step in and watch him walk across the lobby as the doors close.

Wow. This is crazy. I've been warning myself all evening about getting too involved with him, and now we're taking this step. Am I doing the right thing?

I'm exhausted. It's been an emotional few hours. I just want to go to sleep and turn everything off for a while.

Monday morning, I knock on Arlene's office door with my coffee in hand. Talking to Griff about the increased responsibilities she's asked me to take on gave me confidence.

"Good morning." She smiles. "How was your weekend?"

If you only knew. "It was fun." I smile too. "I thought about what you mentioned last week about taking over the school curriculum project. And I'd love to do that."

"Excellent! I have confidence in your abilities, and of course we're all here to help. Can we talk more this afternoon?"

"Of course. My afternoon is wide open."

We arrange for me to come back at two, and I return to my cubicle with a sense of lightness in my chest and an eagerness to get to work. I dive into what's already been done and start making lists of what else needs to happen. Around ten o'clock my cell phone buzzes. I grab it to see a text from Ford. *Coffee?*

I text him back. *Yes, please!*

I grab my purse and head out, checking my phone for any other messages. And yes, there's one from Griff.

Good morning, beautiful. Miss you.

Riding the elevator down, I smile. *Miss you too.*

I step out into the morning air. The sky is blue but tall buildings shade the street as I walk to the nearby Starbucks.

Ford's already there with my flat white, sitting at a table. He looks up from his phone as I approach and slide into the chair. "Hey."

"Good morning!"

"Didn't see you much this weekend."

"You were working."

"Yeah." He rubs his forehead. He looks tired. "We go to court this week. And there are some other things happening with the FBI."

"So mysterious." I tilt my head and pick up my coffee, knowing not to ask questions. "You work too hard."

He rolls his eyes. "Sometimes, yeah."

"I have some good news."

His eyes brighten. "Yeah?"

I tell him about the project Arlene wants me to manage on my own.

"Congratulations! That's fantastic!" He beams at me. "Good for you, Chelsea."

"Thanks. I'm nervous about it, but I can do it."

"Of course you can. You'll be running that organization one day."

"Haha. I doubt that." But Ford's words make me happy. "I already jumped into some planning, and Arlene and I are meeting later this afternoon to go over things."

"There's a Cubs game this weekend," Ford says. "We should go."

"Oh." I nibble my bottom lip. Griff wants to go to a game. "When is it?"

"Saturday."

I hesitate. "I can't. I'm going out Saturday night to a charity gala."

He rolls his eyes. "Another black tie bash?"

"Yes." I smile. Should I tell him about Griff? He's going to find out after that. I can't bring myself to do it. "Not your kind of fun."

"Nope. Ah well. There are more baseball games. The Cubs are in the playoffs."

"Oh, that's good." I wrinkle my nose. "I don't even know that stuff." I pause. "How about a bike ride tonight?"

"Ugh. I'll see. I may be at the office late getting ready for the trial."

"Okay. Let me know."

Ford ends up so busy that week I hardly see him. I hear him come home late a couple of nights when I'm already in bed, and he doesn't even have time for coffee. I worry about him when things get this intense. It's not healthy. But he loves what he does.

I also don't see Griff all week. He's also busy. But that's okay. I'm engrossed with my own work, wanting to succeed with this campaign, and I also have an appointment for a facial, mani, and pedi to prepare for the gala on Saturday, as well as dress shopping at Saks.

My stomach flutters with nerves every time I think about that. On Friday, I call Dad. "Hey, how are you?" I greet him.

"I'm fine. How are you, sweet? "

"Good! I have lots of news for you."

"Good news or bad news?"

"Good!" First I tell him about my work. Then I say, "And the other thing is…tomorrow night I'm going to the HIV/AIDs research fundraiser."

"That's nice."

"I'm going with Prince Griffin."

Silence fills my ear. "Prince Griffin," he repeats. "We met him that night…"

"Yes. I've…seen him a few times since then."

"*Now* you tell me?" His voice is sharp.

"Dad, there's a reason for that. He's trying to keep a low profile while he's here and stay out of the news."

More silence.

"So, we've kept it quiet. But tomorrow night will be very public, so I wanted to tell you before then."

"I see," he clips.

"There's nothing to be worried about," I assure him. "He's a gentleman and a nice man."

"He's a prince. A playboy prince."

"He has been, yes. He's honest about that."

"You're going to get eaten up by the press."

I wince. "I don't know how it's going to go, but I'm aware that there'll be attention on us. I can handle it." *I hope.* "It's just a date."

"Jesus, Chelsea, you move out on your own and this is what happens."

I roll my eyes. "Dad. Please. It's a date. I'm not eloping to Vegas."

"Good god!"

"Calm down. Everything will be fine."

"I don't think you understand what you're getting yourself into."

I sigh. "Maybe not. But I like Griff and I'm going to the gala with him. And I'll deal with the consequences. I'm an adult. That's what adults do."

"Chelsea." I hear his exhalation. "Okay. Fine. I'm here if you need me."

"I know that, Dad. Always." I soften my tone. "I love you."

"Love you, too, honey."

Okay, I've told Dad. I'll deal with everyone else after the fact.

Griff is picking me up on Saturday. Ford is going for a bike ride with some friends around that time, so I tell Griff to come up to the condo when he gets here. I drink a glass of wine as I get ready, doing my makeup and hair, and dressing in my new gown.

My savings account took a punch with this dress, but I love it. It took a long time to find the right thing. I fell in love with a beautiful ivory gown, but it looked too much like a wedding dress. Black felt a little too safe, but a bright fuchsia seemed...flashy.

This one is a soft blush pink, a simple strapless column with a big bow on the bodice. I'm adjusting the bow in front of the mirror when Griff arrives.

I rush to the door to let him in, still in bare feet.

"Wow," he breathes, studying me. You look amazing."

"Thank you!" I turn to show off my dress with a playful smile, my insides feeling like I swallowed a flock of small birds. "I'm almost ready."

"Wait." He reaches out and pulls me closer, smiling down at me. "You don't have lipstick on yet. Let me kiss you now so I don't mess you up."

My eyelids grow heavy and I tip my head for Griff's kiss. "Mmm. You're so thoughtful. You can mess me up later."

He draws back and meets my eyes. "Yeah?"

I bite my lip, looking up at him through my eyelashes. "Yeah. I wanted to...the other night."

"Wanted to what?" His eyes flash a wicked gleam.

My cheeks warm. "I wanted to get messed up." I run a palm over his shirt. He looks amazing in a tuxedo. "I just...got scared."

"I don't want to scare you. Ever." He leans his forehead against mine. "I mean that, Chelsea."

"I know. And thank you. Thank you for being patient."

He kisses me again, slowly and thoroughly. I'm breathing fast when he releases me. "Okay. Put your lipstick on. But I'm not promising I won't kiss it off you at some point during the evening."

My belly flips as I hurry back to my bedroom. I apply soft pink lipstick and top it with a swipe of gloss, then slip my feet into pale pink stilettos.

The door to the condo opens.

I frown. "Where are you going?" I call. "I'm ready."

The door doesn't close. What is he doing? I pick up the wrap and my small clutch purse from my bed and dash out to the living room.

Ford is here. Standing in the open door, dressed in shorts and a tight T-shirt, still wearing his bike helmet. He's staring at Griff and he looks like he's gazing at an apparition—his mouth open, his eyes wide, his face a strange pallid color.

Griff is sitting on one of the stools at the counter. I turn to him just as he slowly stands and, holy shit, he looks as stunned as Ford. He's staring too, their gazes locked across the room. The air around us has gone electric, buzzing with tension, crackling with heat.

I open my mouth to speak, to tell Ford what's going on, to introduce them. But nothing comes out. Because as I look back and forth between the two of them...I know.

They already know each other.

CHAPTER

ELEVEN

10 years earlier
Ford

I'm sitting outside smoking, inside the confines of Camp Durham. The Afghan sun beats down on me, the air hot and dry.

I look up as someone strolls out of the shower block, and my gaze locks onto him. The heat and the dust and the rest of the camp fade away as the sun gleams off his light brown hair, still damp. He runs a hand through it and I can almost feel the thick, silky smoothness on my own fingers.

A smile creases his cheeks. His bone structure is elegantly sculpted, high cheekbones and square jaw lit by the sun, his lips almost pretty in a very masculine face.

For a moment, I sit transfixed, watching him, feeling like something inexplicably good has just happened in this brutally bad place.

As if he feels me staring at him, he salutes me as he walks past, his smile hinting at a smirk, his eyes dancing with humor. He whistles as he walks toward the barracks.

I watch him stride away with an easy, long-legged gait that's confident and careless. His wide shoulders and biceps stretch his T-shirt, his camo pants sitting low on lean hips.

He's not part of our platoon, but Camp Durham is home to not only the United States Army, but also Danish Defense and a squadron of soldiers from Eria who arrived yesterday, and I recognize the beige T-shirt as part of the Erian gear.

I've been the leader of Pathfinder Platoon for about eight months now since joining the 10th Mountain Division's 2nd Battalion, 87th Infantry Regiment. Our mission on our seven-month tour is to dislodge the Taliban from villages in Helmand Province and help the Afghanistan government with security and services.

I'm a young platoon leader, only twenty-four years old. I've learned a lot, but I've also learned how much I don't know. As a leader responsible for every American in the platoon, plus Abdul our interpreter (terp) I have to appear confident at all times. But the truth is, that's the last thing I feel a lot of the time.

I've gotten to know my men and their families. Their wives and parents and girlfriends trust me with the safety of their loved ones. I envy my men that they have family back home worrying about them, but sometimes I think it makes things easier for me, knowing that if I step on an IED and blow myself up tomorrow, nobody will care.

Okay, that's not true. I've made friends since joining the army, sure. In fact, *this* is my family now.

I stub out my cigarette and push up to stand. There's work to do. Now in our second month of deployment, we're into a routine—patrolling, cleaning our weapons, reading intelligence briefs. We write letters to friends and family, chow time breaking up the days. I have access to the computer in the headquarters shack, so I make sure to email my solders' families and let them know how they're doing. We've destroyed a fuck ton of improvised explosive devices but have yet to see close combat.

In the chow hall, I grab a tray and load up with food. Here in

Camp Durham we live in relative luxury compared to some of the bases. I sit at a long table with some of the other officers, and when I look up, I see him again, sitting at my table just down and across from me.

He's listening to someone else talk. He now has his ballistic sunglasses perched on top of his head, his skin a smooth, burnished dark gold, his eyes creased up with laughter. He forks up beef stew and nods as he chews.

"Hey, Sully, you met these guys?" Tommy nods at the Erian soldiers at the table.

We've all got nicknames and predictably mine is Sully, given my surname, Sullivan.

I look at the other solders as Tom names them—Luke, Philip, Marlin, then the guy I saw earlier, Griff. My eyes meet Griff's and I give him an unsmiling chin lift, while my groin tightens.

Turns out Griff and Tommy met in the States at Naval Air Facility El Centro in California. Griff's a co-pilot and gunner for an Apache helicopter, the Erian army's most sophisticated attack helicopter. The Erian Apaches fly missions supporting troops fighting the Taliban, and accompany U.S. Black Hawk medical helicopters during casualty evacuations.

I focus on my food while the others talk shit.

"You know, you can actually get a disease from jerking off too much," Ryan says.

My head snaps up and I lift an eyebrow as I eye him across the table. "No way. You can't catch diseases from your own hand, man."

"Not that kind of disease. It's called Peyronie's disease. It's scar tissue inside the penis. It causes curved, painful erections."

"Nothin' wrong with a curved penis," Jemarr mutters.

I grin.

"Banana dick," Tommy says.

"Boomer wang," Luke adds to more laughter.

"Also known as beater's curve," Ryan says. "That's what it is."

"The amount of jerkin' off people do around here, we're *all* gonna get it," Jemarr says.

"It's not just a curved penis, it's a *painful* curve," Ryan says. "It can stop you from have sex. Or getting a boner."

"Let this be a lesson to you men," Griff says, and his accent, all classy and superior, makes my stomach swoop. "Cut back on the wanking." He gives a cocky wink that tells everyone he has no intention of cutting back.

"Not gonna happen."

"What else are we supposed to do out here?"

This is a solid question.

My eyes meet Griff's again and sparks flicker in my chest.

"Flogging the log is healthy," Philip says, his accent making the expression hilarious, and everyone cracks up again. "Seriously, mates. We must take care of ourselves."

No argument from me. I miss sex. So goddamn much.

I've never had a long-term relationship. Given my life growing up, that was never a priority, even though I'd discovered sex at an early age. I joined the army right out of high school, and while I've had a lot of hookups, army life isn't conducive to a relationship.

After dinner, we all go to the Erian barracks. They've got a nice setup with a huge flag on the wall and a big screen TV and PlayStation. We get into an animated FIFA soccer game. The Erian football team, as they call it, won the FIFA World Championship last year, so they're ragging on us about our shitty U.S. soccer team.

Griff's an enthusiastic player, very physical, jumping up and throwing his arms in the air, uttering curses that make the other guys laugh. We end up side by side, controllers in hand, playing against each other. Soccer's not my sport, but I'm competitive, so I get into it along with the others. I'm aware of Griff's body next to mine, almost touching, but I focus on the game, eyes narrowed, pumping a fist in the air when I score a goal against Griff's team. He and his mates let out a groan of disgust.

"So that's how it's going to be," he murmurs, shooting me a sideways glance and refocusing on the game with increased intensity.

Okay, we're *both* competitive. Things start to get heated as we attempt to kick the shit out of each other. Figuratively, as in, on the screen. In the end, I win. He drops the controller and stands, extending a hand to me. I take it to shake it in a sportsmanlike gesture, and when his fingers close around mine in a bro handshake, heat washes down through me.

"Good game," he says easily, his grip pulling me closer.

I feel off balance. Stupid for reacting like this when he's so casual. But his fingers drag over mine when we release our hands... and with a flicker in his eye I know he feels it too.

Shit.

"You'd never know that dude's a prince," Tommy says to me on our way back to our barracks. "Seems pretty down to earth."

I frown. "Prince? Who's a prince?"

"Griff. Prince Griffin. Next in line to the throne in Eria."

"Shut the fuck up."

"No lie. You didn't know that?"

"What the fuck do I know about Eria?" It's a small European country with a sizeable military presence, but I'm not one to pay attention to royalty and gossip about them.

"You must have heard of him. He got into trouble back in the States last year. And in Europe, I think. Got caught by photographers coming out of a kinky sex club in Berlin. And he was in Florida when they took photos of him having a threesome outside on the deck of a beachside house. It caused quite the uproar for the king."

"The king. His father?"

"Grandfather. Jesus, where have you been? Living under a rock?"

I snort. "Didn't know you were a royal watcher."

"I'm not, but my wife is."

"Ah."

"Anyway, he seems like a normal dude."

"What is he doing here, if he's royalty? Jesus. He could be killed."

"Yeah. Not sure what the deal is."

In my room, stretched out in my small bed, I close my eyes. A fucking prince? What the hell? Why is here? Does he think this is some kind of game?

Yeah, I've vaguely heard of Prince Griffin of Eria. A playboy socialite who does nothing but travel the world partying. Having met him, I can see it—the waywardness in his eyes, the swagger in his step, the slight smugness in the curve of his pretty mouth.

Whatever. He better not be putting any of us in danger with his desire to mix with the commoners or whatever the hell he's playing at.

I meet up with the prince again the next night at The Eagle, which is called a bar, where we watch news from the UK on the big screen TV and drink beer.

"Would you rather lose your arms or lose your legs?" Ryan asks.

"Jesus," Tommy says.

Ryan shrugs. "It's a fair question."

"I'd rather lose my legs," Luke says. "I'm good with my hands."

Everyone guffaws. Black humor. Gotta love it.

They ghoulishly debate the question for a while. Then Tommy changes the subject. "What's the first thing you want to eat when you get back?"

"Prime rib," I answer immediately.

"I want a cheeseburger," Ryan replies. "The biggest, nastiest cheeseburger I can find. Loaded with everything."

"Christ, don't. You're killing me," Jemarr groans. "Do you assholes always have to talk about food?"

"Yes," Ryan answers. "I'm wasting away here in the goddamn desert eating MREs."

Yep. We've all lost weight.

We continue to bullshit, talking about the things we'll do when we get home, but home is a long time away. I look at Griff. "What about you?"

He grimaces. "When I get home, I won't have much choice about what to do."

His reply takes me aback. "I'd think you can do whatever the hell you want to do. You're a prince."

"Ah." He shakes his head, his lips curved. "That's where you're wrong. The royal family has duties. Obligations."

"Right." Obviously, I have no clue about that.

A few days later, Griff and I find ourselves playing cards. We're not alone, but we're far away enough from the other guys that we can talk.

"You sounded like you won't be all that happy to go home," I comment.

He grimaces. "I'm not eager to return to that life. I love what I'm doing here."

"I can't imagine you'd rather be here in the desert than living in a palace."

He laughs. "You would think. But this is important to me." He hesitates. "Here, at least I can be myself."

"You can't be yourself at home?"

"At home, my father's always reminding me how to behave. Sometimes I feel like I'm three different people—Lieutenant Marlow.

Family me, royal me. And the me I can be when I'm with my mates having fun. I've let the family down a few times."

"The threesome in Florida."

"Ha. You heard about that."

I grin. "Yeah."

"I loathed the restrictions on me, the expectations that were now loaded onto me. I acted out. A lot."

He tells me how he likes to ski and play polo, neither which are things I've ever done. I feel like a peasant, compared to his life. But he's not snobby.

"I wanted to play hockey," I tell him. "I loved it, but life got so messed up there was no time or money for it."

"I admire anyone who can do that," Griff says. "It's like polo but on ice with tiny steel blades instead of a horse."

I laugh. "I guess."

"What are *you* going to do when you go home?"

I pick up my cards. "I've been thinking about more college."

Griff nods. "Good on you. To do what?"

I stare into the distance. "I'm not sure yet. But I know I want to do something where I can actually see what I accomplish. Putting criminals behind bars."

"Law enforcement?"

I frown. "No. Maybe law school."

"Jesus. I fucking hate lawyers."

I laugh. "Okay. What about you? What are you going to do until you become king?"

Another surreal moment.

"Fuck if I know." He shuffles the deck. "Hopefully something fun."

"Seriously. You're going to go back to jet setting around the world?"

"No." He meets my eyes. "I'm bullshitting. I've no desire to do that anymore. After this?" He waves a hand. "I guess I want to do something that makes a difference, too. I'll figure it out. At least here, I'm fighting for something."

I snort. "The question is, what?"

"We're fighting against terrorism." But Griff's lips twist.

"Yeah. I know everyone felt that threat, that fear. Everyone wanted to go to war and defeat the fucking Taliban. I did too. I thought I was fighting evil. I thought I was fighting for justice. But now...I'm not so sure." I shake my head.

"I get it. I do. But there must have been moments when you felt you've done good."

"Sure. Some. I feel I've done good when I've protected people who need it. I like helping people who are weaker. I hate it when they get killed." I pause. "Sorry. I hate to sound defeatist. I'm here to do a job, and I'll do it."

"You're not a soldier," he says quietly. "You don't want to just blindly follow. You're a warrior. You want to make things right."

I meet his eyes. He's not wrong. But his ability to read me unsettles me. "And yet we're sitting here playing fucking cards."

"Oh come on. Things don't have to be so serious all the time." Griff grins. "Having a laugh once in a while won't stop you on your mission. Come on. My mates and I are going to teach you Americans how to play rugby."

"Rugby?" I know fuck all about rugby.

"Rugby."

Griff leads the way, rounding up a bunch of guys and, miraculously, a rugby ball, and we head outside into the hot, dusty air.

"Okay," Griff calls. "Obviously each team is trying to gain the most points. Games are eighty minutes—"

A bunch of us groan.

He flashes that charming grin. "But we won't play that long." He starts going through rules. "The ball can never be passed forward, only backwards or perpendicular."

"That makes no fucking sense at all," I mutter.

He sends me a wicked glance. "But while you cannot throw a ball forward, you can kick it forward at any time."

I roll my eyes. "You can throw *and* kick the ball?"

"Right." A team can only advance by passing or kicking the ball. Any team can win the ball at any time, but it's usually done by the forward pack."

"This is bullshit," I say. "You're just making stuff up."

He pretends to be offended. "What? You doubt my integrity? Okay, you score tries by carrying the ball into the opponent's try-zone. A try is worth five points." He runs down the yard. "This is the try zone."

We start playing but honestly all of us are completely lost about how it's supposed to go. Somehow Ryan gets the ball and passes it to me. I start running and out of nowhere, Griff leaps and tackles me, taking me hard to the dirt. I grunt, stunned.

We lie on the ground, his arms wrapped around me, his face nearly in my junk. He grins devilishly up at me. "This would be better if you were wearing tight shorts."

What the fuck? I stare at him, more dazed by his words than the tackle.

The other guys come running and we scramble up. I don't bother trying to dust myself off. I meet Griff's eyes and grin. Okay, he's sparked my competitive instincts. I still don't know what I'm doing, but I'm going to have fun taking him down.

Maybe life doesn't have to be all serious, all the time.

We're on the road again for a patrol behind Arandar Ridge. Our prophet section has been listening to the enemy's radio chatter and based on what they've been hearing, something's afoot.

Cory Lansing, my driver and radio specialist, steers our Humvee, one of five, down the dirt road then through a deserted village. On the other side of town, we pick up speed, headed toward the series of ridges and hills. Soon we're sweating under the sun. We drink water and Gatorade, and eat beef jerky and potato chips, but in this burning hellscape you can't replenish all the fluids we're losing. I have a faint headache, and dust coats my face and hands.

I'm just opening a bottle of water when a tingle starts down my spine. I pause, scanning the landscape. Then Tommy's Humvee in front of us explodes. Orange flame flashes, and dirt and smoke belch from beneath the vehicle.

Cory hits the brakes, throwing us forward.

"Tommy!" I stare in horror.

Another explosion detonates behind us, shaking the ground, followed by the rapid pops of machine gun fire. Cory grips the steering wheel.

This is accurate, aimed fire. They're shooting at us. Fuck!

I reach for my radio handset. "This is Mountaineer Three Seven."

I hear Ryan's voice. "Three Seven, this is Three Eight. We gotta get outa this kill zone!" There's garbled static, then "We're getting fucked up back here!"

My mouth is as dry as the desert, my heart in my throat.

We're in a kill zone bordered on our right by a drop off into a ravine, on our left by the ridge. I see muzzle flashes in the trees on the hill that separates us from the base. The enemy orchestrated a fucking ambush.

We need artillery. We need aircraft. We can't drive out of this.

Another explosion bursts near Tommy's Humvee and a round strikes out windshield, the ballistic glass turning into a spiderweb of cracks. I switch the radio to my platoon net. "All elements, this is three seven. We're blocked. We're going to have to fight this out."

Up on the hill, I spot more muzzles flashes. Goddammit, they're on both sides of us!

Tommy's voice comes over the radio. He's alive, thank fuck. Okay. *Okay.* This clears my head a bit. I need to think.

I'm the leader. I need to lead. I need to do this. In combat, men measure up. Or they don't. One of our captains lost his men the time he froze and couldn't make a decision. That can't happen.

I grab the door handle and step out of the Humvee.

CHAPTER
TWELVE

Ford

"Sir, what the hell are you doing?" Cory yells.

I stand under the brilliant sun, surveying the scene. An RPG strikes the rim of the ravine and I instinctively duck beneath the wave of heat that rolls over me. A bullet ricochets off the Humvee. I eye Tommy's rig, so close and yet so far. What if he's injured? What the hell will I tell his wife?

I have to get him.

Hunching down, I sprint toward him, carrying my rifle by its scope. Bullets spray dirt around me. My lungs are burning as I race uphill, my ACUs drenched with sweat. I slam my hand against the door of the Humvee and yell, "Let's go!"

I keep running, praying that Tommy will follow. If he didn't... would I go back and get him? Jesus Christ. My heart's ready to explode out of my chest as I reach the cover of a row of conifers. I look behind me to see Tommy running toward me. Relief nearly takes me out at the knees.

Not only is he with me, the rest of the Pathfinder platoon is as well—Ryan, Jamarr, Hux—gunners and drivers staying in the vehicles.

Energy rushes through my veins. Jesus fucking Christ. I suck more air into my lungs. As Jamarr arrives, I say, "Use your 203 and knock out those positions over there." I gesture at the ridge. Without a word, Jamarr jogs to the side of the road and hunkers down.

We organize into a perimeter and the men start shooting. Jamarr finds a target and shouts with glee. "Take that, motherfuckers!"

I run back down the hill, the weight of my equipment almost sending me ass over elbows. I reach the Humvee where Cory is waiting and grab the radio again, letting them know what's happening and where exactly we are.

Then I hear it. The sound of choppers. I pause and tip my head back, listening, It grows closer, the whomp whomp of the blades like the sweetest symphony.

The Apaches rise above the ridge and float toward us. They start firing at the enemy.

Captain Alcott's voice tells me, "We picked up an enemy intercept. They're withdrawing to the west."

"Copy that."

For hours we work, fighting the enemy, the gunfire of the Apaches taking out shooters and providing us cover. As dusk nears, the firing finally dies down and the artillery barrage lifts. The Apaches follow the enemy as they withdraw and we clear the enemy's fighting positions, finding spent shell castings, empty water bottles and blood-crusted dirt. We find the spot on the hill where the RPG team had left behind their reloads and several launchers, which we bring back with us.

Then we drive back to the base. Amazingly, all our Humvees still function, but we can't continue the patrol we set out on only that morning.

At the base, we're greeted with a loud, jubilant celebration—bear hugs, back slaps, and high fives.

When the Apaches return to the base, the Erian soldiers meet with the same reception. Griff strolls in his graceful, long-legged gait across the dirt toward us and our eyes meet.

I walk toward him and grip his hand. "Thanks, man."

His hand is warm and strong and a lot cleaner than mine, but he holds on anyway. "You had that under control."

We lift our chins in mutual respect.

I walk over to the tactical operations center to greet First Sergeant Deseo. Captain Alcott appears, and I spend the next half hour giving him a full report of everything that happened. When we're done, I say, "I am fucking starving. Breakfast was a long time ago."

"I kept the cooks to make sure you guys got something to eat when you got back," Deseo says.

"Appreciate that."

When I walk into the chow hall, I see my platoon already seated and eating. Silence falls. I stop and eye them. Tommy stands and walks toward me, his face grim. "Sir."

I arch an eyebrow, not sure what's going on.

"You did a great fucking job out there today."

A smile breaks across my face and a laugh bursts out of me as the other men applaud. Pride swells in my chest as I walk over to the squad leaders' table. Griff is already sitting there, and once again our eyes meet, the corners of his crinkled with warmth, humor, and...admiration?

The mood is triumphant. I feel almost euphoric. But later in my bed, I remember...I saw a man get blown up today. I remember the shreds of flesh and bone. The scent of blood and smoke. We were victorious. What more could I want?

I want to be a warrior. I did what I had to do. The adrenaline rush of survival and triumph bonded us. But it also changed me. Into what, I don't know.

Sleepless, I climb out of bed and pull on pants and boots. I wander out into the dark Afghan night. I light a cigarette and stroll.

A shadowy form walks toward me. I can't see the face, but I recognize the shape and the way he moves. Griff.

"Lieutenant," he says in that smooth accented voice. "What are you doing up?"

I lean against a wall and take a drag of my smoke. "I don't know."

He turns his back to the wall and leans, too. "The adrenaline rush is hard to come down from."

"Yeah. I guess that's it."

"You did a brilliant job out there today."

I don't answer. Then I say, "So did you."

Watching those helicopters dip in and out of the valley, unleashing their firepower, being shot at themselves, had been a welcome and awesome sight.

"Thanks, mate." He reaches out, plucks the cigarette from my fingers, and lifts it to his mouth. I watch him close those lips around the tip and pull, and something tightens low inside me. "This was your first combat as platoon leader?"

"Yeah." I scrub a hand over my face. A combat leader did not show weakness. Today, I had to set an example for my men. I had to be confident and strong. But here, in the dark, I admit, "I was scared shitless."

He lets out a low laugh. "We all are."

"I don't know. Some of those guys seemed to be enjoying themselves."

"We're all human. Everyone's afraid of dying. We just hide it."

I drop the cigarette butt to the ground and crush it with my boot. "Yeah."

"That's what you train for. So your training takes over. But we need fear."

"Christ."

"Seriously. It alerts us to danger. Gives us that adrenaline flood that we need." He pauses. "The problem is when the fear doesn't go away even when the threat does. If your brain doesn't go back to normal." His gaze grows distant.

"You've experienced it."

"I've seen it in some of my mates." He doesn't meet my eyes. "It's rough."

I've changed my opinion of Griff. I thought he was playing at being a soldier, using his position to get here and shoot guns. We've been spending more and more time together, talking about things I don't talk to anyone else about. And I think he's the same, sharing stuff about his life no one else knows.

After today, I see he's a courageous, highly trained professional. Maybe we would have made it out of that ambush without him and the other helicopter pilots. But I'm glad they were there.

"I heard what you did out there," he says. "Running to get Tommy. Taking control."

I swallow, heat spreading through my chest. "It's my job." I pause. "Have you read Gates of Fire?"

"No."

"It's historical fiction by Steven Pressfield. About the Battle of Thermopylae." I sense Griff's surprise at my literary knowledge. "A lot of it is about Spartan society, especially the military training program Spartan boys had to complete to become citizens of Sparta. There's a quote in it... 'A king does not require service of those he leads, but provides it to them. He serves them, not they him.'" I pause and meet Griff's eyes. "I serve my men."

He stares at me for a stretched-out moment. "You are bloody amazing," he says hoarsely.

The air around us is thick, electric. He moves closer. He showered and I can smell the sharp scent of soap. His face is smooth and sculpted by shadows. We're the same height and his face moves closer to mine...and a longing swells up inside me, sharp and raw, a craving for human contact, for pleasure and life and connection. It's not just that, though...it's Griff.

From the moment I set eyes on him, there was something about him that attracted me.

His nose brushes mine. I should move away. But instead I tip my head so our mouths are a breath apart.

Griff kisses me.

Fuck.

His mouth is hard, his tongue wet, rubbing against mine. Christ. I open to him instinctively, and Griff shifts closer, running his hand over my chest, my shoulder, my neck. He lifts his mouth off mine, tilts his head and dives in again, deeper, hotter. I grab his shoulders and yank him closer, our kisses going on and on, deep, sliding kisses, tongues licking, teeth nipping. A groan rumbles from Griff's chest and I feel it right in my groin.

We pull back and stare into each other's eyes in the darkness, his glittering, his mouth wet and shiny.

"Combat makes me horny," Griff whispers.

I can't resist. I can't. I let out a low sound of surrender.

Griff turns me and pushes my back against the wall, leaning into me. He sucks my tongue, bites my bottom lip, kisses across my stubbled jaw to my ear, then buries his face in my neck when I find his ass and grip it. We're both panting and straining against each other, hot and desperate.

Griff shoves a hand under my T-shirt, and his rough fingers on my skin send shivers cascading down my spine. My cock throbs and I push against Griff, feeling the outline of his stiff prick. I rub against him there and he groans into my mouth.

Rubbing over my pec, he finds my nipple and catches it in his fingers briefly. My entire body twitches hard against his. Heat rushes through me, excitement building, pounding in my veins. My dick aches.

"Yeah," Griff mutters. "Christ yeah. That feels good, Ford."

"Fuck." I pull back and close my eyes. My chest rises and falls as I struggle to breath. "I should go back in. Get some sleep."

"Come to my room."

My body flares to life, pulsing in time with my quickened heartbeat. White hot need jolts straight to my groin.

Silence swells around us as we stare at each other with focused intensity.

"I've never been with a man before."

"Why not?"

"Jesus." I swallow. "I never thought about it when I was younger."

"But you're thinking about it now."

He wasn't wrong. My entire body is pulsing and aching.

I like girls. I like sex. There was a girl in high school I really liked… but I couldn't bring her home. I couldn't have that kind of relationship. When I enlisted, I was living in a hyper-masculine environment and the talk was all about pussy, and I was fine with that. But then I started thinking about guys. Maybe it was the lack of sex when we were deployed.

"Yeah." I huff out a harsh laugh. "That sounds like any port in a storm, right?"

"I don't know. Maybe."

"It's insulting, though. Lowering your standards, fucking anything that moves, male or female…"

"It's not lowering your standards. It's expanding your horizons. It's called bisexuality."

That shuts me up for a good long moment. "Is that what you are?"

"Yeah." He lifts a shoulder. "I've always known it. Always been attracted to boys and girls. I've never acted on the boys much, though, because holy shit, if my grandfather found out the future King of Eria was queer, he'd die of apoplexy. I know I have to get married some day, and it's going to have to be to a woman if he's still alive."

His words feel like a fist driving into my gut. But it's crazy to let that bother me. It's not like we can have any kind of real relationship.

"You can't be gay in the U.S. Military."

"That's ridiculous. You can't change who you are because of laws."

I laugh. "I know, that's not what I'm saying. What I'm saying is, fucking a man is breaking the law. The rules of the Uniform Code of Military Justice outlaw any form of gay sex."

"Don't ask, don't tell."

"I know. You can do it, just don't get caught. It's a big risk though."

"Fuck that. The Erian Armed Forces actively recruit gay soldiers. They don't care."

"We're not there. Yet. I don't know if we ever will be. Too much homophobia. And as a leader, I have to enforce the rules. Any rule."

He gives me a long, silent look. "So that's a no?"

I stare back at him. A sense of inevitability throbs between us. I let out a low groan. "No. That's a yes."

CHAPTER
THIRTEEN

Ford

In Griff's room, we both know we have to be quiet. Griff silently strips off my T-shirt then unfastens my pants and lets them fall to the floor. I toe off my boots and kick away the pants. Then he pushes me down onto his bed. I watch him take off his own clothes, revealing his sculpted body in the shadows. His dick is long and thick, his gaze fastened on mine as he gives himself one slow stroke. The air is hot and vibrating around us.

He lowers himself onto the narrow bed next to me, lying on his side, propping himself on one elbow. His other hand rests on my belly. I curl my arm behind his neck and our mouths meet in a carnal, rapacious kiss. I have to swallow the noises that rise in my chest, the pleasure almost unbearably acute.

I grip Griff's shoulder, then loosen my grasp and slide my palm over smooth skin. His hand moves on me, too, caressing my abs, my chest, sliding around to my waist to pull my closer. Our mouths slide and bite and taste.

After long moments, unable to stop myself, I roll onto my side toward him, getting more aggressive. Griff's arm slides beneath me and his other hand comes to my face, holding me there as our kisses become rougher, frantic. His leg hooks over my hip and my thigh slides between his, our cocks rubbing together.

His mouth bruises mine, his tongue invades me, his kisses dark and brutal. Then he rolls me, flat onto my back, and he moves over me, straddling one of my thighs. He watches my face and I stare back in fascination at the dark, hungry expression on his, the utter beauty of his bone structure, the erotic curve of his wet mouth. Leaning down, he kisses my chest, dragging his tongue over the ridges of my abs, then his breath lands hot on my throbbing dick laying against my belly.

I clench my teeth. I want to say his name. I want to beg him for more. I want to cry out.

He parts my thighs and kneels between them and when he takes my dick in his hand I nearly weep. Christ. Jesus fucking Christ. He lifts it to his mouth, licks all over, then releases it to grip my hips as he teases the sensitive head with his tongue. He looks up at me, his eyes dark and liquid as he licks.

Hot sensation races up my spine, sizzles through my brain, then shoots down to the base of my spine.

He takes me deep, deep enough that his nose presses to my groin, and sharp need slams into my balls. He lets his mouth slide off, careful to do so quietly, then curls his hand around my slick shaft and pumps me up and down. Fuck...that feels so good.

He pulls off, licks the head again, then taps it against his flattened tongue. Electricity licks over every nerve ending in my body, tightening every muscle. After more long pulls of his mouth, he pushes my dick against my belly and slides his tongue over my balls.

He uses his tongue and teeth and lips to torture me, sucking my balls into his mouth, teasing me and licking me. He even uses his finger, slipping it into my ass. I stifle the gasp that rises to my lips, more sensation shooting up my spine. Then Griff takes my shaft into his mouth, right to his throat. My hips move instinctively, fucking his mouth, and a groan climbs my throat again.

Holy fuck. Holy holy fuck. Sensation pounds through me, relentless, scorching hot, my balls so tight at the root of my cock as Griff tongues them again. Pressure builds inside me.

His hand continues to jack me while he licks and sucks my balls. I'm gripping the pillow on either side of my head, every muscle taut, my jaw straining with the effort not to shout. He sucks my cock like he's starving for it, like he can't get enough, and fuck, that makes me insane.

Then he flips me over onto my belly. I squeeze my eyes shut, my hands in fists. I hear some soft rustling noises as he moves off the bed then back on. My body tingles with anticipation, my mind blank, sensations overloading me from behind, where I can't see, only feel, every nerve ending on alert and on fire.

Coolness hits my ass, then Griff's fingers smooth over it, between my cheeks and down over my hole. *Aw, fuck.* I press my mouth into the rough blanket, pushing my hips up intuitively. He shifts away from me, then he's back, the head of his cock sliding up and down, in the crack of my ass, over my perineum, then lingering on my entrance. I tighten up and he smooths a hand up my back. I think I hear the word "relax" float in a whisper.

Relax. Sure. Right. I'm dying. Burning. Blazing.

He pushes at my asshole with the blunt crown of his dick. Pushing, pushing...fuck...intruding...penetrating. My eyes sting and I quiver. It's uncomfortable, but it's not unfamiliar—I admit I've experimented when I jerk off. My body tenses, though.

He taps one butt cheek. *Relax.*

I bear down, and fuck me, he slides into me and splits me in two. I can't stop the whimper in my throat, and he taps my ass again. And then...holy mother of god, I think my body lifts off the bed. Pleasure slams into me.

. . .

My thoughts spin out of control, all I can do is feel, letting him fuck me, the sensation of him inside me hitting that exquisite pleasure point. I grit my teeth at the thrill that pours through me. My skin burns and tingles all over, my balls drawing up tight.

Then Griff pulls out. I breath heavily into the blanket but he grabs me to flip me over again. On my back, I stare up at him, his face carnal and beautiful.

He pushes my legs up and back and eases slowly into me again. I look down where we're joined now, intimately, perfectly, and Griff pushes in deeper. I lick my lips, dazed and overwhelmed.

I reach for my cock, the need to come building fast and dark. Now we can see each other, it's more intense.

Fully seated inside me, Griff slides his hands up my body, over my abs, my pecs, then he curves his fingers over my shoulders and holds on as he begins to move. His eyes meet mine and we stare at each other, moving together slowly. Then he lowers himself over me, sliding an arm beneath my head, and he kisses me, hard and crushing. Griff's hips rock into my body, slowly and steadily, the bed bouncing as he fucks into me, his jaw set, mouth open, eyes unfocused.

I lift my arms and grip Griff's ass, helping him move against me. Our mouths slide together again, then Griff lifts his mouth a breath away to look at me, both of us panting, soft noises escaping our throats, heat building.

He kisses the rough stubble on my jaw, opens his mouth on me and grazes my chin with his teeth. He kisses and sucks the skin on the side of my neck, buries his face there, and breathes hard as his pace quickens. He kisses my shoulder, my chest, finds a nipple and sucks it into his mouth. My body jolts and I pull in a sharp breath. I lift my arms and fold them behind my head, watching Griff as he kisses and sucks. It's so fucking hot I'm going to combust.

Griff kisses his way back up, all the way to the underside of my arm, tracing the tattoo there with his tongue. He curls his hand around the back of my head, kisses my ear, sucks on my earlobe. Then he pushes up, straightens, and grips my thighs. I'm so close—dark pressure gathering, my skin buzzing. I fist my cock and stroke, jerking in brisk movements as Griff increases the pace and fucks me in a fast, hard rhythm. The mattress bounces beneath us.

Sensation builds and twists, hot and fierce. It slams into me, hot and bright, electricity racing up and down my spine, the backs of my thighs tingling, sensation exploding inside me. My cock jerks with each pulse of semen, draining me.

When my vision clears, I watch in awe as Griff's face contorts. He pulls out, yanks the rubber off, and comes in wrenching pulses, his semen mixing with mine on my stomach. We're making noises, we can't help it, harsh breaths that are nearly sobs, groans that aren't quite muffled. Emotion swells in my chest, my heart pounding, my breathing jagged. *Holy fuck.*

Our eyes meet and something passes between us, something amazing and powerful and moving. And Griff once more stretches out over my sweat-slicked body to kiss me.

Then he collapses beside me, pulling my face toward him for another kiss, this one longer, lingering, tongues sliding. He pulls back and strokes my face. "My warrior."

My chest swells with emotions. Words rise to my lips. I know they sound ridiculous, over the top, melodramatic. But it's the truth. So I choke them out. "My prince."

"Why did you join the army?"

Once again, Griff and I are hanging out. We know we have to be careful. But the pull between is so fucking strong, it's hard to stay away.

I hesitate before answering his question. I always feel I should have some noble answer, like I want to right wrongs, punish evil, save the world...but the truth isn't very noble. "I had nowhere else to go."

Griff eyes me, his eyes curious but warm.

"My dad was in jail. My mom was dead. I was homeless. I managed to finish high school without getting on social services' radar, but once school was done, I had nowhere else to go. I went down and enlisted."

"Christ."

"Yeah. My life growing up was shitty." I glance at him again, embarrassed to be telling a prince about my fucked-up childhood. He would never be able to relate to this and it's humiliating.

"Tell me."

I tell him about my drug-dealing parents who ended up stealing from their suppliers, the abuse my dad laid on me and my mom, how my life felt out of control and terrifying.

Griff makes a rough noise in his throat.

I tell him about the day I might have killed someone. The memory is still painful. "At first, I was hiding in the bedroom, trying not to cry. I almost couldn't breathe. Then I cracked open the door and I saw my dad on the floor not moving. I thought he was dead. Then that asshole was moving toward my mom, unbuttoning his pants."

"Fuck, no," Griff growls.

"I grabbed a baseball bat and went at him." I'll never forget the sickening crunch as the wood made contact with the back of the guy's head. My mom sat there, blood and tears running down her face, staring at the body on the floor, telling me to run. "I don't know if I killed that guy."

"Fuck, Sully."

"Ever since...I've tried to be...good. That sounds stupid." I shake my head. "I've tried to make up for maybe killing a man."

"You did the right thing. He was going after your mother."

"Yeah, but—"

"Life's not all black and white, Sully." He eyes me evenly. "There are lots of shades of gray. You're here. Sometimes we have to do hard things to do the right thing. To defend the people who need it."

I stare at him and something unlocks in my chest. A cold fear. Heavy guilt. "Yeah. You're right."

I tell him about my mom's overdose, my dad getting arrested, and being homeless.

"What happened to your dad?"

"He ended up in prison."

"Is he still there?"

"Yeah. He'll be there for a long time."

"Do you keep in touch with him?"

"Fuck no. I don't want anything to do with him."

Griff's hand on my shoulder is warm and solid. I've never told anyone about this; in fact, I've lied and told people both my parents are dead.

"So...like I said. I had nowhere else to go."

He nods somberly.

"That's a far cry from your life, I'm sure," I say.

"Yeah." Griff sighs.

"Why are *you* here? You're a fucking prince."

"It's what I want to do. It's what I've always wanted to do." He exhales sharply. "Christ, I had to battle just to get here. The Palace did *not* want the second in line to the throne to be in a war zone."

Second in line to the throne. Just hearing him say that makes this whole conversation feel bizarre.

"If it's okay for the other guys to be here...putting their lives in danger...why's it not okay for me? I'm not special. Those other guys out there are. *You* are."

I shake my head. "It's just hard for me to imagine. I'm here because I had nowhere else to go. You obviously had so much. Who's the hero in that scenario?"

He closes his eyes. "I don't feel like a hero."

"How did you get them to agree to let you come?"

"I kept pestering my father. We got the Erian press to agree to stay quiet about it. He wasn't convinced they'd live up to their word, and frankly I'm not sure they will, but so far they have. Nobody here gives a shit who I am."

I lift an eyebrow.

"Seriously. The lads won't respect me if I don't do my job, and I do it bloody well. The locals...they have no idea who I am. When the enemy is shooting at us, they have no clue who's in the chopper above them."

"True." Respect rises inside me.

I look into his eyes and a connection expands between us, invisible yet palpable, reaching right into my chest and wrapping around my heart. This is way past "any port in a storm." My feelings for this man are...complicated. Huge. Terrifying.

I drag myself out of my cot one morning, weeks later. I dreamed of Griff, hot sex dreams, but also his smile, his warm eyes, his regal head tilt.

I've never been in love before. But I think this might be it. It's fucking crazy and stupid—what the hell am I doing, getting involved with someone here, not to mention another man, and he's goddamn royalty from another country. If there was ever a hopeless situation, this is it.

And yet...an unfamiliar feeling of exhilaration fizzes inside me, something unusual in this hellish desert. I'm energized. The sun seems less harsh, more radiant; the mountains less threatening and more magnificent.

I head to the chow hall for breakfast, a spring in my step, grabbing a coffee first, then a bagel and a bunch of grapes. I sit at one of the tables, next to Tommy and Ryan. "What's up, ladies?"

"Griff's gone."

I freeze. I stare at Tommy. "What?"

"He left before dawn this morning. He's gone back to Eria."

I am ice, cold and rigid. I drop my gaze to the bagel on my plate so nobody sees the confusion and panic on my face. "Why?" I manage to squeeze the word out between stiff lips.

"Word got out that he's here." Tommy shakes his head. "And the fucking Taliban threatened his life."

My head snaps up to gape at Tommy. "Fuck off."

"Nope. It's true. They talked to Reuters and said they were going to either kill him or kidnap him."

I look away again. My gut churns nastily. I haven't even taken a mouthful of food, but I feel like I'm going to puke. What. The. Fuck.

"They had to get him out of here fast." Tommy shrugs. "Sucks, man."

"It's crazy," Ryan adds.

"It's crazy they let him come here at all," Jamarr says. "He could have been putting our lives in danger."

I give him a sharp look. "*That's* what you're worried about?"

He eyes me. "Uh…"

"We weren't in danger," Tommy says with a sigh. "Shut up, Jam."

I can't think. I can't talk. I sure as fuck can't eat my breakfast. But I have to sit here and pretend nothing's wrong while my heart splinters into cold, painful shards.

CHAPTER

FOURTEEN

Present Day
Chelsea

My head spins with incoherent thought fragments. I don't understand what's happening. My wrap falls to the floor from loosened fingers, and I glance down at my purse. My legs have the strength of cotton candy and I wobble a few steps to a chair and drop onto it.

Ford and Griff know each other? How? And why don't they seem happy to see each other? What is this thick tension about?

"Ford...you're back," I say inanely.

He turns his hard eyes on me, his eyebrows drawn down. "What...?"

I'm not the only one who can't form an intelligent sentence.

I feel like a band is tightening around my chest.

Griff's fingers on the edge of the counter are so rigid his knuckles are pale. His Adam's apple pushes out as he swallows. "Sully."

Sully?

Ford, getting somewhat of a grip, steps into the apartment, letting the door fall closed behind him with a sharp crack. He yanks off his helmet, still staring at Griff. "What are you doing here?" he demands.

So yes, they know each other.

"I don't understand..." I attempt to speak again. My voice is shaky.

"Neither do I." Ford whips his gaze over to me again. "What is going on?"

"I wanted to tell you," I say. "It was—"

"*Tell me what?*" A muscle in his jaw ticks.

"About Griff...and me..." I trail off.

His eyes turn on me, cold and bleak. "Griff...*and you?*"

I blink rapidly, my fingers twisting together. Now he seems angry. Why is he angry? Like my dad, is he worried about me? "Y-yes. We've been seeing each other."

"What. The. Fuck." Ford swings back to Griff. "You're in Chicago."

"Yes." Griff lifts his arms to his sides, attempting a small smile. "I am indeed."

I endure another stare down between the two of them. My stomach is simmering, a sick feeling rising inside of me. This feels terrible, but I don't understand why.

"We're going to the fundraiser," I say in a tiny voice.

Ford's head moves slowly from side to side. "I see."

I stand, hurrying to Griff's side. I curl my hands around his upper arm through his tuxedo jacket. "I wanted to tell you," I say to Ford in a rush. "But Griff's trying to stay out of the tabloids while he's here, so we've been—"

"Lying," Ford snaps, focusing on me again. "You've been lying."

I close my eyes, my heart sinking. I suck air into my constricted lungs. "There was a reason."

I hate the way he's looking at me. Like he hates me. It's killing me, like a knife being twisted in my heart. "Ford, I'm sorry." I let go of Griff's arm with one hand and extend it. "Don't look at me like that."

"Ford is your roommate," Griff murmurs. "That's a right cock up."

"Okay." I try to breathe again. "Someone tell *me* what's going on. You two obviously know each other."

"You didn't know," Ford snarls at Griff.

"I did not." Griff meets his eyes with a lifted chin. "It appears we're all...surprised."

Ford gives a rusty laugh. "Surprised. Yeah." He rubs his forehead. "Fuck me."

I'm still waiting for someone to answer me. A large fish flops in my belly and my heart pounds unevenly.

The two men exchange a long, loaded look again.

"We knew each other in Afghanistan," Griff finally says. "We both served at the same base at the same time."

I nod. "Okay." I believe the Erians were fighting alongside American troops there, but they're acting like they were fighting against each other.

"Right." Ford clears his throat. "Years ago."

My gaze flicks back and forth between Griff and Ford. Griff's biceps under my hand are hard as granite. I watch him curl and uncurl his fingers.

"We should go." Griff stands.

Ford looks like's been punched in the stomach.

"I..." I don't want to leave Ford like this. He's angry with me and I hate it. And I'm still confused by all this. "I guess we should." I meet Ford's eyes. "We can talk later. Okay?"

The corners of his eyes tighten and his mouth firms. "I'll be in bed when you get home."

"Tomorrow, then."

He gives me that grim look. "Sure." Ignoring Griff, he walks past us and down the hall.

My eyes wide, I gaze at Griff. "I-I'm sorry," I whisper. "I had no idea…"

"Neither did I." He exhales sharply. "Let's go. We can talk more on the way."

I pull my bottom lip between my teeth and cast an unhappy glance down the hall. "I hate leaving him like this."

Griff's eyes narrow. "You said you're just friends."

"We are. But we're good friends. Best friends. I…care about him."

He purses his lips and nods. "I'm sorry this happened."

"I'm still not even sure what just happened." I start to the door.

"Hang on, Chelsea."

I turn. Griff is there with my wrap and my purse.

"Oh. Thank you." My brain feels like scrambled eggs. "I don't know if I can do this."

"It's fine, love." He kisses my forehead. "Everything is fine."

But his eyes are shadowed and a tightness at the corners of his mouth tell me everything is not fine.

In the car, I have a million questions, but I stay silent, replaying what just happened, trying to make sense of it. Finally, I say, "So… you and Ford are friends?"

"Yeah."

That was…minimal.

"I told you about my time in Afghanistan," he adds. "We fought alongside the Americans."

"Right."

"I met lots of good guys. Ford's one of them."

"He is a good guy." I look down at my hands in my lap. My throat tightens. "I hate that I lied to him. I hate that he's mad at me."

"I'm sorry." He rubs my arm. "I'm sure he'll understand when you explain more."

"I hope so."

"I appreciate that you've been so discreet," Griff says somberly. "I truly do."

"I understand. I just wish...I didn't feel like I was sneaking around. I told my dad yesterday, so he wouldn't flip shit if he sees pictures, or someone asks him about it."

"How did that go?"

"Not great." I try smiling. "He worries a lot about me."

"He loves you."

"I know."

We arrive at the Field Museum. Climbing the grand stairs to the entrance, I tell Griff, "When I was little, I didn't understand why it was called the Field Museum. It's not in a field and it has nothing to do with fields."

He quirks a brow.

"It's named after Marshall Field," I tell him. "A benefactor of the museum."

"Ah. I love the neoclassical style."

"I forgot your interest in architecture. You'll love this building."

We enter Stanley Hall. The gleaming white marble, soaring ceilings, arched doorways, and gracious columns create an elegant ambience, while the big African elephants, hanging gardens, and flying pterosaurs add whimsy. Tables have been arranged throughout, gleaming with silver, topped with tall flower arrangements.

We obtain drinks and I resist the urge to toss back an entire glass of wine. I feel rattled, off-balance. Then I tag along with Griff as he mingles, greeting people he knows. I know several people here, too, mostly through my father, some through work. I try to keep a smile on my face and focus on making conversation instead of thinking about Ford looking so dumbfounded at seeing Griff and what that means.

I feel eyes on us, all the time, curious and avid. Pictures are taken, some candid, some posed with Griff. One of the photographers asks for my name and how to spell it. "You two make a gorgeous couple," she says to me, with an expectant air.

I just smile. I'm not giving them anything more than pictures.

I keep up the act all through dinner. Then Griff asks if it's okay if he gets shown around the museum by someone who works there. "Of course!" I say, smiling. "I can see how interested you are."

This is my chance to escape, and I head onto the terrace. The evenings are cooler now, so the event isn't being held out here, but the doors are unlocked so I sneak out and meander over to the stone wall. I tuck my wrap closer around me and sip my wine. Lights gleam on the harbor water and the city skyline glitters. I inhale a few deep breaths of fresh air, suddenly so exhausted I'm not sure I can stand up. I lean on the wall and close my eyes briefly.

I know I had to keep Griff secret because of who he is. I did it for him. But this is just a fun, once-in-a-lifetime fling, and if I've destroyed my friendship with Ford because of it, I'll never forgive myself. Ford has been the best of friends. He's in my life for the long haul. Or I thought so, anyway. Even when he was dating someone, he included me, and we kept our own relationship as friends. He even invited me to live with him. We have so much fun together. I almost told Griff I love Ford, but stopped myself, because I was afraid he wouldn't understand. It's friendship love. I care about him.

My eyes sting and I tip my head back to stare up at the night sky. I can't have lost Ford. I'll talk to him tomorrow and explain every-thing and I'll make him understand. It'll be okay. It *has* to be okay.

"Hey." Griff's soft voice comes from behind me.

I turn. "You're back. Was that fascinating?"

"Yes. Very. Are you okay?"

"I'm fine. Just getting some air. Actually..." I finish my wine. "I'm super tired."

"Do you want to leave?"

"Could we?"

"Of course." He crosses to have a word with Jac, standing discreetly just inside the doors, then comes back to me. "Shall we?"

I take the arm he offers, and we re-enter the hall. Music now fills the space with a few couples on the dance floor. I remember dancing with Griff at the gala where we met, and a sadness fills me. We should be dancing and laughing and having fun, but I'm not having fun tonight, and I don't think Griff is either.

Despite my flirty promise earlier about letting him mess me up, Rhys drives us straight to my place. This afternoon I was excited about tonight being the night I would finally sleep with Griff, but now…it just doesn't feel right.

Griff walks me into the lobby. "Do you want me to come up?" he asks as we pause at the elevator. "In case Ford is up? I can be there for support."

I blink at him. "For some reason, I think it might be better if you're not there."

His mouth tightens, but he nods. "You may be right." He tips his head. "Clearly he was jealous."

My jaw loosens and I gape at Griff. "Jealous? Are you kidding me?"

"No."

I shake my head violently. "No. Absolutely not. We're friends. He worries about me."

"Like your father."

"Yes." I frown momentarily, as I question what it is about me that makes these two men in my life protective of me. A flame of anger ignites in my belly that they see me as weak. Naïve. I want to be a strong, independent woman. I don't want to be coddled and sheltered and…and confined.

And yet, once again I've messed up.

I cover my eyes with one hand.

"Hey," Griff says gently. "It's okay, lovely."

"I don't know if it's okay." I choke out the words. "Ford is my best friend. I've fucked up." I don't usually talk like that, but I don't care.

He presses my face to his chest. "It'll be fine. Tomorrow's a new day. Get some sleep."

I nod against him. "Yeah. Good idea."

He cups my face in two hands, so gently, and kisses me softly. "We'll talk tomorrow, yeah?"

I nod with a tiny smile. "Okay."

Someone else is coming into the building and we step apart. Griff lowers his head as he walks out, and I push the elevator button.

I'm usually the one staying positive, so I needed to hear those words from Griff. Still, I'm not convinced right now that everything will be fine.

CHAPTER

FIFTEEN

Griffin

Ford and I have to talk. This is a dog's dinner.

I'm so fucked up about this, I can barely function. Seeing Ford again after all these years is gobsmacking enough but learning that he's Chelsea's friend and roommate—holy shit. And seeing his face when he looked at her—he's in love with her.

And she has no idea.

What the hell do we tell her? I close my eyes and bang the back of my head against the couch. I'm sitting in the living room of my borrowed house Sunday morning, feeling like shit after a sleepless night. Around one in the morning I got up and drank a good portion of a bottle of gin. That didn't help.

I've no way of reaching Ford unless I go over there, which is what I'm going to have to do. And Chelsea will be there. Fuck.

I see Ford's face again. Christ. He looks older, a little hardened, but he's still beautiful with his dark hair, square jaw, and deep-set pale green eyes beneath thick eyebrows. Those eyes...watchful. Alert. Penetrating.

Never in a million years would I have thought of reconnecting with him when I came to Chicago. I knew he was from here, but I completely lost touch with him when I left Camp Durham, hustled out of there that morning without even a chance to say goodbye. Or to tell him I was falling in love with him. So I had no idea if he was still enlisted, still fighting overseas, back in America...or even dead.

I press a hand to my chest where my heart is bumping and jarring.

I'm falling in love with Chelsea. I know I shouldn't be. But her sweetness and optimism and intelligence captivated me from the moment I saw her. She has a delicate fragility that tugs at something inside me, and yet there's a touching inner strength. She's perfect. Okay, she lacks a little self-confidence and maybe she's a wee bit naïve, but I've fallen arse over tits for her. I can't get enough of her.

But seeing Ford brought all those feelings I had for him roaring back. Holy shit. I'm a mess.

I stand up and walk over to the big windows overlooking the park-like back yard. Rain is pissing down outside, the sky low and foggy. The leaves on the trees drip water, and crystal droplets glisten on the flowers and shrubs.

I press the heels of my hands to my eyes. I need to figure out what to do.

"Hey, boss, you okay?" Jac asks behind me.

I turn. "Your highness."

He scoffs. "Right. Your highness."

We've been friends for years. He's more than my bodyguard. He's the best there is at his job and I never want to lose him. He knows more about me than even my mother. "A bit of a situation has developed," I say carefully. I head to the coffee maker on the kitchen counter. Another hit of caffeine might help. "Coffee?"

"I'll make it." He bumps me aside and busies himself.

"I can make coffee."

"I know you can. What's up? Is it Chelsea?"

"Yes. And no. Hell." I run a hand through my hair. "I may have developed feelings for her."

"Ah."

"Which is bad enough, right? I'm going home next month."

"Take her with you."

"I'd basically ruled that out."

"Why?"

"She's American."

Jac shrugs. "So?"

I don't know how that would go over with the family. Or the people of Eria. I mean, Jesus, I'm not thinking about marriage! Not that fast. So why *does* it matter?

I sigh. "Last night I met her roommate. Her friend."

He nods, leaning against the counter as the coffee brews. He crosses his arms, stretching his T-shirt across his broad chest, biceps bulging beneath the short sleeves. "Ford."

"Yes." I pause. "I...knew him. In Afghanistan."

"You knew him." He lifts an eyebrow.

"Yeah. We were lovers. And friends. I...cared about him."

Jac has mastered the art of keeping a poker face, but the faint twitch in his eye tells me his reaction. "Inconvenient," he murmurs.

"To put it mildly."

He hands me a mug of coffee and pours one for himself. "Clearly Chelsea doesn't know that."

"No. And I don't know what to tell her. Ford and I were both so stupefied at seeing each other all we managed to say was that we'd met in Afghanistan."

"If you're serious about her, she needs to know."

"But am I? Serious? Fuck. I don't know." I rub my forehead, then gulp some hot coffee. "I'm confused."

Jac narrows his eyes. "Do you still have feelings for Ford?"

"How the hell could I? It was ten years ago!"

He gives me a long, level look.

"I don't know," I admit. "I was floored. I didn't expect to see him. All those memories came pouring back."

"Dog's dinner is right." Jac straightens. "I'll take you over there."

I shake my head, one corner of my mouth twitching up. "How'd you know?"

"I know you."

I look down at my faded jeans and navy Henley. I should change. Nah. "Just let me grab my phone."

I have long enough on the drive to make myself crazy thinking about what I'm going to say, how I'm going to handle this. When we turn onto West Ohio, I rub damp palms over my jeans. Only a few blocks more and we pull up at Chelsea's building. Ford's building.

Jac gets out and accompanies me into the building while Rhys goes to find somewhere to park. The outside door is locked of course. I have to call up to get in. I only have Chelsea's number.

Then someone exits the building and lucky for me they're not particular about security, and we duck inside.

We ride the elevator up and approach Ford's door.

Jac hangs back. "I'll wait out here," he says quietly, pulling out his phone.

I nod, then rap on the door.

Seconds later, it's yanked open. "Did you—oh." Ford stands there.

He looks as wrecked as I feel. His hair stands in all directions, the dark stubble on his jaw gives him a dangerous look, and his eyes are tired.

I summon up all my training, my stoic, imperturbable demeanor, deliberately relaxing my tense muscles. "Good morning, Sully."

He stares at me. "What the fuck, Griff."

"I know. May I come in?"

He shakes his head but steps aside so I can enter. I saunter in. Not seeing her, I ask, "Where's Chelsea?"

"I don't know."

My eyebrows shoot up.

"She was gone when I got up." He rubs one eyebrow with his fingertips. "I texted her, but she hasn't answered."

"She's angry."

"I don't know what the hell she is," Ford growls. "Since she hasn't talked to me."

"You look like hell, mate."

"Thanks." Ford gives me a dirty once-over. "You don't look much better."

"I know." I drag a hand over my hair, then my unshaven jaw. "It's just as well she's not here. We need to talk." I walk over to big windows overlooking the city and the lake, a dreary, sodden gray panorama today. "Nice view."

"Thanks."

I turn to face him. "I'm sorry."

His face tightens. "Sorry for what?"

"Well, let's go back to the beginning, shall we?" I take a seat on a chair and cross my ankle over my knee in a relaxed pose. Meanwhile, my heart is banging its way out of my chest. "I'm sorry I left Camp Durham without talking to you."

He shrugs and lowers himself onto the couch. "No big deal."

I focus a steady gaze on him. "Wasn't it? It was to me. I was gutted."

His mouth softens minutely.

"I had no choice, obviously," I continue. "The press got wind of me being over there and the Taliban found out. They threatened to kill me. Or kidnap me. My family panicked and lifted me out of there with no notice whatsoever."

"I heard that."

"I would have talked to you. If I could. I felt like shit."

His face stays aloof.

"You meant something to me, Ford."

"Don't do this," he grinds out, his hands curled into fists. "Just let it go."

"I thought I did." I give him a wry smile. "It took goddamn years, but I thought I did. Until last night."

He stares at me. "Years."

"Yeah."

Ford bows his head, shaking it.

"I'm also sorry for showing up here out of the blue. And I'm sorry that I somehow got involved with Chelsea, because it seems to have hurt you."

Ford's head snaps up. He fixes a hot stare on me. I resist the urge to shift in my chair.

"But I have to be honest with you. I'm also *not* sorry for being involved with her, because she's an amazing, beautiful, brilliant woman."

His mouth thins. "Yeah. She is. What are you doing with her, Griff?"

"Nothing nefarious." I hold up my hands. "We met at a gala weeks ago and hit it off. She's been showing me around Chicago."

"Weeks." Ford's lip curls. "She's been seeing you for *weeks*. And never told me."

I lean forward. "I asked her not to say anything to anyone. I know what the press is like. They go nuts when I smile at a woman. I didn't want her besieged with aggressive reporters everywhere she goes. She's had…" I pause. "I'm sure I don't have to tell you this. But she's been sheltered. She's not prepared to deal with that."

Ford's eyes flicker, acknowledgement of that. "Until last night, apparently. You decided she was ready?"

I force myself to keep my jaw loose, my mouth relaxed. "Point taken. But we talked about it, and she agreed."

Ford gnaws on the inside of his mouth.

"I look after her," I say earnestly. "I have security with me all the time. They watch her, too. I'd never let anything happen to her."

"Good to know," he says dryly.

I watch the set of his shoulders, tense and hunched, his rigid face and fisted hands. Something softens and aches in my chest. I long to move across the room, sit beside him, touch him. Reassure him.

Reassure him of what, though?

"I had no idea you're her roommate," I continue. "Truly. I was just as gobsmacked as you were."

"I could see that."

"We need to decide what to tell Chelsea. About us."

He lets out a short breath. "We told her last night."

"You don't think we owe her more honesty than that?" I study his face. "You care about her, too."

"Of course." His voice is gruff, and he clears his throat. "We're friends."

"Is that all? It looked like more than that to me."

Ford's eyes go blank and he lifts his chin. "That's all. Clearly she only wants to be friends."

I notice the obfuscation there but say nothing. "She knows you're bisexual?"

"Yes. Does she know *you* are?"

"Yes." I shrug.

Ford juts his chin out again. "How serious are you about her? How long are you here? I assume you haven't moved here. What are you doing here anyway?"

"A barrage of questions." I lean back again. "I'm here working on my foundation, an organization dedicated to helping veterans get the supports they need. We're establishing a base here in Chicago to work with American veterans' organizations. I had planned to go back to Eria at the end of September, but it's looking like I'll be here into October."

"And then?"

I drop my gaze to the rug, turning over his question in my mind. "I don't know."

"You're going to break her heart."

"I'm not!" I jerk my head up.

He gazes at me.

"I don't know," I repeat, more quietly. "I'm...developing feelings for her. I don't want to leave her."

"You're going to be King of Eria."

"Yes." I turn to the wet view out the windows again. "It's...delicate."

Ford snorts. "No shit."

This reminds me of the Ford I knew years ago and my heart shifts. Just the way he tilts his head, the way he raises that strong chin, his blunt way of talking...it's all so attractive. I could never look away from him. I wanted to talk with him for hours. I wanted to feel him—

How am I supposed to say that? That I was sure I was falling in love with Chelsea...until I saw Ford. And now I wonder if I'm still in love with *him*.

But he's in love with Chelsea. He denies it...but I saw it.

This is more than a dog's dinner. This is an epic clusterfuck. I want to press my fingers to my throbbing temples. But I have to keep that impassive façade in place.

Ford is one of the few people in the world who've seen me with that mask off. But that was a long time ago.

"So," I say casually. "Is this how it goes? I keep seeing Chelsea. You and I act like we barely know each other. And that's it."

A muscle flicks in Ford's jaw. "Sounds good to me."

My back molars grind together. "Seriously?" My control is slipping. I surge up out of the chair and cross to stand in front of Ford. "That's bullshit."

He stands too. His nostrils flare and he shoves up the sleeves of his sweatshirt. Tendons in his forearms stand out and it's so fucking sexy I'm nearly undone. "This whole thing is bullshit!"

"The fuck it is!" I suck air into my lungs. "It's happening and we need to deal with it!"

"I don't know how to deal with this! I don't know why you're here! I don't know why you're with Chelsea. I don't know...I...don't..."

I slide a hand around the back of his neck and jerk his head closer. For sharp, brilliant seconds we stare into each other's eyes. And then...our mouths crash together. I close my eyes as our mouths fuse, exerting pressure on his head to keep him in place...but he's not trying to pull away. Our mouths open hungrily, and a groan rises in my chest from deep within me.

"Fuck you, Griff," he mutters against my lips.

I kiss him again, tilting my head, biting at his lips, sweeping my tongue into his mouth and fuck, he tastes so good, just like I remember.

"What...?"

The soft, breathy exclamation startles us apart and we turn horrified eyes on Chelsea, standing in the door.

CHAPTER
SIXTEEN

Ford

"Chelsea." My voice croaks. My head empties and all the air feels sucked out of the condo.

The door swings behind Chelsea with a soft click. Silence expands in the room.

She stares at us, her mouth open, eyes as big as my bike tires, her hand pressed to her chest.

Griff moves first. "Chelsea. Love." He strides toward her.

She throws up a hand. "Stop."

He stops.

She turns her head slowly from side to side. Her chest rises and falls quickly, delicately, with her breath.

Okay, none of us knows what to say.

"I knew there was something," she says slowly, her voice so low I almost can't hear it. "I felt it." She swallows. "You two weren't just friends, were you? You were lovers."

Griff shifts his body so he can look at me, then back to Chelsea. "Yes."

"It was a long time ago," I add, taking a couple of steps closer.

Griff nods.

Her still-big eyes dart back and forth between Griff and me. "You were just kissing. Two minutes ago. That's not a long time ago."

I grit my teeth. Shit. We could have been completely honest with her and told her things were over between Griff and me a long time ago. But she walked in on us kissing.

Which meant nothing. I tell her that. "That didn't mean anything."

Griff turns to me with a raised eyebrow, and I shoot him an icy glare. "Right, Griff?"

"It was a mistake," he says. "I'm sorry you saw that."

I can see Chelsea's struggling to find words. "Wow. I did not expect this."

"I know." I keep my voice low and gentle.

Her face takes on a frozen look as she focuses on me. "How could you do that?"

"Chelsea. I—"

"Never mind. I'll leave you two to it." She hustles past us, down the hall, and into her bedroom.

"Chelsea, wait," Griff calls to her.

I open my mouth, but don't bother saying anything as her bedroom door smacks shut.

Griff turns to me and drops his head back, eyes closed.

"Well, we fucked that up, didn't we?" I say.

"Oh yeah. Absobloodylutely. Christ."

I want to lash out and blame him for it, but the truth is, I was all in on that kiss. He was right—it was a mistake. But in the moment, it was...incredible. "You should leave," I grunt. "I'll talk to her when she's settled down."

"What are you going to talk to her about?" Griff fixes his gaze on me.

"I'll apologize. I'll tell her that..." I clear my throat. "You care about her and what was between us was in the past. What just happened was a mistake and she should talk to you about it, too."

His rigid features relax, and he studies me for a long moment. "You're still an honorable man, Ford."

My chest burns. I say nothing.

Griff nods. "Okay. If I don't hear from her, I'll try calling her tonight."

I nod and watch him walk out of the condo.

I lower my ass to the couch and bury my face in my hands. I'm not sure how I'm going to talk to Chelsea and convince her that everything is fine when I can't figure out what the hell just happened myself.

The things I know are—Chelsea has been seeing Griff for weeks and seems to have feelings for him. He says he cares about her too. Whatever the reason for that kiss, it really was nothing. We were both angry, frustrated...and there's more that I don't even want to admit to myself.

But I'm not going to come between Chelsea and someone she cares about. I could never do that. I would never want to hurt her. So I'll do whatever I have to, to make sure she and Griff are okay.

My chest feels like an M1 Abrams tank is resting on it.

Griff better not be playing with her.

I know his history. Maybe he's settled down since he left Afghanistan, I don't know. I haven't followed his exploits since then; that hurt too much. Maybe he does have feelings for her.

I thought he had feelings for *me*, all those years ago.

I rub my eyes and go into the kitchen for a bottle of water from the fridge. I guzzle it down and eye the nearly empty bottle of tequila on the counter. Yeah, better not get into that again.

I need to go into the office for a while. But there's no way I can leave now. And I doubt I can concentrate on work, anyway. I need to give Chelsea some space for a while before I try to talk to her. I'll clean out the fridge.

My fridge is typically spotless and organized, but with Chelsea here, things tend to get a bit messy. I find restaurant leftovers from I don't know how long ago, a packaged salad that's turning brown, and something sticky has spilled on a shelf. Normally, that irritates me. When I spill something, I clean it up, for Chrissake. But with Chelsea, her slightly sloppy habits get only a mildly put out shrug.

I empty everything and scrub the inside of the appliance, including the drawers. I inspect some condiments, checking for best before dates. I haven't been paying enough attention; the ketchup and a bottle of hoisin sauce have to go.

Creating order calms me and I survey the clean and tidy fridge when I'm done.

"You're so weird."

I jump and turn.

Chelsea stands at the island with raised brows.

My lips twitch. "I'm not weird. You're weird."

She almost smiles. "Cleaning the fridge? Seriously?"

"It needed it. FYI, your leftovers are in the trash."

"They were probably still fine."

"If by fine, you mean fine as a science experiment, then yeah."

"They weren't *that* old."

My heart expands and relaxes at our usual ribbing. I pull in a long breath through my nose. "Can we talk?"

"I don't know." Her eyes look bruised and her mouth droops. "I don't want to talk. I'm pissed at you."

"Well, I'm pissed at you, so we're even."

She stares incredulously. "You're pissed at *me*?"

"Hell, yeah. You were going out with someone for weeks and never told me. And that someone happens to be Prince Griffin of Eria."

Her head drops. "I know. I'm sorry." Then her head snaps up. "Wait. You kissed my boyfriend! What the hell, Ford? Who does that?"

"I'm sorry, too. I really am. Please. Let me talk. Please listen."

She swallows as she meets my eyes. "I'm afraid, Ford."

I frown and drop the towel I'm holding, taking three big steps around to her. I clasp her upper arms and hold her in place. "What are you afraid of?"

"I'm afraid of what you're going to say." Her voice is a thin whisper.

"No, no. Christ, no." My heart lurches painfully.

"Last night...after you came home and saw Griff...you seemed so angry. I didn't tell you about him because of who he is. I truly wasn't trying to hide something from you or be sneaky. I hated that I couldn't tell you everything." She pauses and her bottom lip quivers. "How much fun I was having. How special he made me feel."

I nod, my throat squeezing. She *is* special.

"I was so afraid I'd hurt you by keeping that from you, and that y-you wouldn't want to be friends anymore."

"Fuck."

"I thought about it all evening. And I was so scared. This morning I went for a long walk because I was afraid to talk to you."

She's doing a lot of talking for someone who didn't want to talk, but I don't point that out.

"What else are you afraid of?'

"Now..." She turns damp eyes up to me. "I'm afraid Griff still wants to be with you...not with me."

My eyelids clamp down as a wave of pain and guilt washes through me. "That's not true," I grind out. "Not at all. He cares about you. "

"Th-then why were you two—" She hiccups. "Why were you kissing?"

I ease her away from me and down onto one of the stools at the island. I sit on the other one, facing her. "I don't know," I say honestly. "We were arguing and...it happened. I'm sorry."

Her lips are pouty like she's trying not to cry. She presses them together and swallows again.

"Look." I keep my tone low and gentle. "Griff and I had a...thing... in Afghanistan. We got to be friends and hung out and then...it changed into more. It didn't last long. He got yanked and had to go home to Eria and it ended. That was it." I pause. "I'm so sorry, Chelsea. I would never betray you like that."

It also feels like a betrayal to describe what happened between Griff and me so casually. I don't want to hurt Chelsea. I also don't want to dishonor Griff and what we had. I'm stuck between a giant boulder and a steel plate. And I'm feeling the squeeze.

"I knew he was with other men," she whispers.

"Does that bother you?"

"No." Her answer is immediate. "Only if...if he wants to be with another man *now*. Instead of me."

"That's not the case." I make my tone firm.

Her head is down, her long dark hair hanging over her face. Her fingers twist and turn together. "This is really...wow."

"I know. Crazy coincidence."

"I guess I do need to talk to him."

Something fractures in my chest. I manage to croak, "Yeah. You should do that."

I do end up going to the office in the afternoon, and when I get home Chelsea's gone. I assume she's with Griff. With a boulder lodged in my gut, I make myself a ham sandwich for dinner. Opening the fridge and seeing how clean it is should make me happy. But it doesn't.

I eat mindlessly, picturing Chelsea and Griff together.

Yeah, they make a beautiful couple. Griff's golden good looks, his aristocratic bone structure and sensual mouth...Chelsea's long, shiny dark hair, slender curves, and sweet, engaging smile.

I imagine them talking. Kissing. Fucking.

I close my eyes at the stabbing sensation I feel in my heart. My gut churns unpleasantly. I shouldn't have eaten that sandwich.

This is bugging the hell out of me, and I need to get over it.

I lock myself in my bedroom and try to watch TV to avoid seeing Chelsea when she gets home.

Monday evening, I stop at Whole Foods on my way home from the office. After the refrigerator cleaning, there's not much left in there. I get some basics and a couple of prepared meals. Chelsea loves the chicken tinga enchiladas here, so I pick up some. I make one other quick stop. I don't even know if she'll be home, but whatever.

I'm grouchy and drained. I trudge into the condo with my bags. I immediately know Chelsea is here. I don't know how. I just feel her presence. Her scent. Her energy.

Her bedroom door is half open, so I call out, "Hey! I'm home and I brought dinner."

She appears a minute later, looking like she's just changed, probably out of her work clothes and into a pair of leggings that end above her slender ankles and outline the perfect shape of her legs and ass. She tugs a sweatshirt down into place.

"Hi." She leans on the counter.

I'm unpacking the things I bought and studying her face surreptitiously. She looks as tired as I feel. "Chicken tinga enchiladas." I hold it up the package.

"Ooh yum!"

"And I picked up these." I slide a package of M&Ms across the counter to her.

She closes her eyes briefly as she picks them up, her smile tremulous. "Thank you."

Her pleasure hooks something deep inside me. "I'll heat them up." I turn away.

"Go change. I'll put things away and get these in the oven."

"Okay. Thanks."

In my room, I hang up my suit and toss my shirt and underwear into the hamper. I pull on gray sweats and an old T-shirt, and head back to the kitchen. Chelsea's opening a bottle of water. She takes a big drink of it.

"Did you talk to Griff?" I ask, attempting a casual tone.

"Yes." She walks into the living room and gazes out the window. "We talked."

That's not telling me much.

"I told him we probably shouldn't keep seeing each other," she says to the window.

I clamp my teeth down on my bottom lip.

"He didn't agree," she continues.

"Why do *you* think that?" I ask.

"It's going to end anyway. Now the media has got hold of it, they're going to blow it up into a big thing—they already are! And with the history between you two...it's probably best."

"But Griff doesn't agree?"

"No." She turns to face me. "He...still wants to see me."

A fist twists my guts. "Of course he does."

"We're going to keep it low key. Although it's a little late for that. Everyone was freaking out at work today because they saw pictures of us from the gala."

"Understandable."

"But I'm still not sure it's a good idea." She sighs and wanders to the couch, sitting with her legs curled under her.

I walk closer. "You know you don't need to worry about me and Griff. Right?"

She turns big eyes on me. "We can't ignore that."

Well, shit. I rub my mouth. "True. But like I said, it's in the past." I hesitate. "Are we okay, Chelsea?"

Her eyes grow glossy. "I don't want to lose you, Ford."

Aw fuck. She might as well have my heart in her soft little hands for the tug I feel on it. "You won't," I rasp out.

She nods, ducking her head. "Good."

It's not that easy, though.

Griff arrives on Thursday evening to take Chelsea out for dinner. He comes up to the condo and I let him in. I get a whiff of his cologne, something he never wore in Afghanistan, mingled with his own unique scent that still has the power to tighten my groin. I move away from him quickly. "Chelsea!" I call. "Griff's here."

I'm affected by him, but I swear to Christ if he gives me even one look that hints the same, I'll punch him in his beautiful face for disrespecting Chelsea.

She walks out wearing wide-legged jeans and a snug sweater that hugs her tits. She slings her purse over her shoulder, dressed casually but as always with that air of refinement and class. "Hi." She greets Griff with a tentative smile. "I'm ready."

He walks over to her and drops a light kiss on her mouth. I can't help but watch in a sort of fascination, my dick stirring.

"Good. Let's go." He shoots me a smile. "See you later, Ford."

As they leave, I'm left standing alone in the apartment. With a sense of longing so intense I feel it like a pain in my chest I close my eyes and swallow hard through the thickness in my throat.

This is so fucked up.

Thinking about them together has become an obsession. I have to fight it at work, digging deep to focus and not screw up my career. At home I can let my guard down and torment myself imagining them, where they are, what they're talking about, what they're doing.

I have to put those walls up when Chelsea's around, though. The last thing I want is her feeling sorry for me. She can't know the complicated mix of feelings I'm having.

But walls are designed to keep people out, and as I turn down opportunities to spend time with Chelsea or make up excuses to be out when Griff comes by, I feel Chelsea's disappointment. That's not what I want; in protecting myself, I'm hurting her. And I don't know what to do about this.

My growing frustration and longing make me angry at myself. My temper is shorter, my guilt makes me surly. I know it and I hate it. I snap at Chelsea when she leaves dishes in the sink and irritably ask her to turn her music down.

And when she comes home excited to tell me about what she accomplished at work, her new project challenging her, I want to tell her how proud I am of her and tell her how amazing she is, but I hold back. I'm an asshole.

Friday night, Griff arrives for another date. Chelsea got home late, so I offer him a beer while she's getting ready. He accepts and we take seats in the living room. The sun is setting, the sky a deep midnight blue, the lights of the skyscrapers glittering outside my windows.

"I do love that view." Griff gestures at the windows.

"Yeah. Definitely attracted me to this place."

"How long have you lived here?"

"About four years."

"Chelsea says you're Assistant U.S. Attorney. You got a law degree after you came home."

"Yep." They've talked about me.

"That's great, Ford. I always admired your drive. Your honor."

I meet his eyes and see the sincerity in them, then quickly look away. "Thanks."

I admired those things about him, too. Especially because he's a prince. He didn't have to be in Afghanistan. I did.

Heat rises into my face. In my agitation I gulp a mouthful of beer, then choke on it. That pisses me off.

"Are you okay?" Griff asks, a notch between his eyebrows.

I nod, giving one last cough to clear my airway. "Yeah. Fine," I snap. I wipe the back of my hand over my mouth and glance toward Chelsea's bedroom. What is taking her so long?

"What kind of cases do you work on?" Griff asks.

I don't want to sit here and make conversation with Griff. I want them gone. This show is getting old. And annoying. I blabber some general stuff about what I do. Chelsea's still not here and I jump to my feet. "How's your beer?"

"I'm good." He holds his up.

I stride to the kitchen and grab another, tempted to shoot the entire thing straight down my throat. Then I walk up to Chelsea's door and rap on it. "Hey. What are you doing in there? You're as slow as turtles fucking in molasses."

The door is yanked open. She looks amazing in a sleeveless pink dress and pointy-toed shoes, her hair long and loose and glossy. She stares at me with a mixture of annoyance and amusement. "Excuse me?"

One corner of my mouth twitches despite my aggravation.

"He's telling you to hustle your tits," Griff calls.

"I got that." She arches a brow.

"Scooch your cooch!" he adds. "He wants to get rid of us."

She meets my eyes. "He always does, these days."

I frown. "Scooch your cooch?" I repeat. "That's not very respectful."

"And telling her she's as slow as turtles fucking in molasses is?" Griff walks toward us with his graceful, long-legged stride.

My jaw tightens. "Taking fucking forever."

"What the hell is wrong with you?" Griff demands. "She's getting ready to go out."

Chelsea looks between us. "I'm almost ready," she says, her tone placating.

I roll my eyes and try to move past Griff to go back to the living room.

"Wait." He stops me with a hand on my shoulder. His hand burns through my T-shirt. I flinch before I can stop myself. "What's your problem? I thought we were all good."

"We're great," I mutter, pushing him away.

"Clearly, we're not." He grabs me again.

Oh fuck. He's putting his hands on me. With more force, I grab him and shove him again.

He doesn't let go of me. I don't let go of him. We're wrestling in my hallway, stumbling toward the living room.

"Stop!" Chelsea cries. "What are you *doing*?"

I bash Griff into the wall and he lets out a grunt. "Fucker," he mutters.

"Call me that." I take a swing and almost connect with his face, but his arm comes up in a lightning-quick move, blocking my fist. His other hand connects with my jaw. I reel back, stars twinkling in front of my eyes.

Rage explodes inside me, white hot and incandescent. *You left me.* "Asshole." I swing again and land a hit. His head flies back. Gripping my shirt, he swings me around and we careen into the open space of hardwood floor. *You're fucking Chelsea.* I feel myself losing my balance, going down, and fuck him, he's coming with me. We land hard on the floor. A burn flashes from my hip through my body.

"Stop!" Chelsea screams. "You idiots!"

She lands a kick on my ass with a pointy-toed shoe. I yowl.

That gives Griff a chance to roll me under him. He's lean but strong. Pressing me to the floor, his weight pinning me, we stare at each other, panting, sweating.

Christ. Jesus Christ. His body on mine, lean and muscled, feels familiar even years later. I can't stop my own body from reacting and I squeeze my eyes shut on the hard twist of lust.

"Yeah," he grunts. "Idiots."

"Get off him!" Now Chelsea hoofs him.

"Fuck!"

I push up and roll him now, trying to land another blow.

"Oh my god!" Chelsea cries. "Just stop!"

I get Griff under me, ready to drive my fist into his nose. My eyes meet his. Heat erupts around us, between us. Our mouths are close. His lips part, his chest pumping with his breath, color staining his cheeks.

"Do it," he breathes. "I fucking dare you."

What's he daring me to do? Punch him...or kiss him? I want to do both.

I roll off him and onto my back on the floor. I close my eyes and my lungs strain for air.

He doesn't move either.

Then Chelsea makes a strangled noise and her high heels click rapidly down the hall. I feel the slam of her bedroom door vibrate from the floor into my body.

"Fuck," Griff moans.

"Yeah. Fuck."

CHAPTER

SEVENTEEN

Griff

"What the fuck just happened?" I ask the ceiling of Ford's condo.

"You're an asshole."

"I already know that." I roll my head on the floor to look at him, still breathing fast. "So are you."

"Not gonna deny it." His face looks like someone is pulling his fingernails out with pliers. He rolls to his feet and stands, heading straight to Chelsea's room.

No surprise there.

I follow him, shaking my throbbing hand.

He knocks on the door softly and leans on it. "Chels. Come out."

"Fuck you. Both of you."

He glances at me, grimacing.

"We're sorry, love," I call through the door. "Come out."

"I never want to see either of you again! You are both dead to me!"

"Dramatic," I mouth to Ford with a "yikes" face.

169

He leans his forehead against the door. "Chels. Talk to us."

He looks defeated—slumped shoulders, pained expression. My heart contracts sharply. "Does the door lock?" I ask quietly.

He scowls. "No. But we're not going in there without her permission."

"Of course." Yeah, I did think of it. Yeah, I'm an asshole.

Suddenly the door flies open and Ford nearly falls into the room.

Chelsea glares at us. Her face is pink, her eyes damp. She's taken off the sexy stilettos and stands in bare feet. "What the hell is wrong with you?" she demands. "Both of you!"

Ford reaches out and takes her hands. "I was pissed."

"At who?" Her gaze bores into him.

He rubs his forehead. "I don't know. Nothing. Everything. I'm..." He shakes his head. "I'm messed up."

"No shit!" She plants her hands on her hips. It's so fucking sexy, blood rushes south. She looks at me. "And you?"

"I was pissed too." I slant Ford a hot glance. "Still am."

"Why?"

"Because...for Chrissake. Let's just get this out in the open." I look back at Chelsea. "He's in love with you! Can't you see it? And he's fucking jealous!"

Chelsea's face slackens. Her mouth hanging open, she swivels her gaze to Ford.

His cheeks stained with red, he gives me a murderous look. "I'm not jealous!"

"Yeah, you are. Just fucking admit it."

"No," Chelsea says in a near-whisper. "That's not right. We're friends."

I narrow my eyes. Holding Ford's gaze, I say, very deliberately, "He's in love with you."

"That's ridiculous."

"Just tell her," I snarl. "Be honest."

"No!" Ford shouts back at me. "Are you enjoying this?"

"What? No! What are you talking about?"

Ford looks at Chelsea. "You're in love with Griff, aren't you?"

Her bottom lip parts from the top lip and pushes out. Her eyes flicker to me, then back to Ford. "Ford. Don't."

I'm pretty sure Chelsea has feelings for me. I know I do for her. But we haven't said those words to each other. "What a fucking mess," I mutter, grabbing the back of my neck.

Chelsea crosses the room and plops down onto her bed. She stares down at her bare toes. "I don't understand any of this."

Ford steps into her room and I follow him, keeping our distance from Chelsea.

She lifts her head. "*Are* you jealous, Ford?"

He doesn't answer right away.

"Or maybe I should ask...*who* are you jealous of?" Chelsea continues, an edge to her tone. "Because I definitely get the impression you still have feelings for Griff."

Ford doesn't look at me.

My breath stalls in my throat and my heart picks up a wild, uneven beat. And I have to admit the truth to myself—*I'm* jealous. I'm jealous that Ford lives with Chelsea and she cares about him so much and that he's in love with her.

This is insane.

And listening to the bitter inflection in her voice, it sounds like Chelsea's jealous too. She's jealous that Ford might have feelings for me.

I swallow, ideas crowding my brain, crazy, fantastic, absolutely batshit ideas.

I turn to Ford. "Yes, Ford. Who are you jealous of?" I take a step closer to him.

He backs up. "What is this?"

I take another step. He does, too. Closer to Chelsea, watching us with wide eyes. So beautiful. So precious.

"Answer us." Now I crowd him, bumping my chest to his. We're right by Chelsea, still sitting on the side of her bed. The air in the room is thick and hot, making it hard to breathe. My skin is burning.

"Fuck you."

I smile.

Ford's eyes blaze into mine. He looks at Chelsea and his expression softens.

"Ford...?" She stares into his eyes.

He reaches for her hand again.

I take her other hand.

Her eyes slide back and forth between us.

"Fine," Ford scrapes out. "Chelsea, I care about you. As more than a friend."

Her breath catches. "Oh." She takes a long breath. "Really?"

I see the agony on Ford's face. I hate it and I love it. "Really."

She takes a shaky breath. "And what about Griff?"

Ford meets my eyes. His gaze is steady. I pushed him to this, but he's not backing down. He's brave and honest. "I cared about Griff, too, a long time ago. Seeing him again brought all that back."

Emotion fills my chest. I reach for Ford's free hand and grip it. "Me too." Our gazes hold for a stretched out, vibrating moment. Then I turn to Chelsea. "You, my beautiful girl...I *am* falling in love with you."

Her fingers twitch against mine. Her eyes well with despair. "I don't understand any of this!"

"Yeah, you do." I smile. "You care about Ford, don't you?"

"Yes." Her tone is hushed, and she flicks him a shy glance. "I do. He's my best friend."

Ford's eyes flicker and the corners of his mouth tighten.

"Just a friend?" I ask gently. "Nothing more?"

"He...*you*..." She meets Ford's eyes. "You *couldn't* be anything more. You had a boyfriend. I knew...*thought*...you would never be interested in me. Then we were friends, and roommates, and...we couldn't..."

"Chelsea." Ford goes to his knees on the floor next to her. "What are you saying?"

Her eyelashes flutter like a hummingbird's wings and she nibbles her bottom lip. "I-I'm saying…" She casts me an agonized glance.

"It's okay." I squeeze her hand, my confidence growing. "Tell him."

She swallows. "When I first met you…that night…remember?"

A smile flits over Ford's lips. "Yeah."

"I thought you were so attractive."

Ford's chest rises and falls faster.

"I was disappointed when I saw you with a man. But…I still wanted to be your friend. Things clicked with us."

"They did." He holds her gaze steadily.

"After I moved in here, I started having…sex dreams about you."

"Ah." One corner of his mouth hitches up.

"It was embarrassing." She ducks her head. "That was why I started dating. I figured I needed…er, sex. Oh!" Her head jerks up.

"What, sweetheart?" Ford caresses her hand.

"Why did you break up with Jeff?"

His face takes on a look of sad resignation.

"Not because of me." She draws back, her teeth sunk into her bottom lip, eyebrows elevated.

Ford closes his eyes, tipping his head back. "Partly."

"Oh god." She shuts her eyes too, her mouth strained. "Oh, Ford."

"Don't. You didn't know."

She gives a slow nod. "Then I met Griff."

"Did that change your feelings for Ford?" I ask her quietly.

Again she looks distressed, like she's worried she's going to hurt me. "No. But Griff…I care about you, too. You know I do."

"I know. So, you see? You do understand how Ford can care about two people. Because you do, too. And…so do I."

"Christ." Ford's fingers grip mine tight enough to snap bones. "Griff…"

"I know. It's fucked up. But it's also kind of…extraordinary." And I, too, drop to my knees next to Chelsea.

Her breath lodges in her throat and she blinks rapidly. "Griff… don't…"

I know what she's saying. I'm the future King of Eria and I'm on my knees before a woman. But it feels right. "I need to do this."

Her lips tremble. Her eyes shine. Then she lifts her chin. "I care about both of you. I don't want to lose either of you. But I won't be lied to." She meets my eyes, then Ford's. "I won't be used or taken advantage of." The strength in her voice humbles me and makes me proud.

Ford and I turn to each other. I see Ford's regret and I feel my own like a hard knot in my chest.

"I promise." I bow my head and kiss her hand, still clasped in mine.

"I promise, too," Ford says quietly. "I'm sorry, Chelsea."

I watch her face and see the change as she realizes her power. And I love it.

"I can't choose between you," she says. "I *won't*. If you make me choose, I will hate both of you forever."

CHAPTER
EIGHTEEN

Chelsea

"Get up," I command.

Both men rise and sit beside me on the bed. My heart is racing, my hands shaking.

Ford...oh my god. Ford said he cares about me as more than a friend. I'm still trying to make sense of that and...I admitted I'm attracted to him. And I admitted I care about Griff. And Griff said he's falling in love with me.

Griff is right. This is a mess.

"I won't choose between you," I repeat in a whisper.

But what is the other option? They care about each other. I have to walk away and let them be together. But the thought of that breaks my heart. I'm pretty sure that's what that splintering sensation in my chest is.

"Christ." Ford mutters.

"What if you don't have to choose between us?" Griff says, his accented voice like velvet.

I search his face.

"What if you can have both of us?" he adds.

My eyes widen. My heart ricochets around in my chest.

"Griff. We're not one of your debauched games," Ford growls.

"I know." Griff is calm. Or he seems calm. But I can see the heat in his eyes, the tightness at the corners of his mouth. "That's not what I want."

Is he talking about having a threesome? Or is he saying I should see both of them…separately? But then…what about them?

I rub my temples.

"I feel like this is meant to be," Griff adds, still in that low, lush tone. "All of us. We all care about each other."

I glance at Ford. His eyes burn into mine. His cheeks are flushed. I've never seen Ford like this—shouting, fighting, angry, and passionate enough to punch someone. It's a little scary, except I know he would never hurt me, but it's also enlightening. His reactions show how much this means to him.

How much *we* mean to him.

My heart knocks against my breastbone again. I hold his gaze, sensing his unspoken question. His concern for me soothes my frantic heart. I'm safe with this man.

I turn to Griff. His gaze is earnest. Sincere. He believes what he said. *This is meant to be.*

I know what he means. There's a sense that our paths have converged in this way, at this time, for a reason. "You're going to have to be very clear with me," I say slowly. "I'm not…experienced… at things like this."

Am I interpreting this wrong? I'll be mortified if I am.

"Please tell me what you mean," I add.

Griff glances at Ford.

"It's up to her," Ford says in a low voice.

"All three of us," Griff says. "Together."

I swallow. "For sex." I can't even process that idea. Two men…at the same time. I swallow and my pussy clenches again. I squeeze my thighs together.

Griff's face pinches up. "I feel like this is more than sex." Once more, he looks at Ford. Their connection is thick and loaded. Then they turn their gazes back to me.

I'm actually considering this. No—being totally honest, I *want* this.

This could be the stupidest thing I've ever done, and I've been hoodwinked a couple of times. I want to believe this, that these two men really care about me, that this isn't some twisted way for them to be together. My head is telling me I'm being incredibly gullible. That men use women for depraved, selfish reasons all the time.

My heart looks both these men in the eyes and...trusts them.

Am I losing my mind?

And my body? My body craves this, with a burning intensity, a deep aching need I've never felt before.

Slowly, I nod my head.

I sense the air around us lighten and soften.

My eyes flutter closed as they both lean in to me and kiss my cheeks. So gentle, so careful...so sexy. Their faces are so close together as their mouths move closer to mine...I open my eyes and meet Ford's eyes.

We've never kissed. For a moment, I'm lost in his green tea eyes, feeling a little like I'm sliding slowly down a tunnel, everything disappearing behind me, fading around me. "Ford."

"Chelsea." His smile is so tender and intimate, and I'm consumed by it. My eyes close again as our mouths meet, his warm and firm. He licks along my bottom lip then slides his tongue inside. My belly is flip flopping, electric tingles buzzing over my skin as I kiss him back, opening to him, tasting him so deeply. His hand slides into my hair and twists, holding my head in place as our mouths cling.

He kisses me like a man who's been locked in a closet and was running out of air. His entire body strains toward me, hot and vibrating, inhaling me. His lips move on mine with soft licks and gentle nips.

He draws slowly back, and Griff moves in, taking my mouth in another kiss. I know his kisses, I know his taste, the feel of his tongue, and I want to lick inside his mouth and devour him.

As Griff and I kiss and kiss, Ford lifts my hair and opens his mouth on the side of my neck. Sensation trickles down my spine. I love having my hair touched, and my neck is so sensitive…a shiver works through me. The sensation of both these men touching me like this is nearly overwhelming. I'm melting, my bones dissolving.

Then, their faces still only a breath away, they turn to each other…I stare in helpless fascination as their eyes meet…hold…and their eyelids lower as their mouths meet too. Their kiss is hard but tender. Hungry but cautious. They each lift a hand to the other's face, Griff's thumb rubbing along Ford's jaw.

Emotion clogs my throat, watching them and the obvious yearning they have for each other. I can't be jealous because it's beautiful and pure. It's also hot. More heat pools low inside me and my heart explodes into an excited rhythm.

They draw apart and turn back to me.

"So sweet, Chelsea," Ford murmurs. "I love the taste of you. Finally, I'm tasting you." He gives me another lingering kiss. "Want to taste you everywhere."

"Oh." My breath all leaves my lungs.

They take turns kissing me again, and while one has my mouth, the other kisses my neck, my shoulder. Their hands move over my body, flattening on my stomach, caressing down one arm and back up, then cupping a breast. I swell into Griff's palm through my dress, my nipples tightening.

"Perfect," he mutters. "Goddamn perfect."

Ford's hand lands on my bare thigh, edging my dress higher, stroking my leg, getting closer to my aching center. Griff reaches over to run his hand over Ford's chest, then up to the back of his head, into his hair, pulling his head closer for long, scorching kisses that I watch in awe.

I move my hands to their thighs on either side of me...both strong, Griff lean, Ford thickly muscled from his cycling. My fingers curl over them and squeeze and I want to move higher. I want to know if they're aroused. But I'm hesitant. What if they're not? Is me grabbing their crotches getting a little presumptuous?

I've had sex but I'm not very experienced, and holy jumping Jesus on a jet ski, I've never had sex with two men at the same time. I feel like I'm in a dream and this isn't real.

"I don't know how to do this," I whisper, my eyes closed, head tipped back.

Griff sucks on the skin at my throat. "We'll take care of you."

"This is for you," Ford adds, kissing my shoulder. His hand is shaking when he covers my breast. "Christ, Chelsea. So soft..." He squeezes me gently, leaning his forehead on my shoulder.

I want my dress off.

As if he reads my mind, Griff reaches behind me and finds the tiny tab of the invisible zipper at the base of my neck. Slowly, he tugs it down and the fitted dress loosens around me.

My skin tingles everywhere as their hands move over me, both of them easing my dress off, lifting me, tossing it aside. I'm sitting in my strapless bra and panties, both pink.

Griff and Ford both bend to kiss my shoulders, the side of my neck, my jaw. As Ford tugs my earlobe between his lips, Griff's mouth drifts lower, opening on the upper curve of my breast above the edge of my bra, then between my breasts. Then he tugs the soft cup down to reveal my nipple. Shock ripples through me, but in a good way, flowing straight to my pussy. A deep inhale lifts my breasts and Griff slowly takes one sensitive nipple into his mouth and sucks.

The noise he makes—pleasure and pain combined, I think—inflames my senses. My head falls back, my hands still clamped onto their thighs. While Griff sucks my nipple, Ford kisses his way down there too, but he reaches behind me for the clasp of my bra and flicks it open. Then they're both sucking my nipples. The sensation shoots me straight up into the exosphere. My entire body trembles as sensation engulfs me. I've never felt this much. Every delicious, dirty feeling—it's almost unbearable.

I squirm with need as they play with my breasts, licking, sucking, cupping, and squeezing. Ford draws back to admire me, using his fingers to pluck the nipple and draw it out, and that's so hot I'm dying.

"Look at you," Ford whispers. "So pretty."

Griff tugs my bra away. Ford lifts one of my legs and lays it over his, Griff following with the other leg. I'm spread wide for them, my pulse racing, my core throbbing. Griff trails his hand down over my stomach and then over the front of my panties, cupping my pussy. I pulse against his palm.

"Hot." He rubs gently. "And wet."

I whimper because I can't speak. I know I'm wet.

"Are you aching, sweetheart?" Ford asks.

"Yes."

Ford shifts behind me and slips his arms around me so he can cup both breasts at the same time. He plays with me while Griff strokes and rubs my pussy, teases the sensitive skin of my inner thighs, and then curves his hand over me and squeezes possessively.

"What a hot little pussy," Griff says.

Behind me, a groan rumbles in Ford's chest. He pinches my nipples, sending sensation arrowing straight to my core. I slump back against Ford's chest, my arms and legs limp.

Griff slides off the bed to his knees again, hooking his fingers into my pink panties, and drawing them down my legs. I bite my lip in anticipation of being revealed so intimately. I'm nervous but so wound up I don't care, I just want more. So much more.

"Jesus," Griff breaths, studying me. He touches his fingertips to my flesh reverently. "So pretty."

He and Ford keep exchanging looks, communicating without words, and they do that now. Ford grasps my waist, lifting and turning me so I'm further on the bed, arranging me across his lap. Griff climbs back on, pausing to unbutton his shirt and shrug out of it.

"Oh yes." I reach out a hand to touch his chest, then his abs. His skin is lustrous gold, a dusting of light brown hair on his chest, and he's lean enough that the ridges of his abs show. I look up at Ford. "Take your shirt off, too."

Smiling, he helps me sit up while he reaches behind his neck to grab his T-shirt and pull it off. I settle back into his arms and now I get to feel him up, his muscled pecs and firm abs. I press my fingers over his collarbone then curl them around his strong shoulder.

They kiss me again, one after the other, then each other, all our mouths so close we're practically all kissing at the same time. It's magical and erotic and I'm floating, all heat and light and wanting.

Griff reaches out to touch, too, laying his hand over Ford's heart. Then he lifts my legs so I'm sideways on the bed, parts them and moves between them.

"Oh god." I try not to tense and clamp my thighs together.

"Relax," he whispers. "You're beautiful. I want to taste you. I want to feel you all over my face. My tongue. My lips."

A moan leaks from my lips and my knees fall wider. Ford bends and kisses my mouth, hot, wet, sliding kisses with tongue, his hand molding one breast, tweaking my nipple and then, oh! Griff's mouth lands on me in a soft, closed-mouth kiss. Tingles radiate from deep inside me, an achy knot of need tightening.

He kisses up and down the seam, kisses where my leg meets my groin, nips at the tendon in my thigh. He presses his nose to the triangle of hair I asked the girl to leave when I got waxed for the first time a week ago, breathing me in. "You smell incredible," he groans. "My cock is so hard I think I'm going to black out."

A soft huff leaves my lips, all the laugh I can muster, I'm so breathless.

"You and me both," Ford mutters.

Yes, now I can feel his erection. He's definitely hard. "I like that," I mumble.

"You like that you're making us hard?" Amusement colors Griff's voice.

My lips lift faintly. "Yeah." I really do.

"You only have to look at me and I'm hard as a fucking fire hydrant," Ford mutters.

"I didn't know that." I look up at him, my chest filling with something soft and fizzy.

He smiles down at me, his hand smoothing down my stomach and back up to my breast. "Now you know."

Griff's kisses progress to open-mouthed, sucking, nibbling on my flesh, his tongue sliding all over me. "Smooth. Soft." His tongue probes deeper. He groans again. "Fuck me. Your taste...Chelsea..."

"Christ." Ford grips my right breast. "I want that too."

"Patience," Griff mumbles. He slips an arm around my leg and splays his hand on my lower belly, draws back, and slips his fingers through my wetness. He watches this intently, his face hungry.

Ford kisses me again, and I drift on sensation, melting, becoming boneless. Griff's tongue flicks over my clit and my body jolts. He does it again, and again, and everything inside me tightens. He slides a finger inside me, then another, bending them and massaging a spot inside me that magnifies every sensation. I feel like a band is tightening around my womb.

"I want to make you come, baby," Griff murmurs. "Come on my face. My tongue." And he closes his lips around my clit and sucks.

I'm so lost I can't do anything but that as sensation takes over, a hot coil twisting up inside me, up and up to a peak of pure ecstasy bigger than anything I've ever experienced. I shudder through it, soft cries filling my bedroom along with the slick sounds of Griff's mouth and fingers on me and in me. Ford holds me, cradling me in his arms, murmuring soft words of praise, kissing me.

I quiver and close my thighs on Griff's head, unable to bear any more. He rises, his mouth wet, his eyes gleaming. "Bloody hell. That was...spiritual."

Ford laughs softly and I attempt a smile, snuggled lethargically against Ford. "I agree. I think I saw angels."

"That was my talented tongue." Griff kisses me softly, that talented tongue sliding over my bottom lip, tasting faintly of my own essence.

"Cocky," I say.

"Indeed." He presses his hand to the front of his pants where a definite bulge is straining the zipper.

"What do we do now?" I ask, although I sort of feel like sleeping.

"Whatever you want, pet."

"I want you to take your clothes off."

They exchange a grin.

"Happy to oblige." Ford settles me on the bed and rolls off to strip out of his jeans and underwear.

Ford. I'm seeing Ford naked. I've imagined Ford naked, but this is real life. My languor disappears and is replaced with excitement as I take in the thick muscles and defined angles of his hips and legs and...his cock.

Oh yeah, he's hard. Broad and heavy. Pulsing with veins.

My lips part as I watch him kneel on the bed. I want to touch him so I stretch out a hand and feel his...knee. Not quite brave enough yet.

Griff also takes off the black dress pants he's wearing. His body is long and lean and elegant, his cock just as beautiful, similar to Ford's but uncircumcised, which intrigues me.

"Let's move you." Ford again picks me up with ease. Griff pulls down the covers and Ford lowers me to the sheets, a pillow beneath my head. They lay down on either side of me and tug the covers up over us.

I'm imagining both those cocks inside me, but how will this work? I feel so innocent, even though I'm having very dirty thoughts. And I'm in bed with two men.

Holy shit. I'm in bed with two men.

Okay, it's too late to freak out. And surprisingly, while it's a bit surreal, it feels right. I also feel a sense of agency. Griff and Ford are so attentive and eager to please me with their touches, their looks, their kisses. It makes me feel strong and secure and in control.

It's what I've always wanted.

CHAPTER
NINETEEN

Ford

My dick is so engorged I think I might burst. God, how long have I wanted this?

To be with Chelsea, yes. On top of that, I didn't realize how goddamn much I missed Griff.

Watching them together tormented me. Yeah, I've been jealous. But not how you'd think. I wanted them both.

Greedy much?

I've never cared about anyone else like I've cared about these two people. I still can't believe we all ended up together like this. I'm still not sure if it's bad luck or good.

Right now, we have to make this good for Chelsea. Griff and I both know that. Right now, this isn't about us. She's sweet and good and taking probably the biggest risk of her entire sheltered life.

Watching Griff's head between Chelsea's legs, licking her, pleasuring her, was like my own pleasure. Holding her as she came was humbling. She's beautiful and brave.

She lays between us, eyes closed, mouth curved into a soft smile. I can't resist touching her and I roll onto my side, prop my head up on one elbow, and trail my fingers down her arm.

Her smile deepens.

I meet Griff's eyes across her body. He, too, pushes up and leans over to kiss me. Our mouths meet in a jolt of heat that radiates through my body. I slide my tongue over his bottom lip and taste Chelsea, and my dick twitches.

When we move apart, I look down at Chelsea to see her watching us. Her lips are parted, eyes hazy. "You guys…"

"What, sweetheart?" I push hair off her forehead.

"I want you to be happy."

My heart squeezes. I glance at Griff. I don't know what to say to that, because this is a fucked-up situation and I have no idea what the hell we're doing. "I'm happy right now."

Her smile quavers.

I caress her stomach, then slide my hand up between her breasts and let it rest there.

"We want *you* to be happy," Griff says.

"You just made me very happy," Chelsea says with a tiny smirk, surprising me.

"You want more of that?" I ask, moving to cover one of her sweet tits with my hand. I give a gentle squeeze.

"More orgasms are never a bad thing."

Griff chuckles and I grin.

"Not gonna argue with that," I say. I glance at Griff again. What's our plan here?

"Do it," he says quietly to me.

"We have all night," I answer.

"All weekend," he counters, one corner of his mouth lifting. He looks at Chelsea. "We might exhaust you, love."

Her eyes flick between Griff and me. "You two think you have enough stamina to do this all weekend?"

"Oh! A challenge," Griff says. "I love a challenge." He kisses her.

"Me too. Chels...have you got condoms?"

"I do." She gestures at the dresser across the room and rolls her eyes.

I throw back the covers, swing my legs over the side of the bed, and walk over to the dresser.

"Not that I've needed them," she adds.

I've assumed that Chelsea and Griff have been fucking. I turn and shoot Griff a sharp look. "Haven't you two...?"

"No," they both answer.

Chelsea nibbles her bottom lip. "I wanted to."

"Oh Christ, me too," Griff adds with a groan.

"It just never...worked out," Chelsea adds.

A rush of emotion roars through me, so intense it almost drops me to my knees. This is the first time for me and Chelsea, but also the first time for her and Griff. That makes this feel even more momentous.

"Top drawer," Chelsea says.

I pull it open and see the box. I bring the whole thing, because hey, apparently we're going to be here a while.

Standing beside the bed, I open a package and roll the rubber onto my aching cock, acutely aware of both Griff and Chelsea watching me with heated gazes. My dick swells even more, and I give it a fast, hard stroke.

We take turns kissing Chelsea, long and sweet, lush and wet. And in between we kiss each other.

We cup her breasts, dipping our heads to take her sweet nipples into our mouths in hungry draws. Chelsea's hands slide into our hair, holding us in place as we lick and nibble, soft breathy sounds tumbling from her lips. Our heads are close together, so close we can touch—and we do, exchanging heated glances and then joining our mouths in scorching, brutal kisses.

We caress her body from shoulder to hip, over her thighs. I part them and find her wet pussy and growl my appreciation. "So wet, sweetheart."

"Mmmm."

"Doesn't she have the prettiest pussy?" Griff asks.

I push down the covers and move between her legs to see. With gentle hands I open her thighs wider and study her glistening pink folds. My dick hardens even more. "So pretty. Need a taste."

I bend my head as Chelsea moans, "Oh please, I need more. I need you inside me."

"Getting impatient, love?" Griff says with a wicked smile.

I could sink between her thighs and stay here all night, inhaling her scent, tasting her arousal. But I want to be inside her, too, so I lick, tease her clit, kiss her belly, then rise up onto my knees.

Griff sits up too. "You fuck Chelsea. I'm going to fuck you."

My heart bounces hard and my dick jumps. This is new for Chelsea, but it's new for me too. I mean, being with two people.

"I want to fuck you both," Griff adds in his elegant accent.

I bend to give Chelsea a soft, lingering kiss. "You're amazing."

She sucks in a breath and gazes up at me with eyes full of trust. I want to deserve that trust. I want to look after her.

Griff walks around the bed and grabs another condom. He holds it out to me. "Put this on me."

His voice holds all the imperiousness of a prince. Or a king.

"Yes, your highness."

He snorts and my lips twitch. I take my time rolling the thin latex down his shaft, admiring his shape and the velvety softness of his skin. I brush my fingertips over his balls and he sucks in air.

"We need lube," he murmurs, looking to Chelsea.

"Same drawer." She lifts her chin.

"Perfect." As I glove up, he moves away and returns with a small bottle. He squeezes silky liquid into his palm, then strokes it over his dick. I clench again, thinking about him penetrating me. My dick throbs and I grip it, sliding it up and down through Chelsea's slit, slicking it up. I meet her eyes as I find her entrance and she gives a tiny nod and pulls her knees higher.

"Please," she breathes.

I ease in gradually, inch by excruciating inch. Her body's a tight glove wrapping around me, and a groan climbs my throat. When I'm seated fully inside her, throbbing against her snug channel, I lower myself over her and bury my face in the side of her neck. I breathe in her scent, fighting the need to come. "Okay?" I ask hoarsely.

"Yes." She grabs my thigh with one hand, digs her fingers into my back with her other. "God, that feels good. So deep."

Griff moves behind me, grips my hips, then rubs against my ass. Every nerve ending in my body tightens and I shudder against Chelsea, sliding my hands into her hair. She pets my back as Griff rims my hole with a lubed-up finger. My balls throb and tension builds at the base of my spine. Then he pushes inside me, past the tight ring of muscle, and I let out another long groan.

"Yeah," Griff murmurs. "Feel that? Feel good?"

I can only grunt.

Griff's finger slips out to be replaced with the thick head of his cock pushing at me.

"Tight, Jesus, fuck," Griff mutters.

"Christ." I shudder again, heat pulsing through me. I go still, electricity sizzling over my skin, my cock swelling and pulsing inside Chelsea.

"Okay, Chelsea?" Griff rasps.

"Yes...it's good. I feel you...your weight..."

I feel it too. The three of us joined like this. So intimate. Our bodies. Our souls. Our three hearts. So much beauty and perfection.

Chelsea cries out as we both move, Griff fucking me from behind, pushing me deeper inside her. Pleasure scrapes over that sensitive spot inside me, fire spreading through my body, coiling up tight inside me.

"Fuck, not gonna take long." I find the rhythm with Griff. "Inside your tight pussy, Chelsea...and Griff in my ass. Christ..."

"Fuck, me too." Griff groans. "Chelsea...?"

"Close." She shifts her pelvis beneath us, and I shift too, rubbing against her clit.

Griff and I push, me into her, him into me. I'm nearly out of my mind with the dual sensation on my dick and in my ass, and when Chelsea's fingernails dig into my back and she wails, I let myself go, ripped apart by sensation, wild, hot, exquisite. I grunt and shout through my release, hearing their cries through a dark roar in my ears. Griff's fingers bruise my hips as he presses his groin to me, tensing against me. Then he falls over my back, arms outstretched, fists pressed into the mattress. He kisses Chelsea, lifts and turns his head and manages to kiss me too.

We collapse into a damp tangle of sweaty limbs, heaving chests, and pounding hearts. I try to keep my weight off Chelsea and after a moment, Griff and I move and try to extricate ourselves, bumping elbows, his foot landing near my junk. It's clumsy and awkward and yet I laugh. "Jesus, Prince Charming, watch yourself."

"Better I hoof you than Chelsea."

She laughs too. "I agree."

CHAPTER
TWENTY

Chelsea

We do in fact pretty much spend the weekend in bed, except it's not my bed. Saturday morning, Griff convinces us to go to his place, or rather the house he's borrowing, so his security dudes can be there and there's more room. Also there's a king-size bed, which is a good thing with two big, tall men. And also a Jacuzzi tub outside!

We stop for brunch on the way to Griff's house although I get a bit jumpy because this restaurant is so close to my dad's place, I'm worried he could walk in. Sitting in the sunny café with Ford next to me and Griff across from us, eating my poached eggs and toast, I have another wave of *is this for real?* I've always been comfortable with Ford, until recently, and I slide back into that, leaning into his shoulder when he makes a bad joke, teasing him, stealing some of his hash browns. And Griff watches us with such amusement and heat, it gives me the confidence to flirt with both of them.

Both. Of. Them.

For the moment, I can pretend this is all fine. I can push away any misgivings and have fun. I can indulge in the attention of two men who seem to find me attractive and who flirt back.

We go for a walk. I lead the way to the nearby park, where I often played as a child. As we stroll, Ford and Griff talk, sharing memories from when they were in Afghanistan together. I listen intently. Ford doesn't talk about that time to me, and I'm eager to learn more about him and his past.

And about Griff's, too. I can tell from how he speaks about his stint there that it was important to him. And it sounds like he was good at what he did—flying Apache helicopters.

"He saved my ass," Ford says to me, relating the story of how he and his platoon had been under fire and Griff swept in with his helicopter.

"Eh. I was doing my job," Griff says, faint color rising in his cheeks.

"You didn't want to leave, did you?" I ask quietly.

"No. I was pissed." He makes a face. "But obviously I couldn't risk the lives of anyone there. My family was worried about me, but I was worried about what the Taliban would do if I was still there."

My stomach tightens at his talk about his life being at risk. But of course it was. Everyone who was there risked their life to be there. Including Ford.

I feel such a sense of respect and admiration for both of them. Seeing the walls they'd put up coming down fills me with happiness as they share memories and make jokes and talk about things they've done since they were together.

I can see the affection they have for each other under the quips. There's a connection between them that seems to have survived miles and years apart, but also to have survived their fight about me. It tugs at my heart, filling me with a strange yearning. I care about both these men, but I've never had someone love me that powerfully, that immensely. Seeing them together is beautiful and heart-warming, but also saddening as I long for that kind of love.

Because this is fun—wicked, erotic, dangerous fun—but this can't last. Obviously. While I push that knowledge to the back of my brain and enjoy myself being wanton and wild and reckless, it's always there, teasing at the edges of my consciousness.

I lie on my side in the bed, Ford in front of me, kissing me. Griff presses against my back, kissing my shoulder, my neck, my ear. I cup Ford's face and Griff's hand slides over Ford's upper arm and shoulder.

"Love this," Griff murmurs. "Feeling you between us."

Ford's mouth moves down my throat. My eyes closed, my mouth falls open, fighting for breath as both men nuzzle and kiss me. Ford licks my throat and cups one breast as Griff caresses my butt. I'm sandwiched between them, their mouths and hands moving over me. Ford finds my mouth for more long, deep kisses and I reach behind me and feel for Griff's cock. He groans, his mouth near my ear. I stroke up and down and his hands slide around me and cup both breasts.

"You feel amazing." I stroke Griff's cock. "Both of you. I can't believe this."

"I know." Ford lays his lips over my heart. "I know."

Griff pulls my hair back and nudges me more in front of him so he can lean under me and kiss Ford. With soft nipping kisses, Griff and I kiss, Ford and I kiss, Ford and Griff kiss. My head is swimming, spinning, my blood filled with carbonation.

The air sparks and snaps around us. My nipples are tight and tender, Griff's harsh breath in my ear, Ford's lips on mine. It's messy and awkward, and also sweet and sublime. I'm lost in the sensation. I can't think, can only feel, two men against me, hard muscle, sleek, hot skin, strong hands, warm mouths.

Griff shifts back and once again they're both nuzzling my hair and ears, kissing my cheek and jaw, and Griff's hand slips between my butt cheeks. Leaning into Ford, I kiss him and run my hands over his pecs.

Griff rolls away for a few seconds. As Ford kisses me I'm barely aware of the rustling sounds of Griff donning a condom, then he's back, sliding his hand up and down my slit, finding me slick. The head of his cock replaces his fingers, pressing at my entrance, a pinching sensation fading into fullness as he enters me. Ford kisses me, his hand caressing my arm, then Griff's, then back to me. Ford's erection swells against my thigh as the three of us press closer together, Griff fucking me from behind, their arms around me and each other, their breathing harsh and guttural in my ears. I hold onto Ford's shoulder, Griff's slow thrusts pushing me into Ford. Griff holds onto Ford too.

"Does she feel tight?" Ford asks.

"Yes." Griff presses his mouth to my shoulder. "So fucking tight. So fucking juicy. We make you wet, love, don't we?"

"So wet." I lift an arm behind me to find Griff's head and thread my fingers through his hair. He kisses my upper back with open-mouthed kisses, his tongue lingering on my skin. Ford kisses me then Griff leans over my shoulder to kiss Ford. Once more, Griff draws my hair back and kisses my shoulder, fingers curled around my upper arm, sliding in and out of me. Ford's arm goes over me and clutches Griff's ass, pulling all of closer still. It's all a jumble of mouths and hands, kissing, stroking, fucking.

Ford moves away, shifting to his back. With a smile, I push the covers down to reveal his enormous erection. I want to touch him. I want to taste him. My mouth longs for it. So I do. I curl my fingers around him and lean down to kiss the tip. Griff's still moving inside me and I push my butt back against his hips as I lick Ford's cock all over and then take him in.

"Christ, your mouth." Ford slides his hand into my hair and drags his fingers over my scalp. "Suck me…like that. Fuuuck."

I rest my cheek on his abs, working with my mouth and my hand to jerk him, hands caressing my waist, my hip, my shoulder. I hear their breathing behind me, their murmurs and guttural noises, their kisses.

Ford shifts away and moves to the foot of the bed where he kneels and leans in to lick me right where Griff's cock is fucking me. "Oh yeah. Look at you. Look at him stretching you there. Gorgeous."

Heat blazes through me as his tongue slides over my clit, but also over Griff's shaft. He lifts my leg over Griff's hip and Griff slides his hand around my neck, pulling me around to face him, cupping my jaw, kissing me as Ford licks, teasing my straining clit. My entire body is seized with electricity, quivering, straining with need.

Hand on my throat, Griff lifts his head to look down at Ford, watching him. He reaches down to glide his fingers into Ford's thick hair. His cock slips out of me and Ford lays soft kisses over it as he guides it back into me.

Hot. Beautiful. Moving.

Ford's mouth on me combines with the sensation of Griff's cock inside me, a tight coil inside me twisting up. Then Griff pulls out of me and rolls me to my back. I gasp at the emptiness, pulsing on nothing, but he climbs over me and pushes inside again, this time fucking me hard and fast. I can't stop the noises that fall from my lips as he drives into me, my orgasm so close to the surface that I climax, crying out, sensation rocketing through me. I am fucked senseless.

Griff reaches for Ford's cock and jerks him, and he comes, shooting onto my belly. He groans and collapses beside me, finding my mouth in a long, hard kiss as Griff climaxes with a shout, holding himself tight to my pussy, pulsing so deep inside me.

A moment later, Griff stretches out on the other side of me, the opposite of how we started, but I'm still between them.

"You're a goddamn queen," Griff mutters. "I can't get enough of you. And Ford. I want to fuck you. And fuck you. And fuck you."

I'm already limp and spent, but his words seep into the depths of me and melt my soul.

~

"I saw in the news that your grandfather had passed," Ford says to Griff. "I'm sorry."

Griff nods. "Thanks. I loved him. He was a good king. And a good grandfather."

"Which means you're now next in line to the throne."

"Indeed." Griff sighs.

I remember him saying that he'll become king even if he doesn't want to. "You'll be a great king."

"I can never be as beloved as my grandfather. Even my father, who is king now. When I got back to Eria after Afghanistan, I tried my best to do my royal duties and play the part of the heir to the throne." He pauses. "I was fucking miserable."

My throat squeezes. "I'm sorry."

He shrugs, looking a little shamefaced. "I shouldn't complain. I know what a privileged life I lead. But the formality and rules and conventions make me feel like I'm smothering. I at least felt somewhat better when I started my foundation. Then I had something meaningful to work on—a way that I could do good, in a very real, tangible way. Something I was responsible for, myself. And I was so happy to get away and come here for a time."

"You figured it out," Ford says in a low voice. "We talked about that...back then. About how you felt trapped in your life."

Their eyes meet and I watch the understanding pass between them, a connection that shows me the value and strength they get from each other. Without judgment.

"How you felt trapped in *your* life," I say to Ford.

His gaze slides to me and he nods. "Yeah."

"Well, I think you've both done remarkable things to deal with that." I lean over and kiss Ford, then Griff.

"Amazing girl," Griff says, his voice rough. He curls a hand around the back of my neck and pulls me in. "You're doing amazing things to deal with feeling trapped in your life, too."

"They don't seem very amazing." I pause. "Other than this."

"You're doing things that are hard for you. That's wonderful."

My chest heats at his praise. I consider that. I've been trying. "Having a threesome wasn't exactly the way I planned to do it."

They both chuckle.

"In a way, though, it's a big step," Ford says. "Doing what you really want even though it's...risky."

More pride swells in me.

"And taboo," Ford adds.

"And with a prince," I add cheekily. "What could we do that could make it even more shocking?"

"Go public." Ford gives a twisted smile.

I laugh and meet his eyes. He shrugs. He's joking. We could never do that.

This is definitely stepping outside my comfort zone. Taking a risk. Holy hell. It's like a smack in the face, realizing how much of a risk it is. Not even so much for me—nobody cares about my sex life. Except my dad. Not that I'd tell him about my sex life, but...oh my god, he'd have a stroke.

But Griff—he has a lot on the line here. His playboy past is supposed to be just that—in the past. He's going to be King of Eria. And Ford? He could be president someday. His reputation as an upstanding citizen if he wants to run for office is definitely at risk.

"What are we doing?" I whisper, pressing my hands to my cheeks.

"Easy, lovely." Griff slides his arms around me and pulls me against him. "Don't think about it too much. Let's just enjoy these moments, yeah?"

"Exactly." Ford kisses the back of my neck.

This can't go anywhere. This is crazy. But I'm distracted from my panicked urge to run by two sets of hands on me, spoiling me, competing to give me orgasms, giving me so much pleasure I'm drowning in it.

CHAPTER
TWENTY-ONE

Griff

"Wanna fuck you," I whisper against Ford's mouth.

Ford groans and our kisses turn hard, savage.

We're in my bed, Sunday afternoon. We've taken turns with Chelsea, fooled around a lot with each other, and I fucked him while he was inside Chelsea. But this time I want him. Just him. "Face to face," I growl.

Ford rolls to his back and holds out a hand to Chelsea. "Come here, sweet girl."

She smiles. "This time is for you two," she whispers, scooting herself up onto the pillows. She leans over to kiss Ford and then shifts toward me. I kiss her mouth, hard and grateful, knowing what she's doing. "I'm here,"

I meet her eyes. "Queen," I whisper.

She smiles.

Ford and I haven't been together, alone, since Afghanistan. This isn't alone—but it's the two of us, face to face. I move over him, kissing him with deep, devouring kisses, holding his face in my hands. He grips my shoulders, caresses the back of my neck as our mouths crush together. I move my mouth off his and stare into his eyes, nose to nose.

Something like a jolt of electricity passes through me. For a moment, I'm outside my body, filled with that insatiable hunger I've felt since that night I spent with Ford in Afghanistan. Nothing and nobody has ever been able to fill it...like this.

I kiss my way down his body, licking his nipples. I pause to play there, tugging one tight nub into my mouth, making him jerk with pleasure. His thick cock rises against my leg. I pinch and suck, then move back up to his mouth again in hard, eating kisses. I slide my lips to the side of his neck and suck his skin into my mouth. He makes urgent, rough noises, hands moving over me, his knees coming to the sides of my hips. We kiss and I rock against him then lift up and stare down into his eyes again.

"You feel it," I whisper.

His hazy eyes brighten and his lips quirk. "Not yet. Fuck me, for Chrissake."

"You know what I mean." I kiss him once more, hard, then slide down his body, kissing his chest, his abs, then shifting lower. "I always remembered those nights with you," I murmur against the tender skin just above his cock. I brush my lips over the trail of hair.

"Me too," he groans. "Christ. That was my first time with a man."

Chelsea makes a small noise from beside us.

"My first time with a prince," Ford adds.

I huff out a laugh and lick over his hip bone. "You've been with other princes since then?"

Ford's lips quirk, his eyes closed. "So many."

I hide my smile against his pubic hair, inhaling his scent—musky, male, aroused. I curl my hand around his cock and stroke it, then bring it to my mouth. As I close my lips around him, I look up at him and our eyes lock. He slides a hand over the top of my head, strokes my cheek. I let his cock slip out of my mouth. It lays thick and heavy on his belly, and I run my lips from root to tip.

I slide my hand under his balls and squeeze. "Fantastic," I mutter. "So full."

He makes a low, strangled noise. I suck him, lick him, rub the head of his cock around my lips and suck him again. I love the feel of him in my mouth, the pulsing heat, the meaty weight of him on my tongue. "Perfect."

I move lower still and push Ford's legs up so I can nuzzle his balls, and I lick and suck there, too, tenderly.

"Oh god," Chelsea breathes. I glance at her and she's wide-eyed, open mouthed, her finger playing between her thighs.

I move back up over Ford and lick his mouth. "Chelsea."

"Yeah?"

"Can you get us a condom and the lube, love?"

She quickly stretches out and yanks open the drawer, tosses the bottle onto the bed then holds up a condom.

"Put it on me."

She obeys, efficiently wrapping me up, though I have to grit my teeth at the sensation of her soft fingers on me. I squeeze liquid into my palm, drizzle more all over Ford's cock and balls, then rub it in, making both our cocks slick and shiny.

Ford breathes hard and unevenly, watching us. He slides his hands beneath his knees and pulls them back toward his chest, his cock pulsing on his belly as I move between his legs on my knees.

"Oh yeah," I said. "Gonna fuck you now. Gonna fuck you so hard."

"Yes. Do it."

Chelsea's eyes widen as she watches, her breath quickening even more, back with her fingers between her legs.

"Perfect girl. Good girl," I say. "Touch yourself. So sweet but so dirty."

I rise up and grab Ford's knees, pushing them higher still. I slide a hand under his ass and lift, yanking a pillow down and stuffing it under his hips for a better angle. Then I push into him, slowly, watching his face. He grunts and his jaw tightens, eyes closing, his mouth open on jagged breaths.

Heat runs through me, right to my balls. My throat clogs with emotion as I slam back into the moment. I am here. With Ford. Again. At last.

I push one hand into the mattress on a straight arm and slide the other around the back of his neck, grind my mouth into his, and start moving, slowly, then faster. Harder. His groans fill my ears. He grips my ribs and my ass flexes as I fuck him, bouncing the bed. Holding his legs up, his chest and hard-packed abs gleaming with perspiration, his face tight and intense, I pound into him.

The feel of him around my dick, that tight ring of muscle, has hot sparks crackling over my skin, my balls pulling up tight.

He jerks his own cock, his face tight with pain "Gonna come," he mutters thickly, head moving on the pillow. "Fuck me, I'm gonna... ungh." His words turn into a growl, and he pulses in his own hand, so alive, so hot, white jets of semen spurting onto his belly. I shout, too, holding myself against Ford's body, my fingers gripping his legs. Pleasure explodes and races up my spine, blazing in my chest, and I gush into the tight heat of his ass.

We collapse together on the bed. I vaguely hear Chelsea's whimpers as she comes too, and then she's there with us, laying kisses all over our faces. I pull her between us and we all peace out into luscious bliss.

~

"Now what happens?"

Ford and I look at each other. Ford's jaw tightens. I drop my gaze and rub the back of my neck.

It's Sunday evening. Ford and Chelsea have to work in the morning. I have meetings, too. Do we go back to life as it was before this weekend? Do we *want* to go back to that?

I sure as hell don't.

Now that I've been with both of them, I can't image not being with both of them. "I don't suppose I could convince you two to stay here?"

Now Ford and Chelsea exchange glances.

"That's a long commute," Ford says slowly.

"It is," I agree. "But people do it."

"True. My dad, who lives so close to here, for one," Chelsea says.

"You need your men to chauffeur you around," Ford says. "And there isn't room for them at my place."

"Right you are," I reply sadly.

"Okay," Chelsea says. "Ford and I will go home. You'll visit when you can."

They turn to me. Ford's lips lift into a tiny smile.

"Taking charge, queen?" I say.

She rolls her eyes.

One corner of my mouth hooks up. "What about the baseball game next weekend?"

"Right." She slides her gaze back over to Ford. "We could all go to the game."

For a moment there's silence as we mull this over.

"Why not?" I finally say. "The media has already outed you and me. They won't think anything of a friend being with us."

Ford's eyes narrow and his mouth pinches in a brief grimace. Then his face clears and he nods.

Chelsea sucks briefly on her bottom lip. She's thinking what I'm thinking—that Ford feels like he'll be tagging along with us, since we're a couple in the eyes of the world. "What other way is there?" she asks him.

"I know."

She reaches for Ford's hand and squeezes it, holding his gaze.

"This is fucked," he mutters.

"Yes indeed," I say cheerfully. "We are all literally well fucked."

Chelsea does another eye roll and smiles at me. "You're a bad man."

"I am. I've never tried to hide that fact."

She shakes her head. "No. You try to hide the fact that deep down inside you're actually a very good man."

I gasp with mock outrage. "Quiet! Don't let that get out."

Still holding Ford's hand, she reaches over and grabs mine, too. "I make no promises."

CHAPTER

TWENTY-TWO

Ford

Life is crazy enough with what's happening between Chelsea, Griff and me. But now my work is about to get rough.

Five weeks ago the FBI raided the office of Alderman Dennis Freytag. And I learned that Alderman Freytag is a close friend of Chelsea's father.

Today, I'm afraid to go home.

Just kidding. I love coming home to Chelsea, especially now she knows how I feel about her. And she feels the same about me. And Griff. Yeah, it's complicated. At some point we're going to have to deal with it, but right now we're riding it. We've been to a baseball game, out for dinner, and a couple of long bike rides along the lake shore. Always followed by Griff's security team, of course.

Chelsea's almost always home before me, although I've started getting home earlier. I still love my job, but with something worth going home for, it doesn't seem quite as important that I work late every night.

She's in the kitchen when I walk in, singing to the music playing —a hip hop song I don't know. She's not the best singer but she's enthusiastic and adorable. "We ain't back, yuh. Go suck it in the shack. We ain't back, yuh. Nothin' but crack."

"What the hell are you singing?" I set my messenger bag on the counter, grinning.

She starts and her cheeks redden. "A song! It's Lil Rock."

"I have no clue who Lil Rock is."

"I know. You need to listen to better music than that country shit."

"Country shit." I shake my head. "Sad."

"I'm making dinner and it's almost ready. Good thing you got here now."

"Wouldn't want to keep you waiting."

"Oh no worries, I wouldn't wait. I'm starving." She flashes a cheeky smile.

I round the counter, wrap her in my arms and kiss the breath out of her. We're both panting and blinking by the time we pull apart.

"Whoa," she says.

"I'll go change." I pat her cute ass and head down the hall to my room. Where she's been sleeping since we got back from Griff's place.

Griff's been here a few nights since then, but his schedule has been busy. Is he coming over tonight? I haven't heard from him, but he could have talked to Chelsea.

In a pair of sweats and a T-shirt, I return to the kitchen. Chelsea's lifting aluminum foil off a baking dish sitting on the stove.

"Smells good. What is it?"

"Baked ziti with spinach, mushrooms, and ricotta."

I frown. "No meat?"

She bumps me with her hip. "You'll survive."

"Is Griff coming?"

"Later. He has a business dinner."

We dish up and carry our plates into the living room. Chelsea grabs the remote and turns the TV on. We often eat in front of the TV while watching news.

And there it is.

"Alderman Dennis Freytag, who is chairman of the powerful Finance Committee, has been charged with one count of attempted extortion, according to a criminal complaint filed Wednesday and unsealed Thursday."

Chelsea stops eating and stares at the TV. Her gaze swivels to me.

I meet her eyes and hold her gaze steadily.

The TV news anchor is still speaking. "Freytag stepped down as chairman of the City Council's Finance Committee this morning, according to a statement from Mayor Samuel Slater's office. Mayor Slater said that he spoke with Alderman Freytag who agreed the best course of action was for him to resign as Chairman of the Committee on Finance."

"This is why the FBI raided his office last month," Chelsea says slowly.

I nod.

"You know about this."

I nod again.

"My dad is going to lose his shit."

That is entirely possible. "I'm sorry, Chels."

She nods, looking troubled. Then she sighs and takes a bite of ziti.

We're just finishing our meal when her cell phone rings. She reaches over and picks it up. "Surprise! It's Dad."

She answers and I pick up our plates and cutlery to carry them into the kitchen.

"Hi, Dad. Good! How are you?" She listens. "Yes. Yes, I did." She glances my way. "Oh. Did they? Huh." A longer pause. "Dad. That's his job. No, I didn't know. He doesn't talk to me about his cases." She frowns. "Absolutely not." Her cheeks get pink. "Look, you don't know Ford very well, but I do. And I trust him to do his job fairly and impartially."

Heat spreads through my chest. I quietly clean the kitchen as she talks.

"If Dennis did something wrong, something illegal, then he deserves the consequences of that," Chelsea says. "But I'm sure he'll get a fair trial and a chance to tell his side of the story."

I smile.

"Ford is the most honorable man I know," she says firmly. "Justice and fairness are important to him." She listens. "Yes. Yes. That's right. Because I know him, Dad." She goes quiet, listening again, shaking her head. She covers her eyes with her hand. "Look, Dad—" She pauses, then tries, again, "Dad. *Dad.* I'm not listening to you if you're going to say those things. Let's talk when you're in a better frame of mind."

She ends the call and flops back on the couch, eyes closed.

"He's not happy," I say from the kitchen.

"Nope. He is *pissed*." She sighs.

I dry my hands on a towel, hang it up, then return to the living room. I sit next to her on the couch. "I'm sorry, sweetheart."

She opens her eyes. "Don't apologize for doing your job."

"How did he hear?"

"They mentioned your name in the newspaper as the AUSA who's prosecuting the case."

"Ah. Well. Thank you for defending my honor."

She smiles and reaches out to push hair back off my forehead. "You are an honorable man. I believe everything I said to Dad."

"Thank you."

It's been rare in my life to have people who believe in me. Who'll defend me and protect me. Griff. And Chelsea. Something spins in my chest, hot and soft.

"Are you okay?" She eyes me, a small notch between her eyebrows.

"I'm great. I knew this was going to be uncomfortable. Thanks for being you."

She smiles. "I'm always here for you, Ford."

I lift her hand to my mouth and press my lips to her knuckles. "Thank you."

Not only am I moved by her defending me, I'm awed by her willingness to stand up to her father, who I know is not easy to stand up to. Chelsea is growing into an impressive woman. And I'm so fucking lucky to have her in my life.

"No, you can't trip someone when they have the puck."

Chelsea and I are explaining hockey to Griff as we watch the Chicago Aces. We have a suite to ourselves, which somehow Griff conjured up, and we're sitting right at the wall to watch.

The Aces just took a tripping penalty and Armstrong skates to the penalty box below us.

"So he gets a time out?" Griff asks.

Chelsea laughs. "Yes. For two minutes."

"And they have to play without him?" Griff asks. "Can't someone else play?"

"No. They have to play a man short."

"Okay, I guess that's fair."

We watch the Aces try to kill the penalty, but the Bears get the puck and hold onto it in the Aces zone, cycling between players over and over, until finally Heller shoots at the net and goddammit, it goes in.

"Shit," I mutter.

Chelsea drops her head forward. The first goal of the game.

Armstrong leaves the box and Griff points. "Hey, you said two minutes."

"Unless the other team scores. Then the penalty ends."

"Hmm."

They drop the puck at center ice and the game goes on. Karmeinski goes after Balachov from the Aces and lays a huge hit on him against the boards, and the crowd roars.

Griff roars, too. "What the bloody hell! Can they do that?"

"Yeah, that was a good hit."

"They can't trip but they can do *that*? That guy was laid right out! What the hell!"

I laugh at his outrage. "Um, yeah."

"That seems dodgy. What a cocked-up sport this is."

Chelsea bumps her shoulder against his. "You'll love it. Keep watching."

Of course he's a big fan by the end of the game. I'm surprised at Chelsea's knowledge of hockey. I love the game. Maybe our enthusiasm helped convince Griff it's fun.

After the game ends, we wait until most of the fans have dispersed, then prepare to leave. Griff's men step out first, then Jac comes back in. "There's a crowd out there," he says to Griff.

"What? Ah, hell."

"Somehow they found out you're here. What would you like us to do?"

"How many?"

"Twenty, twenty-five."

Griff sighs and rubs his forehead. "Okay, escort us through them."

We step out, Griff going first. Upon seeing him, they all squeal. They're all women. Young women.

"It *is* him!" one cried. "Prince Griffin! Are you a hockey fan?"

Chelsea and I share a look and follow behind. Nobody's interested in us. I try to use my size to create a barrier between some of the women and Chelsea.

"Hello, loves," Griff says with a cheerful wave as Rhys and Jac run interference for him. "I'm a hockey fan now. Good game by the Aces."

"Prince Griffin!" A young woman rushes at him. Jac attempts to stop her. "I love you! Marry me and I'll have your babies!"

Chelsea chokes on a laugh.

Phones are out, camera's clicking as they take pictures.

Jac is in a bit of a scuffle with the girl, clearly not wanting to hurt her, but she's fighting with him to get free.

Now Chelsea frowns. With a wry look at me, she hurries forward and takes Griff's arm, pressing herself against him. "He's taken, hon," she says with a smile.

The vibe in the air instantly changes to disappointment.

Griff smiles down at Chelsea, a smile full of love and affection, but also a hint of concern.

"Who's your friend?" one girl calls, looking at me. "Is he a prince, too?"

Dammit, I thought I was flying under the radar. I ignore her question as we forge through the concourse area and down the escalator, Rhys in front, Jac in back. The screeching women follow us, still trying to get Griff's attention, still taking pictures.

We were able to park in the area reserved for players, which has secured access, so we finally manage to leave the fans behind. Once in the backseat of Griff's car we all look at each other.

"Sorry," Griff says. "I didn't expect that." He focuses on Chelsea. "I didn't expect you to do that, either." His forehead crimps. "They took pictures of you. It'll be all over social media in...well, probably right now."

"I know." She shrugs. "I was trying to protect you."

"At what cost to you, darling?" He touches her cheek. "You don't have to do that."

She meets his eyes. "Yes. I do."

I take her hand and squeeze it. I know how she feels. I'd do whatever it took to protect Griff, too. And her.

Griff looks at me around Chelsea, seated between us. "There are pictures of you, too."

I didn't even think of that. "Probably not."

"Oh, there are." He shakes his head.

"Does that happen often?" Chelsea asks. "I mean, of course it does. No wonder you've been so careful about where we go."

"I guess it was bound to happen at some point." Griff makes a face.

"It's a little...unsettling," Chelsea says quietly. "They were so...fanatical."

"Yeah. People get bold in a crowd like that. Did it scare you?"

"To be honest, yes."

"And yet you were such a brave girl, stepping forward like that." He presses a kiss to her temple.

She was. I'm sure in her sheltered life, she's never experienced anything like that. I've been confronted by the press a few times after big cases, shoving phones and microphones in my face, cameras recording, but it's not quite the same. Not so personal. It doesn't make me feel like I'm being objectified, my privacy being invaded and violated.

"How do you deal with that, Griff?" I ask in a low voice.

"I suppose I'm used to it. It's part of my life." He pauses. "I hate it for both of you, though."

We fall silent as the car drives through the dark city to my apartment building.

"I won't come up tonight," Griff says when we arrive. "We'll talk tomorrow, yeah?"

I nod somberly. "Yeah."

TWENTY-THREE

Griff

I can't do this to them.

I don't even know what we're doing.

This is a fucked-up relationship—three people? You can't do that! And on top of that, I'm a prince. A celebrity. An "eligible bachelor." Anywhere we go, we'll attract attention. The worst kind of attention. On top of that, I know what the media is like. They'll start digging into Chelsea's background. Chelsea's dad will get dragged into this, since he's well known in Chicago. And if there's any sniff that there's more between Ford and me than friendship...well, I can't even imagine what the fallout from that would look like. He has a career that's important to him. He has big goals. He wants to make a difference in the world.

As do I. But if I fuck things up for myself, I'm the only one who has to live with it. If I cock things up for them...I can't fucking bear the thought of that.

I drag myself through meetings and a tour of a veteran's hospital.

Then I go home to my borrowed house and drink myself blind with gin.

～

A few days later, I go to Ford's place. When I'm not there and I know they're there together, it makes me envious. I want to be there too, with them. But I weirdly don't feel jealous. It's hard to explain the difference, and I've thought a lot about it. Yeah, I'd like to be there with them, but I'm happy they're together. I *love* seeing them together. That convinces me I'm about to do the right thing.

They've made dinner for the three of us, herb and garlic salmon with asparagus and a rice pilaf.

"You're both getting better at this cooking thing," I tell them as we sit at Ford's dining table to eat.

"We are!" Chelsea beams. "It's fun doing it together."

"We've had a few failures," Ford says. "The pancakes we tried to make were a disaster. They were either raw or burnt."

"We just need more practice," Chelsea says.

"And we learned the hard way you're supposed to prick a potato with a fork before you microwave it."

"What happened?" I ask, mystified.

"You poor innocent boy," Chelsea says.

"It exploded," Ford replies. "Actually, it was kinda cool."

They're so cute. My chest cavity feels empty and frozen. I poke at my salmon.

"Griff, are you okay?" Chelsea asks.

My head snaps up. "Of course."

"You seem...preoccupied."

I sigh and set down my cutlery. "Okay, yes, I am. I've been distracted all week. After the hockey game."

She blinks at me and tilts her head. "Why?"

"We can't continue this." I keep my head up and regal, my shoulders square. "I can't put you through the media scrutiny you're going to get—no, you *are* getting—because of me."

She nods. "There was a lot of stuff on social media this week."

"Exactly." I shake my head and throw out a hand. "Look at you two. The perfect couple. Cute. Smart. Ready to take on the world. Me being part of that is putting all your hopes and dreams at risk."

"No, Griff." Chelsea frowns.

Ford makes a rough noise. "What are you saying, exactly? Are you pulling another vanishing act on me?"

I narrow my eyes at him. "I'm here, aren't I? Much as I would have liked to ghost you, I knew I had to face you and be honest with you. So I'm here. And I'm telling you we can't see each other like this anymore."

They both gaze blankly at me. "So...you're done with us?" Chelsea croaks.

I press my lips together. "I wouldn't put it that way. I'm bowing out. Out of concern for your best interests."

"Fuck that," Ford says. "I think *we* get to decide what our best interests are."

"Yeah," Chelsea agrees. "We made it through that little skirmish. We're fine."

"Just wait. We've been linked together more than once now. You're going to get a taste of how the media can destroy someone."

"What?" She gapes. "Nobody's going to destroy me."

"Okay, maybe not. You, darling, are squeaky clean. I know they won't find anything on you. But they'll try. And people will make things up."

Her eyebrows slant downward. "That's crazy."

"It's true." I glance at Ford. "And you could be part of that. I know you have big plans for your future. I don't want to ruin that for you."

Ford's jaw tightens. His eyes are intense and hot as he stares at me. Finally, he says, "I get it. I know what you're saying. But..." He stops.

I know why. How do we defend this? Explain it? We can't.

"Please," I say gently. "Let's just end this. You two can have a life. An amazing, normal life."

"What is normal?" Chelsea bursts out, surprising me. "My life hasn't been normal since my mom and sister were killed standing on a street corner. I've finally been feeling...normal. I mean, I know this is...atypical. But..." She swallows, her eyes going shiny. "I've been *living*. I finally feel like I have a life. That I have some agency." Her voice breaks. "That I have love."

Fuck. Her words rip a hole in my gut. I bow my head. I hate that she was unhappy before and I love that she's breaking out of her shell. But this is the right thing. "I'm sorry. But you and Ford can live."

Ford is watching intently, listening, his lips in a grim line. "No."

"What?" I meet his eyes.

"You walked out on me once before."

"I had no choice!"

"I know. But this time you do. And you're not doing it. Not to me again, not to Chelsea."

"You know I have to leave sometime. This is ridiculous. I have to go home. One day I'll be King of Eria. How the fuck is that going to work?"

"I don't know! But it's not happening right this minute."

"Please don't do this, Griff." Chelsea's wet eyes beseech me. Aw, hell. My cold heart softens minutely. "Please."

I sit perfectly still. The condo is quiet. I feel the tension, the waves of dread pouring off both of them, making the air around us heavy.

"We care about you," Chelsea says. I meet her eyes and she holds my gaze with steady conviction. "And you care about us."

I want to deny it. I want to make up shit about not caring so I can walk out of here and not feel like I'm betraying them. But I can't. I can't deny it. My chest caves in and my head drops forward. "I do."

I hear Chelsea's sigh of relief and sense the shift in the atmosphere in the room.

"Okay," Ford says, his voice solid and safe. "That's it then. None of us knows what the future holds. But for right now...we're together."

I raise my head and meet his eyes. They blaze with love and certitude.

Fuck, I love this man. I have since I set eyes on him.

I slide my gaze to Chelsea, so beautiful, so pure. She too regards me with a staunch devotion.

"I don't deserve you," I whisper. "Either of you."

"Deserve?" Chelsea's lips lift. "Everyone deserves loves, Griff."

I gnaw briefly on my bottom lip. "Maybe. But two times the love? What the hell did I do to deserve *that*?"

She laughs softly. "What did any of us do?"

"I know how you feel," Ford says in a tone as rough as tree bark. "I never felt like I deserved this either."

I draw in a deep, deep breath. And let it out. "Okay. Okay." I still have a worried feeling about this, but if I'm being honest with myself, I don't want this to end right now, either. I know at some point I'm going to let them down. But right now, I want to be with them. More than is sensible. More than is prudent. But also more than is within my ability to resist.

I'm staying.

CHAPTER

TWENTY-FOUR

Chelsea

My project is progressing. Our Communications people have been working on it as well, and today I'm being interviewed by a local TV network for a segment they're doing about increasing turnout among young voters. I'm nervous, but I'm also confident. I've been working on this my entire adult life, I'm passionate about it, and I've been immersed in this project since Arlene assigned it to me.

"Our research shows the young voters like to vote early, either in person or by mail, well before Election Day. But we also found that many young people don't have enough information about voting by mail, so that's a big part of our focus."

Two days later, I get a call from a national television network that saw my segment. They too want to interview me. This is excellent exposure for us, and helps in so many ways, including fundraising, which is hugely important. Without donations, our organization can't exist.

Arlene is thrilled about it. "You did great in that interview. You're very good on TV. It helps that you're so pretty, of course."

"Oh my god."

She laughs. "Well, it does, but you're also very well-spoken and well-informed. Sincere. Engaging. You come across with a lot of credibility."

"Wow. Thank you." This is a huge compliment for me, given my lack of experience and confidence. "Fake it till you make it, I guess."

"There is nothing wrong with that strategy," she says. "I'm going to talk to Kamal

about getting you some media training so we can possibly get you more exposure. That will help raise the profile of your campaign."

Yikes. I don't know how I feel about that. I always saw my role as someone who works behind the scenes. And yet, I enjoyed talking about my campaign and my beliefs. So if this is how I can help, I'll do it.

The media training is set up the next day. Kamal is one of our communications people and he walks me through a bunch of things, including how to handle different styles of interviewing. We watch some clips of Bethany Yang, who'll be interviewing me. He sets me up in a fake interview so I can practice in front of lights and a camera.

"Keep your answers succinct," he tells me. "You're doing a five-minute segment and you have a lot to say. You're never going to be able to say it all, so make sure you keep it simple and short. Keep your sentence structure simple. If you need to buy time to think, use the question to start your answer. And here's a big tip—if you talk to Yang before the interview and then she asks you the same question in the interview, never say 'as I said,' or 'again.' Every question is a new question when you're live."

"Got it."

"Have your key messages prepared ahead of time. I suggest having three bullet points to keep you focused."

Then he walks me through an approach where I answer the question, bridge it with something like "however," or "and," or "what's really important to," then communicate the information I want to share.

The practice and these practical tips help increase my confidence. I'm excited to talk to Ford and Griff about it tonight. Griff is joining us for dinner.

Over pasta with lemon garlic cream sauce, a recipe I found on Pinterest, I tell them everything Arlene said and the training I had. The interview has been scheduled for Friday in a local affiliate's studio. "Now the most important thing," I finish. "Deciding what to wear."

They both laugh. "Of course that's the most important thing."

I smile back. They know I'm joking. Sort of. Kamal also gave me tips on what and what not to wear.

"How was your day?" I ask Griff. "Were you busy?"

"I actually was." He drops his gaze to his water glass, which puts my senses on alert.

"Doing what?"

He pauses, then looks up. "I found an apartment here in the city. Not far from here."

My jaw slackens. "What?"

"You're moving?" Ford asks.

"I guess I am." Griff shrugs. "I'm becoming tired of all the driving. And, while I like your little flat here, it is small. It's awkward for my lads. The place I found has three bedrooms, two and a half baths, twenty-four-hour security, and a parking garage."

Ford rolls his eyes. "This place is too small for your highness."

Griff grins. "I knew you were going to be like that."

"Wow," I say. "But...how long are you staying? You've already extended your stay longer than you planned."

"I'm finding it quite workable to conduct business from here," Griff replies. "So I'm staying...indefinitely."

We all sit in silence for a moment. I glance at Ford just as he looks at me, then we both turn back to Griff.

"I have to say that makes me happy," I say. "But...you will have to leave. At some point."

"Yes." Griff holds my gaze. "But I'm staying right now."

Happiness balloons in my chest.

"Where is this place?" Ford asks.

"Lake Shore Drive," Griff replies.

"Like, around the corner," Ford says.

"Indeed."

I can't stop the smile that breaks across my face. "Not far from here," I quote him. "You couldn't get much closer."

He smiles back. "There were certain amenities I had to have, and this one had all of it. Recently remodeled, furnished."

"And the parking garage and security," I add.

"Yes. I can move in right away."

"Wow." I'm still shocked. But in a good way. "I can't wait to see this place."

CHAPTER
TWENTY-FIVE

Griff

I get the call from my father early Friday morning. This is the day I'm moving to the apartment. Rhys and Jac have gathered my belongings from around this huge house and I'm just packing up my toiletries.

"Father," I greet him. "How are you?"

"I'm well, son." His voice sounds terse.

"Good."

"We need to talk. Do you have privacy right now?"

"I'm alone in my bedroom, so yes." I pick up my kit bag and drop it into a suitcase.

"Good. You need to come home. Now."

I freeze. Give my head a small shake. "I'm sorry, what?"

"You need to come home. You're over there gadding about and behaving indecently. You're goddamn lucky the press hasn't gotten wind of what you're doing. You need to stop that immediately and get your royal ass back here to Eria."

Behaving indecently.

"I've heard what's going on. Griffin. What are you thinking?"

Father's wound up. I close my eyes. "What have you heard?"

After a short pause, he says, "I've heard you're having a ménage à trois affair with a woman and another man. Have you lost your bloody mind?"

I purse my lips. "How the bloody hell did you hear that?"

"Never mind how I heard. It's true, isn't it?"

I don't reply. A heaviness settles in my gut. How could he know that?

"Your flight is arranged for today," he adds roughly. "I've already spoken to Jac and Rhys. They're aware they are to bring you home."

I narrow my eyes, staring blindly across the bedroom. "What the fuck?"

"Was I unclear?" he bites out.

"You've been perfectly clear. You can't talk to me like that. You can't treat me like this."

"Not only are you my son—"

"Your *adult* son."

"You're also next in line to the throne. I am the king and I'm ordering you to return home and end this scandalous behavior before it becomes public knowledge."

My entire body goes cold. I feel disoriented, like I'm experiencing this at a distance.

He's right. He's the king. I'm the future king. I knew from the start of this affair that I was playing with fire. None of us thought ahead to how it would end or what would happen if word got out about it. I know I should have. I've been trying to take my duties more seriously since the time I got in trouble in Florida. And Berlin. And Ibiza.

Why did I do this, knowing all that? Deliberately brushing off those realities for a little fun.

A jagged knife slices through my chest with a burn.

A little fun. Fuck that. This was more than a little fun. This was...

I shut that thought down. I can't go there. I have a duty to my family. To my entire *country*, for god's sake. Millions of people. I can't ignore that any longer.

My shoulders slump as shame washes over me in a hot rush. I've never wanted to let down my country. My people. I thought I'd learned that lesson years ago. My throat thickens.

What have I done?

"I'll be home," I choke out to my father.

"Excellent. We'll discuss this more on your arrival."

I end the call and my hand drops to my side.

Visions drift in front of my vision—Chelsea's smile, her beauty, her intelligent eyes, her courage and growing belief in herself. On that boat tour on the river. The three of us in bed, fucking, laughing... loving. Ford, so honorable, so driven for justice, so stern and fierce and yet able to enjoy a laugh and lighten up and enjoy the ride. I remember the first time I saw him in Afghanistan, handsome, hard, remote—a warrior. Visions of the two of us talking for hours, making love in my dorm...and then I left.

I can't do that to him again. To them.

I have to leave. But this time I have to tell them.

My eyes grow hot and I squeeze them shut. I feel like my heart is being ripped from my chest, like I'm being physically shredded.

I may have taken the easy way out many times in my life, but one thing I resolved after I lost Ford the first time was that I would try to be what I loved most about what I'd lost.

I've failed at that. I've used Ford and Chelsea without thinking about potential consequences for them. Or without *letting* myself think about it, because the truth is I always knew those consequences were possible.

I'm a gormless knobhead. A fucking wanker.

"Jac!" I shout.

He appears in the doorway. "Yes, sir?"

I eye him testily. "You've heard from the king.'"

"Yes, sir."

My entire face feels like it's stiff and frozen. "I have to talk to Ford and Chelsea before we leave."

"Of course, sir."

"What's with all the 'sirs'? Fuck. Never mind. They're both at work. What the fuck time is it, anyway?" I lift my phone and glare at it. Then with fingers that feel thick and clumsy, I send a text message to them both, asking them to meet me for lunch.

Like I could eat lunch.

I ask them to meet me at Millennial Park, thinking that will be easier to keep discreet.

Then I finish packing.

I'm a ninnyhammer by the time we arrive there. Jac parks in the parking garage and he and Rhys follow me to the location I arranged to meet Ford and Chelsea. I'm wearing faded jeans, a hoodie, a ball cap, and sunglasses.

I spot them before they see me. It's a perfect autumn day, bright and sunny, the temperature comfortable. They're sitting on one of the low wooden seats in front of a hedge.

My heart seizes and my feet stop moving. For a moment, I watch them across the open space—Chelsea's hair shining in the sun, her smile for Ford bright. They're both holding ubiquitous American cardboard cups of coffee. Ford's posture is relaxed, leaning toward her, focused on her, his shoulders strong and wide in a charcoal suit jacket.

I can't do this. How can I do this?

I have to do this.

I know I'll never be as good a king as my grandfather or my father, but it's my duty. My destiny. I've never wanted to let people down. And now I'm about to be the world's biggest prick.

I swallow painfully and force my feet to move toward them.

Chelsea spots me and lifts a hand. Even in my disguise she recognizes me from fifty meters away. That makes my heart feel tender... and bruised.

I keep walking, focused on them. Only them. Not the green hedge framing the gleaming skyscrapers, not the girders of the pavilion where we took in an outdoor concert one evening, not the other people walking past enjoying the autumn sunshine.

My people.

I stop in front of them. "Hello."

"Hi." Chelsea smiles, knowing not to stand and hug or kiss me. "How are you?"

"Shitty." I rub the back of my neck.

"What's wrong?" She shifts closer to Ford so I can sit next to her. Her scent tickles my nose. I'll never forget that aroma of flowers over vanilla bourbon. So Chelsea--light and sweet, with undernotes of sultry spice.

I can't get the words out.

Ford sits forward to eye me. We're all wearing sunglasses and I fucking hate it.

"I have to go home."

Well, that's blunt.

Chelsea tilts her head. "Like...for a while?"

"No. For good."

Chelsea flinches and Ford's eyebrows shoot up. "Oh," he says. "Something wrong? Is your father okay?"

"He's fine." I tighten my lips briefly. "He's learned of what's happening here. Between us."

Chelsea's pretty lips part on a gasp.

Ford's jaw tenses. "What?" he growls in a low voice. "How the hell could he know?"

"That's a very good question and I intend to find out." I haven't given that much thought yet since I've been absolutely gutted by what I have to do. "But he knows. He's livid."

"Oh no." Chelsea sets her fingertips to her lips. "Oh my god."

I give a terse nod. "Indeed. I'm leaving later today. My things are packed, because I thought I was moving into the apartment today." Another burn of pain lances through me. Just when I thought we were going to have everything—privacy, more time together. Each other. I take a careful breath, my chest blazing. "I'm sorry."

"It's not your fault," Chelsea says. "I'm just...confused."

"You're not coming back," Ford says roughly.

"No." I stare at the greenery opposite us. "I can't. I have a duty. You both know that." My voice is clipped. "I've let down my father. I've let down my country. And I've let down you. Both of you. I'm sorry."

Chelsea reaches out and curves her hand over my forearm. "Griff."

"I'm pissed," I tell them. "I'm gutted. I'm...ashamed."

"Ashamed?" Ford rasps. "Why?"

"Because...because I tried to be better. I tried to learn from my mistakes. I was a partier. A playboy. I wanted to do something serious and make a difference, but I couldn't serve in the military. I've tried so hard to do something meaningful with my work. To live up to my destiny. And I've failed. I've fucking failed miserably."

"Griff." Chelsea's hand squeezes my arm, her voice clotted with tears. "You haven't done anything wrong."

"Oh, come on." I attempt a smile. "You think this is all fine? Get real, my lovely. Would you be fine with your father knowing about this?"

Her mouth opens.

I continue on. "Of course not. I've royally fucked up and we're only lucky that more people haven't found out about us. I knew there were risks but I downplayed them in my mind. There are risks to both of you, too. Your future, Ford. And yours, Chels. I'm so fucking glad it hasn't gone public, for your sakes. But I have to leave now. Before it does. Before I ruin your lives, too."

"Your life's not ruined," Ford objects.

I sigh. "I'll never have the life I truly want. I'll never have a life where I can be my true self. I know I have immense privilege, but I'll always feel like I'm living a lie. Maybe that's not 'ruined.' But it's…" I stop. My throat has constricted. I can't feel sorry for myself. "I have to make the best of what I've been dealt. I've known my whole life, and for a while I forgot and let myself think I could have everything. And that wasn't fair to you."

Chelsea makes a noise like a sob. Ford's Adam's apple bobs.

I slide my glasses down my nose. I have to see them. I have to be seen. I meet Ford's eyes. "When I lost you the first time, I vowed to *be* what I loved most about what I'd lost. What I loved most about you."

Ford yanks off his glasses and his eyes blaze at mine.

"I vowed I would try to be as brave and honorable as you. That I would try to right wrongs. That I would protect innocent people, not use them for my gain. That I would always try to do the right thing, even if it's the hard thing."

Ford makes a terrible, anguished noise. "Fuck, Griff." His voice is thick. "You were there. You were putting your life on the line for people in that war. You *are* brave. You *are* fucking honorable."

Tears slide from beneath Chelsea's sunglasses.

"I need to be a leader. King. I pledged to myself I would be more serious. That I would stay out of trouble. But I've been a selfish asshole." I turn my eyes to Chelsea. "Chelsea. My love. I'll learn from you, too. I want to believe in the best of people, like you. I want to be patient and kind, like you."

The sob gushes from her lips, her cheeks now wet with tears. I lift the sunglasses from her nose to gaze into her eyes. "Believe in yourself, lovely. You're stronger than anyone knows. You're resilient and you touch a place inside everyone, a vulnerable place where we all want to trust and be honest and open. You've touched that in me."

Her eyes are red-rimmed, her nose pink, her lips trembling. I can't fucking do this.

"Griff. I love you. I don't want you to go."

"I know." I touch her face, then drop my hand. I don't give a shit who's watching but I have to. "I love you, too, Chelsea." I lift my gaze back to Ford. "And I love you, Ford. I always have. I'll remember how lucky I was to have both of you in my life. Despite this shit show, I wouldn't trade that for anything."

Chelsea whimpers and swipes her hands down her face. And fuck me, Ford's eyes are wet, too. I squeeze back my own tears.

"I love you, Griff," Ford says. "I understand what you're doing. I fucking hate it and I'm fucking dying here. But I admire you. And I love you for that. I always have." He pauses, holding my gaze. "'A king does not require service of those he leads, but provides it to them. He serves them, not they him.'"

He said that to me, in Afghanistan. He understands. My eyelids prickle and my heart lodges in my throat. The impulse to grab him and Chelsea and hold them to me is almost unbearable. My chest constricts so tightly it cuts off my breath.

These two people mean so much to me. I don't know how I'm going to actually live without them. I'll survive; I'll go through the motions. I'll do my best. But I won't be living.

CHAPTER
TWENTY-SIX

Ford

"We shouldn't have fallen in love with a goddamn prince," I mutter.

I can't stand the broken look on Chelsea's face. I probably look the same. I want to punch someone or something. I want to blow things up. I want to shout to the sky that it's *so fucking unfair* that Griff can't have the life he wants. That Chelsea can't have Griff. That *I* can't have Griff.

Even as I know I have to accept it, with a deep, dark sense of resignation.

My arm around Chelsea's shoulders, I pull her to me and hold here there as she sobs. "I love you, sweetheart," I whisper. "I've got you. You know that."

She gives a jerky nod and cries more.

This was always going to happen. We knew it. Maybe Griff renting that apartment gave us a false impression that things wouldn't end. It felt so committed. So...enduring.

Yet here we are.

Chelsea shakes against me, wearing herself out. I kiss her hair, fighting back tears myself.

I survived losing Griff once. I'll survive again.

And...what does this mean for Chelsea and me? I feel an uncomfortable pang that the reason we're together like this is because of Griff. What if it's him that held us together? She's devastated by this. What if she loves him more than me? What if now that he's gone, she doesn't want me either?

Jesus, my head is fucked up.

"I can't go back to work," she says thickly.

"I know. I feel the same. Let's go home."

She nods and shifts away from me. We stand and she brushes her skirt down over her thighs. She looks up at me, anguish darkening her eyes, her wet lashes like spiky starbursts. My heart clenches.

We call our respective offices to let them know something's come up and start walking home. We walk across the DuSable Bridge, the river flowing in that unique greenish color beneath us, the skyscrapers on either side creating an urban canyon, then a couple more blocks to our street. Neither of us say much, but I hold her hand as we walk.

Once home, we look at each other.

"Did that really just happen?" Chelsea asks, her hand pressed to her chest.

"Christ. I know what you mean. I can't believe it either." I drop my keys onto the kitchen counter, then scrub my hands over my face.

"What are we going to do?" She moves toward me and takes my hands. "Without him. What are we going to do?"

I gaze at her, my chest full of emotion. Lots of emotions, that I can't even sort out. Disbelief. Sadness. Anguish. Fear. "I want you to know that I love you," I choke out. "I've loved you for a long time. That hasn't changed."

She stares up at me, her beautiful maple syrup-colored eyes

wide. "I love you, too, Ford. I've loved you for a long time, too, even though I didn't realize it."

"This is so fucked up."

The corners of her mouth kick up a little. "It really is."

I pull her into my arms and hold her against me, my face against her hair. "I don't know what we're going to do," I grind out, my throat aching. "But we'll figure it out."

She holds onto me too, and we stand like that for a long time, trying to comfort and take comfort.

CHAPTER
TWENTY-SEVEN

Griff

On the flight home on the private plane chartered for me by my father, I sink into my seat, lost in thought.

I replay the meeting with Ford and Chelsea. I swallow the bile that rises in my throat. And I rehash the conversation with my father.

I've heard what's going on. I've heard you're having a ménage à trois affair with a woman and another man.

I asked him how he heard that. He didn't answer. But then... *I'm ordering you to return home and end this scandalous behavior before it becomes public knowledge.*

It's not public knowledge. So how did he know? Ford and Chelsea sure as hell didn't tell him. That leaves...Rhys and Jac. They're the only two other people who know about this.

My stomach turns to stone. I swallow painfully. What. The. Fuck.

Yes, they're my bodyguards. I trust them with my life, so I

thought I could trust them with anything. I thought they were loyal to me. Jesus fucking Christ.

I jump out of my seat and turn to them, seated at the back of the jet. Standing, a hand on a seat on either side of the aisle, I glare at them.

"Do you need something, Griff?" Jac asks.

I can't speak. My fingers grip the seats and my jaw clenches. Finally, I say, "Which one of you told the king about my relationship with Ford and Chelsea?" I slide my gaze from Jac to Rhys and back. "Or was it both of you?"

They're both very good at keeping their faces neutral. I've known these two men for years. Jac was one of my guards before I went to Afghanistan; he was there when I was having scandalous bacchanals. They've become like family, as many of our personal protection officers do. They're part of everything I do. They're my trusted aides and confidantes, and because they don't actually work for the royal family, but rather the Erian National Police, I've always felt I could be more open with them about my actions and my feelings.

Apparently I was wrong.

Rhys lifts his chin. "I told the king."

I narrow my eyes at him. "Thank you for your honesty."

He gives a tiny nod.

"You're relieved of your duties, of course," I say. "Once we're back in Eria, we will find a replacement for you."

Rhys's face tightens. He nods again. "I understand, your highness."

Jac's jaw tics and he swallows.

"Did you know about it?" I ask Jac.

"No."

I believe him. He's never lied to me before. Or betrayed me.

"I was looking out for your best interests," Rhys says. "You have to know that you were playing a dangerous game."

I want to explode at him, but I can't. I can't show emotion. I'm a

Marlow, member of the royal family, next in line to the throne. "Your intent was admirable," I say quietly. "But misguided. And unacceptable."

I return to my seat. I draw in a few deep breaths, sweat breaking out beneath my clothing. *Fuck. Fuck him.*

I've already admitted to myself that I was an idiot to think I could get away with what was happening. Rhys was right. But still, he betrayed my trust. I can't forgive that.

~

"I don't want to be king."

"Griffin. Don't even say it. There's no point in saying it. Or thinking it. Succession to the throne is determined by descent, sex, and legitimacy. This isn't a choice any of us have. It's the law. The Crown is inherited by a sovereign's children. Male children."

"I'm aware," I bite out. "But that's how I feel. Telling me not to feel that way doesn't help. It doesn't work that way."

"You have a duty. As Head of State, the king undertakes constitutional and representational duties which have developed over one thousand years of history. The Sovereign is the center of national identity, unity and pride. You have a duty to your country."

"The role is symbolic now," I say. "I know there's history. I know it's the law. But laws can be changed. Other countries have done it. Maybe Eria needs to step into the twenty-first century."

"What are you saying?" Father demands. "And it's not just symbolic. There are diplomatic duties as well. When I became king, I promised my people that I would dedicate my life to their service, and I've done so. And you will do the same."

Frustration claws at my insides and up into my throat.

"I have no immediate plan to die," Father says dryly. "It will be some time before you inherit the throne."

"Then why I am I here?" I shout.

"Because you've been taking the piss and have lost the bloody plot!"

I grit my teeth, my hands curled into fists. I turn and stride to the window draped with velvet and stare out at the grounds of the palace. Why am I having this argument? It is futile. I am trapped. Locked into tradition and history and law.

"You want to go back to the United States and continue your debauched little affair."

"It wasn't debauched. And it wasn't a little affair."

Father's head jerks back. "Then what was it?"

I stare at him. "I wish I could explain it. All I can say is…it was love."

"Love." He narrows his eyes. "Please. It was shagging."

My face tightens. I can't deny that. But it was more than sex.

My father knows I'm bisexual. I've been open about it since I knew myself. My grandfather didn't know and wouldn't have accepted it, but he's gone. My parents are at least progressive enough to accept that and to know that my life partner may not be a woman. That's not sufficient to disqualify me from inheriting the throne, although it's never happened before. I mean, absolutely there have been gay monarchs. They just married for show and kept their other relationships private. I never wanted that to be my life. I've always wanted to be who I am. To live honestly and openly.

Of course, I never anticipated falling in love with both a man *and* a woman. At the same time. Apparently, that is *not* acceptable for a monarch. "I know it's not usual, but it is possible to love more than one person at once. It's possible to be in a committed relationship with more than one person."

"You want to go back to that. To your…lovers."

I left thinking it was forever. But apparently there's still a tiny grain of hope deep inside me.

I remember Chelsea talking about hope. How important it is. That it shows a path toward something good. Bitterness sticks in my throat. What good is hope? I can't see any path toward something good. "I love them," I say quietly. "It was a relationship, not me fucking my way around Chicago."

He winces. "Griffin."

I roll my eyes. "You're not even trying to understand. Never mind. Forget that." I slash a hand through the air. "The issues are separate. Whether I go back to the States or not, I don't want to be king. I won't be a good king. I have other things I want to do. Real things. Meaningful things."

"Like this charity you've started."

"I don't like calling it a charity. It's not just giving money to people. It's helping them, in real, tangible ways, making their lives better after they've given their ultimate service to our country."

"That's not being taken away from you."

I nod slowly, suddenly weary. He's right. I can continue my work from here. I can take on royal duties. Father could live another thirty or forty years. Jesus, he could outlive me. There's no point in fighting this battle now.

But...when?

"If we're done, I have work to do."

He gives me a long look, then nods. "We are done."

I leave his massive office and make my way to my wing of the palace. I've been gone for months. I like my own digs. I've decorated the rooms to my tastes—modern and sleek, yet comfortable.

Now I'd give anything to be moving into that little apartment in Streeterville.

I make a call to the head of royal security to tell him I've sacked Rhys and to start the search for someone to replace him. Meanwhile, Jac will accompany me everywhere.

A knock sounds on the door and my mother pokes her head in. I haven't seen her or spoken to her yet and my body tenses.

She closes the door behind her and leans against it. As always, she's impeccably attired in a silk dress and heels. "Griff."

She knows everything. I can tell from the pained expression on her face.

I stand. "Hello, Mother."

She sweeps toward me to pull me into a hug. Her scent hits me, bringing back childhood memories. Roses. I close my eyes and hug her back. "I'm sorry, Mother."

"Are you?" She steps back with a wry smile and swipes her fingertips beneath her perfectly made-up eyes.

"I'm having a hard time figuring out exactly what I'm feeling," I admit, stepping back as well. I gesture to a chair and we both take a seat. "Anger is probably at the top."

"Anger at your father? I heard you two speaking in his office."

"Yes. But also at Rhys." My face contracts. "And at the whole bloody royal establishment."

"Griff." She says my name on a sigh. "What were you thinking?"

I lift my chin and meet her eyes. "I fell in love, Mother."

Her heart is softer than my father's. I've always known that. "Oh." Her brow creases. "But with...two people?"

"Yes." I purse my lips. "I can't seem to put them out of my head."

"You've only just arrived home. Give it time."

"I don't want to give it time. I want to go back." I rub my forehead. "But I know...I know I have a duty. That doesn't make it any less painful right now."

"I'm sorry."

"Thank you." I lift one shoulder.

She leans forward, her face troubled. "I hate seeing you unhappy."

"I suppose, as you say, I'll get over it." The empty cavern in my chest suggests otherwise.

"What can we do about it?"

I stare at her. "What do you mean? I just had it out with Father. He's not willing to consider changing anything."

"I know." She drops her gaze to her lap.

"I understand male preference primogeniture. I've grown up understanding it. I've known my destiny my whole life. Yes, I'm unhappy." I exhale sharply. "But I understand it. I will do my duty." I give a mirthless laugh. "Life is cruel."

"It can be. Yes. I've often thought how unfair it is. As a mother, I've always wanted my children to be happy. And fulfilled. I know I can't always make that happen. There are lessons that must be learned the hard way." Her lips lift into a smile. "Not everyone will like you, no matter who you are. Behavior has consequences. And love doesn't always feel safe; sometimes it hurts."

My chest fills with burning heat. "Yeah."

"There have been many times I've wanted to fix things for you. But I can't fix everything."

"I know."

"This, though...this is something that *can* be fixed."

I blink. "What are you saying?"

"We can end this system where a younger son displaces an elder daughter in the line of succession. It is possible."

I stare at her. "So Catrin would become Queen?"

"Yes."

I don't know what to say. "That's a huge burden to put on her."

"Something tells me she would not be opposed." She tilts her head. "Leave this with me. I can't make any promises, of course. But I do have some influence." She smiles and stands. "I'm happy you're home, Griff. I hate it that you're not happy."

"I love you, Mother."

"I love you too, my precious boy. I know it hasn't been easy for you. You're different. You shine. You pull people into your spell and make them believe in fairy tales. But you're more than just charm. You use that to hide what's really inside you. The pain of caring so much about people. The desire to be your own man, to be free. I admire you for that."

My throat closes up, but I choke out, "Thank you, Mother."

TWENTY-EIGHT

Ford

I've worked so hard to forget my <u>past.</u> I'm not worth anyone's care. I should feel goddamn lucky that Chelsea loves me and not sulk about the fact that I can't have the love of two people.

It's been months since Griff left. We haven't heard from him. I tried to call him once, but his number didn't work. I assume he's keeping a low profile in Eria, being a good little royal. The faint hope I had that maybe he'd be back has faded into acceptance and resignation. We have to go on.

We've been keeping things discreet, laying low. Friends and acquaintances have been curious and she's made light of it, saying that she and Prince Griffin were casually seeing each other while he was here, which was only temporary. Hiding her heartbreak. As have I. But nobody asks me about it.

We've endured media speculation about Griff's departure from the U.S. and his relationship with Chelsea. Chelsea got waylaid one day by reporters asking about Griff and what happened between the two of them. She handled it like the queen she is.

I realize how lucky I am. I have the woman I'm in love with. She loves me, too. I should not be this unhappy. I try to hide it from Chelsea because I feel like it's disrespectful of her. Because I really do love her. But I think she knows. And I think she feels the same.

Which is why I'm here at Chelsea's father's house, sweating underneath my best suit.

Chelsea doesn't know I'm here.

"Drink?" Mr. Alderidge asks.

"Sure, thanks, Gary." I take a seat on the leather couch, remembering my first visit here when Chelsea and I were moving in together. Gary and I have met many times since then. We've been here for dinner. Chelsea has also invited him for dinner a few times, so he could see my place and get to know me and be assured I wasn't taking advantage of his daughter.

He's going to flip the fuck out on me. I tug the collar of my shirt.

He hands me a drink and sits in an armchair, frowning. "What's happening with Dennis Freytag's case?"

Oh yeah. "We're working on it. It'll likely be a year at least before we go to trial."

"I've been looking into it."

I blink. "You have."

"Yeah. Don't worry, it's all legal." He pauses. "I understand there's a lot of evidence. Including wiretaps."

I sip my drink and say nothing.

"I think he's guilty," Gary says unexpectedly, though he still looks pissed. He sighs. "Chelsea was right."

"Uh…"

"About you," he adds. "Doing the right thing."

"I try." I wince inwardly, thinking of what I'm about to tell him.

"She stood up for you. To me."

I bite back my smile. "She did."

"I wasn't happy at the time. But after I settled down, I realized I was actually proud of her."

Now I do smile. "Me too."

"So what's this all about?" he asks. "You wanting to talk to me. Is something wrong with Chelsea?"

"No." I shake my head, although that's not completely honest. "She's fine. I need to talk to you, alone."

He eyes me curiously. "Okay."

I gulp my drink and take a fortifying breath. "When Chelsea and I wanted to move in together, we told you that I was gay."

His eyes narrow slightly. "Oh, Jesus."

He's quick. "That's not totally a lie," I say. "I'm bisexual."

I can see his mind leaping ahead. "You're sleeping with my daughter."

"It's more than that. I'm in love with her."

He shakes his head. "Wait, wait. Back up, buddy. Does she know you're bisexual?"

"Yes. She does."

"Did she know that when she moved in with you? Did she lie to me?"

"No, sir, she did not lie to you. That was what she believed at the time."

"So *you* were the one lying."

"Yes." I keep my chin up and hold his gaze. "I take responsibility for that."

"Jesus Christ!"

"Please hear me out. Chelsea was a friend. I wanted to help her. My offer at the time was truly platonic and with good intentions. I was in a relationship with someone else at the time. She wanted to live on her own and I felt moving in with me was a good option. I could watch out for her. As a friend. She'd made mistakes in the past —naïve mistakes—and I wanted to make sure she was safe. It didn't seem important at the time to clarify that I'm bi."

"So much for doing the right thing," he snaps.

"I *was* trying to do the right thing," I reply quietly. "I was trying to help her."

He looks away, taking a drink from his own glass. Then his head snaps back around. "Does she know you're in love with her?"

"Yes, sir. She loves me, too."

"Oh fuck." He closes his eyes.

"Not the reaction I was hoping for. But not unexpected."

"People who claim to be bisexual are just afraid to admit they're gay."

"That's not true." I pull air into my lungs. "I know that's a common belief, though."

"You were in a relationship with another man."

"Yes."

I can see his mind turning over.

"As I got to know Chelsea better, I started falling for her. I didn't plan that. I had to end my relationship with Jeff, because that wasn't fair to him, but I didn't do anything about my feelings for Chelsea for a long time. It wasn't until I knew she cared about me, too, that we admitted how we felt."

"Fuck," he mutters again.

"I apologize for the lie," I say firmly. "I'm sincerely sorry. But everything you've gotten to know about me is the same. I'm the same person."

He moves his head slowly from side to side. "Why are you telling me this now?"

"Because..." I straighten my shoulders. "I want to marry your daughter."

"What the fuck!" He jumps up, his drink sloshing. "Oh hell, no!"

I chomp down on my bottom lip briefly.

"No. Absolutely not. Get out."

Whoa.

I rise slowly. "Gary, with respect, I didn't come to ask your permission. I came out of courtesy and because I know Chelsea will want your blessing. Chelsea's a grown woman and this is her decision. I—" My voice catches. "I know she loves me, and I hope she'll agree to marry me when I ask her. But it's her decision."

"Not a fucking chance. You're bisexual! You want to be with men and women? How do we know you won't change your mind down the road and decide you want to be with a man? You're not going to ruin her life like that."

"That's not true." I stand my ground. "It's another myth that bisexuals can't be monogamous or be in a committed relationship. I love Chelsea. I want to spend my life with her. I've watched her grow from an innocent young woman to a confident professional who's taking on some of the best TV journalists and becoming known for her knowledge and dedication to voting rights." I hold his gaze. "Who takes on her father."

His eyes flicker.

"I wanted to look after her, and I still do, but she doesn't need to be taken care of. I don't want to take care of her because she's weak. I want to take care of her because she's important."

He stares at me, then closes his eyes. "Jesus Christ."

I don't know what that means.

Then his eyes open and anger blazes. "This is bullshit. I'm not discussing this."

I press my lips together. "That's fine for now. But I'd appreciate it if you'd keep an open mind and think about it."

I set my glass down and leave.

Well, at least he didn't punch me in the face.

What's he going to do? As I drive home, I imagine him phoning Chelsea and flipping a biscuit on her. Christ. How's she going to react to the fact that I just told her dad what's going on with us? She could be pissed at me. Like, livid.

A string of curse words runs through my head as I try to prepare myself.

Chelsea's out on a girl's night with Kallista, Betsy, and Emma. Christ, I hope her father doesn't interrupt that. She takes so much pleasure from outings with her friends.

At home, I change, grab some food, and watch a little TV. Chelsea walks in a while later, relaxed and smiling, and I relax minutely, too.

"Hey. How was your evening?" I ask.

"So much fun."

"Good." I love seeing her happy.

She comes and snuggles up to me on the couch. "And guess what happened at work!"

"What?" I smile at her excitement.

"We got a huge donation! And it was because of me!" She tells me about how a prominent philanthropist saw her on TV and was so impressed by the work the organization is doing, decided to make a generous donation.

My heart expands with pride and love. "That's fantastic. Have I told you how proud I am of you?"

"Many times. But you can tell me again. I'm kind of proud of me, too." She grins.

"You should be."

Well, it seems her dad didn't lose his mind on her. I inwardly sigh with relief. Maybe I'll still get to carry out my plan tomorrow.

Chelsea and I have been taking cooking classes at the Botanic Gardens on Saturdays. After Christmas, this seemed like a good way for us to get out of our funk. It's been fun and we're both improving our culinary skills, which is a good thing.

Today in our hands-on class we learn to make soup. These classes are relaxed and fun and we have some laughs and get to eat our vegetable soup with French pistou for lunch. After, I suggest to

Chelsea that we take a walk in the gardens. It's a mild day, as was forecasted, but it's starting to snow a little.

"Okay, sure. It's so pretty here." Chelsea pulls on a beanie and wraps her scarf around her throat, and we tramp the snowy paths that are kept clear. "The snow really emphasizes the shape of things." She points out rounded shrubs blanketed with white, a low hedge with white lights strung through it that now glow through the icy flakes, the layer of white along the tops of bare branches of trees.

We pause at a wooden bench. I brush snow off it so we can sit.

"You know what I love about snow?" she asks.

"What?"

"How quiet it makes things. There's a special kind of stillness. Like it muffles everything."

"You're right." We sit in utter silence for a moment, appreciating it.

Chelsea turns her face up as gentle flakes float down around us. "This is so beautiful. So calm."

"Can I ask you something?"

"Sure." She smiles at me.

I slide off the bench and onto one knee, pulling the small box from my jacket pocket.

Her eyes widen and her smile turns to an O of surprise. "Ford…"

"I love you, Chelsea. I love you so much it scares me. I know our relationship has been unique."

Her lips quiver into a smile.

"But I truly love you and want to be with you forever. I can't imagine life without you. Since that first night I saw you, you touched something inside me that I didn't know I had. Something… hopeful. Something that made me want to believe in people. And in love. Will you marry me?"

She breaks into a huge smile. "Oh my god. I can't believe this." She covers her mouth with shaking hands wearing gray mittens. "I love you, too. Yes. I'll marry you."

Relief and happiness flood me, lighting up every cell in my body. I can't stop the smile that tugs at my lips and I tug her left mitt off and slide the diamond ring onto her finger. She holds her hand out to admire it, and she's shaking even more now.

"It's beautiful. I love it."

"Thank god."

She leans over to kiss me and I slide a hand around the back of her neck and hold her there as our mouths meet. Our kiss is long, warm, affirming. I smile against her lips, then murmur again, "I love you."

We draw apart, connected in a web of trust and hope and love.

"Get up here." She tugs my hand. "You're in the snow."

I rise, brushing snow off my knee, and sit next to her again. I lift her hand to examine the ring. "It took me two minutes to pick that ring. As soon as I saw it, I thought you would like it."

It's simple and modern, an oval diamond set in satin-finished rose gold.

"Really?" She turns glowing eyes on me. "Well, you were right. It's perfect." Then she nibbles her bottom lip. "This is going to be hard to explain to my dad."

My gut clenches. "Uh. Well. I may have already done that."

She starts, her head jerking around to face me. "What?"

"I went to see him last night to ask for his blessing. I told him everything."

Her mouth falls open.

"Wait, not everything. Jesus. I didn't tell him about Griff. But I told him about us."

"Oh my god." She presses her hands to her cheek. "But you're still alive."

"Yeah. He didn't take it well, though. I'm sorry."

"Don't apologize. We had to tell him some time." She lays her fingers against my cheek. "You were very brave to do that by yourself."

I wince. "He basically said we'd get married over his cold dead-ass body."

"I'll talk to him."

"We both will."

"I can do it."

"I know you can. But you don't have to."

She smiles slowly. "Okay."

"One good thing came out of the meeting. I think your dad's forgiven me for indicting Dennis Freytag."

She straightens. "Really?"

"Somehow he believes Freytag is guilty."

"Wow. Okay. That's good."

"Yeah. And...he's also proud of you for standing up for me to him."

She smiles. "Holy shit."

I grin. "Yeah."

"That's amazing."

We fall silent and she bows her head.

And somehow, I know. "Are you thinking about Griff?"

"Yes." She meets my eyes.

"I know." I wrap my fingers around her left hand, which is getting cold. "I am, too. In a way, I feel like I'm betraying him."

"Yes! I know! But that's so weird. He's not here. He'll never be here."

"I know. And we *are* here. Making a life together."

"And there's nothing wrong with that. We love each other."

"Yes."

We still stare into each other's eyes.

"But..." She halts.

I nod for her to go on.

"I think I'll always feel there's an empty spot in our relationship. That's weird too."

"It's...unusual. Yeah."

"But I don't ever want you to think that's about you!" She touches my face with her mittened hand, staring earnestly into my eyes. "I love you."

"I know." I cover her hand with mine. "I know exactly what you mean. I think it's something we both feel. We both understand. So it's not weird. It's...us."

"Right." Her smile holds a hint of sadness. "I'm so glad you understand."

"I'm glad you do, too."

TWENTY-NINE

Chelsea

After being interviewed by an Emmy-award winning political journalist with a reputation for aggressive questions and not backing down, talking to my dad about me and Ford is going to be as easy as falling off a log. Not that I've ever been on a log, but if I ever am, for sure I will fall off.

I told Ford again that I'll talk to him myself and I meant it, but I also have to admit that I love how he has my back. And he's right that we need to be united in this.

So Sunday afternoon we arrive at Dad's place for brunch. I'm wearing my ring, which I can't stop staring at. I let us into the foyer and call out, "Hello! We're here, Dad."

He appears down the hall to the kitchen. He's scowling. That's okay. He scowls a lot. I used to be intimidated by him, but now I know myself. I know what I'm capable of. I know I'm loved.

I walk up to him and hug him. He's stiff at first, then his arms come around me and he gently squeezes. "Chelsea."

"I love you, Dad," I whisper pulling back, holding his gaze. "No matter what."

He closes his eyes and tilts his head. "Shit."

I laugh. "What does that mean?"

Ford moves up behind me and helps me take off my coat, then hangs our jackets in the closet as Dad says, "I guess I'm supposed to say the same to you. I love you, too. No matter what." Then he lifts his eyes to Ford and squints. "Him, I don't have to love."

I take Dad's arm and turn him back toward the kitchen. I shoot Ford a smiling glance over my shoulder and his lips twitch. "Are you angry at him for lying to us?"

"Hell, yeah. Why aren't you angry about that?"

"It didn't seem like a big deal to me. We were just friends at the time."

We all stand at the big kitchen island.

"I didn't try to hide it," Ford adds. "It didn't come up until Jeff and I broke up and I thought you should know."

Memories of him and Jeff give me a tiny pinch of jealousy. Which is so weird, because I was never jealous of him and Griff.

Dad makes a rough noise in his throat. "You're too trusting, Chelsea."

"Yes, I am." I sigh ruefully. "I know that's gotten me into trouble in the past. And I'm learning to be more careful. But I don't *want* to be hard and cynical. I want to believe the best of people."

I feel the warmth of Ford's admiration and affection.

"What can I do to help?" I ask, looking around the kitchen.

"Set the table." Dad moves to the oven. "I'm heating up an egg pie."

"A quiche," I say teasingly.

"Egg pie," he argues. It's been a joke between us my whole life because of the whole "real men don't eat quiche" stupidity. I catch his eye and we share a smile. His is a tiny, reluctant smile. But it's a smile.

Ford and I set the table, then I toss a salad. "Where did you get this?" I ask Dad.

"You don't think I made it?"

I laugh. "Nope."

"I picked up the quiche and the salad at the Glass Onion. They're very handy for meals."

We sit and serve ourselves slices of the ham and cheese quiche, which smells delicious, and salad. I let the subject of Ford and me drop for now and we talk about some current events in the news.

Then Dad spots my ring. He points and looks at me with lifted brows.

"Ford asked me to marry him yesterday," I say quietly. "And I said yes."

Dad's face tightens and he stares hard at his plate. "You said you were going to do that," he mutters.

"Yes, sir, I did."

"I'm having a hard time with this," Dad says, with unexpected honesty.

I swallow. "I know. That's okay. I know you're not homophobic."

He lifts his head, eyebrows knit together. "Of course not." He glares, then his face softens. "Maybe I just have some things to learn."

I pull in a long, shaky breath and let it out slowly. This is progress. I nod and glance at Ford, whose face registers mild surprise.

Dad adds gruffly, "I want the best for you."

"I know." My nose stings and I rub it. "And I am happy. And... Ford *is* the best."

He gives me a crooked smile. "Don't fall over in shock, but...I agree with you."

I blink at him.

"You've grown and matured since you moved out. You're confident and smart, and you're killing it at that job of yours." He clears his throat. "I think he's good for you."

My nose stings and my throat constricts. I drop my head briefly, then say to Dad, "Thank you."

"Thank you, sir," Ford adds.

"You said something, Friday night when you were here." Dad looks at Ford.

I wait. So does Ford.

"You said...you don't want to look after Chelsea because she needs to be looked after. You want to look after her because she's important."

My eyes widen and I touch my throat, my gaze sliding to Ford.

He meets my eyes steadily. "Yes. That's right."

I pull in a shaky breath, sensation unfurling in my chest, hot, soft, vibrant. This man...I love him with my whole heart and soul. He knows me. He sees me. He's perfect...for me. I blink back tears, smiling at him.

Dad clears his throat. "I know I've been overprotective at times," he continues gruffly. "But Chelsea, honey, I want you to know it was never because I thought you were weak. When Ford said that..." He swallows, and I see how hard this is for him. "I know you thought that. But it was only because you're important. To me. The most important thing."

More tears well and spill. "Oh, Dad. Thank you. I love you."

"I'm proud of the woman you've become. I'm sorry if I held you back."

"Maybe it made me stronger," I manage to choke out.

Ford's eyes crinkle up warmly.

"What about Prince Griffin?" Dad asks.

I jerk back to cold reality. Glancing at Ford, I say, "What about him?"

"I thought you cared about him."

"I did," I say quietly. "But it was never going to be something long term."

Dad nods. "Okay. I just want you to be happy."

"I am happy." I smile reassuringly at him, ignoring the faint hollowness Griff has left in me.

Damn. Dad's come around.

I can do anything. A feeling of pride and strength swells in my chest.

"When is the wedding?" Dad asks.

I look at Ford and we both shrug.

"We haven't talked about that yet," he replies.

"We can have it at the club."

I wince. "I don't think I want a big wedding, Dad."

"Nonsense! You have to! There are so many people who need to be invited."

I bite my lip. "Well, we're in no rush. We can talk about that later."

I'm totally avoiding it because I don't want to argue anymore, but I definitely do not want a big wedding. I get the appeal for Dad, with all his political and business friends, but...that's not me.

In the car on the way home, Ford squeezes my hand. "I'm behind you on whatever you want to do for our wedding. We can go to Vegas and do it next weekend if you want."

"That idea has a lot of appeal."

He laughs softly. "I get it. But if you want a big blow out with a princess dress, we can do that, too."

"Let's ponder it. There's no rush."

"I want to marry you tomorrow."

I grin, a little thrill running through me at his words. "We could do that."

"No. I'm kidding. Sort of. You think about what you want."

"I love you."

He smiles. "Love you, too."

I admit I did have teenage fantasies about getting married. Dad took me to a couple of weddings that were big society shindigs and I got swept up in the fairy tale fantasy with the beautiful dress and Prince Charming waiting at the front of the church and all the guests watching with tears in their eyes as they said their vows.

And there's a part of me that still envisions that. But when I think of the reality...all the work, all the money, all the attention... ugh. Dad will be disappointed if we don't do that, and it would be nice to make him happy since this has been a bombshell for him, but...I really don't know what I want right now.

But I do know I'm in love and Ford loves me and we're going to be together forever. Even if there's that peculiar, indescribable void in our relationship.

I won't commit to a huge wedding, but I agree to let Dad throw an engagement party for us. We manage to keep the guest list reason-able, although it's still more people than I'd like. But I invite my boss and coworkers, and Bethany Yang, who I've gotten to be friends with. Ford invites some of his colleagues and friends. Neither of us are social butterflies, so our friends lists are modest. Dad of course includes the mayor, the governor, a few aldermen, and some of his business friends, along with their partners.

Dad rents a private space on the second floor of one of his favorite restaurants, Babylone. It's a beautiful old space with original wood floors, brick walls, and arched windows. There's even a fire-place, and the coffered ceiling and amber chandeliers create a chic and warm atmosphere.

Ford's happy he doesn't have to wear a tux. Standing next to me in one of his business suits, he's handsome and impressive as we greet guest after guest and make small talk. I have a new dress, which took me forever to decide on. I wanted to blow Ford away. But

I was also considering what Griff would think, remembering the night I met him at the gala in the dress that was so different for me, the dress that made me feel sexy and confident enough to talk to a prince. Finally Kallista and I found this dress at a boutique off Michigan—it's short and low-cut, but has long sleeves, with ruffles and layers of black chiffon that flutter around my wrists and thighs.

Someone takes a picture of us, and Ford and I pose with our heads close together, arms around each other.

"Did you get formal engagement photos done?" Bethany asks.

"No, we didn't."

"You should have had a photographer there when he proposed," she says.

"I guess that's the thing now, isn't it?" I see professional, posed engagement photos on Instagram all the time.

"It is! Where did you propose, Ford?" she asks.

"At the Botanic Gardens. It was outside, at the end of January, so I was kneeling in the snow."

She laughs. "That sounds lovely."

"It was perfect," I say. "Soft snow falling, just us. I wouldn't have wanted a bunch of people there."

"Especially if you'd turned me down," Ford jokes.

We mingle until dinner is served, then sit down to enjoy the meal. We're at a round table with Dad, Kallista and Aaron, Ford's friend Ayan and his wife Christa, and a friend of Dad's—Pat. He introduces her as a friend, but I get a distinct feeling they're more than friends. Interesting. It would be wonderful if Dad found someone to love.

"Can we leave after this?" I ask Ford, keeping my smile in place.

"I wish."

"It's lovely, and everyone's so happy for us. I need to be more enthusiastic about this."

"The engagement? Or the party?"

I nudge him, laughing. "Stop. You know what I mean."

"Yeah, I do. We can handle one fancy party, though."

Someone pops up in front of us to take another picture and we smile and touch our wine glasses together.

"This is making a good case for a Vegas quickie," I say as the photographer moves away.

"We don't have to go to Vegas for a quickie. We could have one right here." He leans in to nuzzle my ear. "I hear the bathrooms are really nice."

"They are," I whisper back. "There are velvet couches and chandeliers."

"Tell me more about the couches."

I bite my lip, my insides heating as I imagine Ford and I disappearing into the bathroom and fucking on the plum-colored couch beneath a chandelier dripping with crystals. "Stop."

"What are you wearing under that dress?"

"Not much," I admit. "A thong."

He groans, and I look around the table quickly. Nobody seems to have heard.

"Later," he murmurs.

Obviously we can't leave our own party until everyone else does. Dad has already gone home and finally the last guests wave goodbye.

Ford looks at me with a raised eyebrow. "Come on."

"Home?"

"No." He takes my hand and tugs me down the hall to the ladies' room. "I want to check out this velvet couch."

My belly flip flops as I trip after him excitedly in my high heels.

CHAPTER
THIRTY

Griff

This is truly happening.

And it's actually happened quite quickly. The bill has been debated and approved by Parliament, and today my father will give Royal Assent, making it law. The Act on Succession amends the Erian Constitution and ends the system of male primogeniture, under which a younger son can displace an elder daughter in the line of succession.

I will still have the title of prince, but my elder sister Catrin will become next in line to the throne.

She is jubilant.

I've always known she thinks the system was unfair, as a staunch feminist. *I've* always thought the system was unfair. And we both know she'll be a better monarch than I ever would.

I'll have no official royal duties, but in reality I will of course undertake some assignments. This will leave me free to concentrate on my non-profit organization.

And to return to the States.

I'm apprehensively excited about this. I haven't been in touch with either Ford or Chelsea since I left. A clean break was needed. And through this process, as my hope grew, I was afraid to contact them and give them any hint in case it never came to pass.

But today it is happening.

I have a bottle of champagne at the ready.

Although the king has to provide royal assent, that's merely a formality, so it's basically a fait accompli at this point. But because of the history of the monarchy and the constitution, it has been decided that Father will appear in Parliament to grant his approval.

And tonight we celebrate as a family.

Celebrations will be done privately—the country doesn't need to know how happy I am about this. They see me as being stripped of my title and many are irate on my behalf. Our royal communications team has been carefully controlling the messaging around this change as a desire to move into the present and do away with archaic, sexist rules, but still people have formed their own opinions. Some see it as a punishment for my youthful escapades, some see it as deserved, some see it as unfair. Many are happy with the change. I mean, in this day and age, it makes sense.

I change for dinner while I drink champagne in my apartment, unable to stop smiling. Wearing a suit and tie for dinner became foreign to me while living in the U.S. Wistfully, I remember casual evenings with Ford and Chelsea—making easy dinners, having animated discussions about politics or whether crunchy or smooth peanut butter is better, ending up in bed. All three of us.

God, I want that again.

That empty longing, that intense desire, that sense of missing something so important...I've lived with that for months now. It's hollowed me. It's cold. It's terrifying. I've been lonely before, but this has felt like I'm facing a cliff with no way to turn around. I've tried so hard to conjure Chelsea's hope, and in the last week, contemplating the possibility of going back, of having that again—that love, that partnership, that intimacy and trust, that ability to be my true self—that hope has burgeoned.

I carry my champagne glass brashly downstairs to the family sitting room where Catrin and Simon have already arrived. Catrin is glowing, wearing an organza dress in watercolor shades of blue.

"Griff." She greets me with a heartfelt hug.

I return the embrace, so goddamn happy for her. We draw apart and smile at each other. "Now my bossy big sister will be queen for real."

She pushes fondly at my chest. "Bossy."

"You are. Admit it. An excellent quality for a queen."

"I don't think I'll get to boss anyone around." One corner of her mouth lifts. "I know I asked you before...but are you really okay with this?"

We had a long talk once Mother had convinced Father to actually consider this. We were both honest and I assured her that she wasn't robbing me of anything. That I wanted this.

"You know I am." I smile down at her. "And you?"

"I'm...overwhelmed. Still a little in shock. But yes. I'm ready for this."

"I know you are."

My father's not entirely happy about it, a bit set in his ways and enamored of tradition, but Mother understood her assignment and has convinced him this will be best for everyone—for Catrin, for me, for the entire country.

"Hello, Simon." I greet my brother-in-law with a handshake. I like Simon. He won't be king, but this will certainly change his life. I hope he's up for it as well, but I know he loves Catrin and he already does some royal duties, so it should be a smooth transition.

"Griff."

"Father." I greet him. "I assume it's a done deal now."

"It is indeed. I see you're already celebrating."

I lift my glass cheerfully. "I am."

"Let's all have champagne," Mother says. "Dinner will be ready soon."

"Um. No champagne for me," Catrin says.

At first, I don't react to this, my thoughts so occupied with my own victory. But Mother goes still, and my head snaps up to stare at my sister.

She grins. "I'm pregnant."

My mouth drops and I throw my arms out to my sides. "Aaaah!"

"Yes."

No wonder she's glowing.

Lightness fills me and I watch joyfully as Catrin tearfully hugs Mother, then Father.

"Congratulations, man," I say to Simon

"Thanks." He beams.

Then I get my own hug from my knocked-up sister.

And it sinks in what this means. Right now, I'm second in line to the throne. But this baby will become second in line—whether a girl or a boy or however they want to identify—pushing me further down the line.

Fanbloodytastic.

I feel like the champagne is fizzing in my bloodstream as we sit down to eat, discussing some of the other bills Father granted assent to, chewing over some parliamentary gossip, and listening to news from Catrin's job, which she will continue at for now.

I can't wait. I'm filled with a sense of urgency. I need to see Ford and Chelsea. I need to talk to them. I need to make plans! Immediately!

I force myself to sit with the family the rest of the evening, teasing Catrin about gaining weight, for once enjoying myself with them instead of feeling the weight of their expectations.

When I finally return to my chambers, I pick up my phone. Sinking my teeth into my bottom lip, I unlock it and scroll. What should I do? Should I reach out to them? Should I make my plans first?

Instagram is open and my thumb moves idly over the screen. An image of Chelsea and Ford slides past and I stop, scrolling back to it. I smile at the picture of them, their heads close together, apparently at some kind of formal dinner. Then I read the caption.

Chelsea Alderidge and Ford Sullivan celebrate their engagement at a party hosted by Chelsea's father Gary Alderidge at Babylone. Chelsea's ring is a gorgeous two carat diamond set in rose gold. The happy couple hasn't decided on a wedding date at this time.

I swipe sideways for a close-up pic of Chelsea's hand, wearing a diamond ring.

My stomach heaves. My shoulders sag. I drop into a chair staring sightlessly at the patterned carpet on the floor.

They're getting married.

I swallow hard against rising nausea and chew on my bottom lip.

Of course they're getting married. That's what couples in love do.

"Fuck!" I hurl my phone across the room and bury my face in my hands. My stomach clenches so hard it hurts, and my chest has a tight band cinched around it, getting tighter and tighter. I can't breathe. I can't think. I'm a mess of emotions—disappointment. Dread. Despair.

Hopelessness.

After all this. All this time. All this work to make this happen. To make some kind of future possible for all of us...and now I see this.

They're a couple.

Of course they are. Fuck.

I squeeze my eyes shut on a wave of anguish, pain sucking a crater in my chest.

I can't move. I'm burning hot, then shivering cold.

I don't know how long I sit there, head bowed, hands clenched. Maybe hours. My heart has shrunk to the size of a walnut, hard and shriveled. Eventually I stumble over to my bed, pulling my clothes off, and throw myself down there.

My head is fuzzy and thick. Thoughts circle uselessly. I sleep a little, then awaken to an emptiness that despair rushes to fill.

Rolling onto my back, I try to clear my mind. I try to think.

They're getting married.

When I left, I knew it was for the best. They could have a normal life. They could fulfil their aspirations—Ford maybe entering politics and changing the world, Chelsea with her fundraising and advocacy for voting rights. They make a perfect couple. I knew that and when I left, I wanted them to have that.

I got my stupid hopes up. Stupid, stupid, stupid. What was I thinking? I can never go back to them. We can never have that kind of relationship. It's inappropriate. Unsuitable. Indecent.

It's not possible.

And I'm a fucking knobhead.

Hot tears slide from the corners of my eyes down into my hair. I put my family and my entire country through this for my own selfish obsessions—for nothing.

Nothing.

I press a hand to my stomach, another over my heart. A dull ache fills my entire body.

What is my life going to be now?

THIRTY-ONE

Ford

"Oh my god."

I look over at Chelsea, curled up on the couch, reading on her phone. "What?"

She lifts huge eyes to me. "Griff."

My heart jolts. "What about him?"

She blinks and gives her head a small shake. "He's not going to be king."

I frown. "What?"

She holds up her phone, a small crimp between her eyebrows. "I just saw this in the news. That Eria has passed a new law that changes the succession to the throne."

I gape. "Seriously?"

"Yes." She bends her head and reads aloud. "'The Act of Succession amends the Erian Constitution and changes the rule of succession from agnatic primogeniture to absolute primogeniture.'" She pauses. "I don't even know what agnatic means."

"I think we can figure it out."

"Yes." She reads more. "'This makes Erian Princess Catrin Crown Princess and strips Crown Prince Griffin of his place as first in line to the throne. He will retain his title of prince but will not be expected to perform royal duties.'"

"Where are you reading that?"

"It's in the Times."

"Holy shit."

"Right?" She lifts her head and gazes at me again. "Wow. I can't believe that."

"When did it happen?"

"Um...whoa, it was nearly two months ago."

"Huh." We haven't heard a word from Griff and, respecting his obligations, neither of us has reached out either. Other than the one time I tried to call him, and found his number wasn't working anymore. What does this mean?

I rub the back of my neck. Possibilities race through my mind. Is he free to live here now? No royal duties...I would think so. He's still in line to the throne, of course. Maybe that makes a difference in what he can do?

"I wish we could talk to him," Chelsea whispers, her eyes full of anguish. "I wish I knew he's okay. This is huge. I want to know how this impacts him. Is he happy?"

"Yeah." I'd like to know that, too. "But apparently he doesn't want to talk to us."

Her bottom lip quivers. "Yeah." She drops her gaze. "I haven't seen anything about him in the news, until this. He must be laying low."

I don't know. I have no fucking clue what he's doing. And in that instant, I'm pissed. Because we care about him. Don't we at least deserve to know he's okay? This *is* huge. You'd think it would be something he'd tell us about.

I stand and pace over to the window. It's spring in Chicago, the trees green and leafy, the lake an endless blue, dotted with boats. Adrenaline surges through my veins, making me feel like I have to *do something*.

"What are you thinking?" Chelsea comes up behind me and slides her arms around me.

"I'm pissed."

"At who? Why?"

"At Griff! He couldn't even tell us about this? We haven't heard a fucking word from him."

"I know. I didn't expect to. Though...maybe I hoped. But that kind of died a long time ago." She sighs.

"I'd like to know if he's okay, too."

Silence falls around us for a long moment as we both gaze out the window. Then Chelsea slides around to face me. "Let's find out."

I meet her eyes. "Are you thinking what I'm thinking?"

"I don't know. What are you thinking?" Her lips twitch.

"I'm wondering how much a flight to Eria costs."

Her smile breaks free. "Me too!"

"Really? Do you want to do this?"

She sinks her teeth into her bottom lip. "Could it cause problems for Griff? I don't want to do that."

"We never heard from him how his father found out about us. But there's never been anything, anywhere about it. That we know of."

"You know what I think? I think it was either Rhys or Jac. Or both of them."

"Motherfucker. Of course it was." I shake my head. "If they're still his bodyguards, I guess if we show up it could be bad."

"They're not his bodyguards," Chelsea says confidently. "If they snitched to his father about us, I'm sure he fired them."

I purse my lips, thinking. "I have no idea how we'd get to see him when we get there."

"Me either." She hesitates. "But we could figure it out."

"Fuck it. Let's go."

She laughs. "I have some vacation time I haven't used."

"Me too."

We're above the Atlantic Ocean, neither of us sleeping, although we've tried.

"I think we should talk about a few things," I say to Chelsea.

She shifts to face me in the dim cabin light. "Like what?"

"What do we want to get out of this visit? Are we seriously hoping that Griff will come back to Chicago?"

She nibbles her bottom lip. "Is that crazy?"

"Probably, yeah."

She thinks. "I guess that is a hope, though. At the least, I want to know how this came about and is he happy about it."

"And what if he did come back? What then? Do we pick up where we left off?"

Her eyes are big and shadowy. "Yes."

"And then what? We all knew that long-term, we couldn't have a relationship as a threesome."

"People do it."

I give a small snort. "Like who?"

"I met these people once at a fundraiser. They live in a ménage à trois relationship. All three of them love each other and are committed to each other. They have a child together. It works for them." She pauses. "We could talk to them. I have Kassidy's name and number."

"Seriously?"

"Yes."

I ponder that. "Huh." But... "Still, if I were to ever run for office, I doubt that voters would accept something like that."

"You don't know for sure until you try it. Also, that's what polls are for."

I nod slowly. "True."

"Maybe people are more accepting than we think, if you're a good candidate and try to give them the things they want. Things that are important to them."

I don't know if I'm that candidate. People have talked about it to me. I know there's interest in the party to have me involved. But maybe not if they learn I'm living in such an unconventional relationship.

Then what? Do I give up that dream?

Chelsea squeezes my hand as I spend a long few moments, thinking about that. If having Griff come back to us meant giving that up. Would it be worth it? Would I do it?

I look at Chelsea. She loves him, too. Having Griff in our lives would make her happy. It would make Griff happy. I think. Making them happy would be enough for me. Yes, I have bigger goals and ambitions, but having the two people I care most about in the world happy...that's the *most* important thing to me.

I know this.

"What about you?" I ask Chelsea eventually. "What if it impacted your career?"

"I doubt it would. Honestly, I've enjoyed being the face of the organization and helping raise more money. But I always saw myself as more of a behind the scenes person."

"If you're raising money, they'll love you."

She laughs. "You are right. Probably same goes for you."

"Yeah. But I think I can make a difference behind the scenes, too, if that's what has to happen. I wouldn't be giving up all my goals. Just achieving them in a different way."

"Right."

Our eyes meet and hold.

"I think we're in agreement," Chelsea says softly. "If Griff will come back, we'll make it work, even if it means adjusting our lives."

"Yeah."

We share a smile. We don't know what's going to happen in Eria, but at least we're together on this.

~

In the morning, we arrive in Wingate, the capital city of Eria. The country is small, very green, and currently it's pouring rain. That's okay.

We take a taxi to the hotel we booked, a nice one that's fairly close to the royal palace. In fact, we drive by the palace on our way there. Chelsea stares out the window at the castle dating back to Norman times, stone walls interspersed with square towers and an impressive gate at the entrance.

"I can't believe he lives there," she says in a low voice.

"Right?"

She turns away from the window. "What are we doing? This is nuts. He's a *prince*, for the love of goats."

"He's our prince."

She squeezes her eyes closed. "I so want to believe that."

Our hotel is great, very old and smallish, but nicely decorated. Neither of us slept well on the flight and are immediately overcome with fatigue at the sight of the bed, so we crash for a couple of hours.

"Should we go explore?" I ask when we're both awake and cleaned up.

"It's still raining." She casts a dubious glance out the window.

"It might never stop. We can't let that hold us back."

"True. Okay. I packed umbrellas."

We wander the ancient cobblestone streets down to the Bryn River. "I remember Griff telling me how they've cleaned up the river and developed the area around it. It's lovely." There are stone paths, shady trees, and places to sit and enjoy the view. On the opposite bank, the city is modern and businesslike, with tall glass and steel buildings. We explore a small market, our steps eventually returning us to the palace.

We walk slowly along the wet sidewalk next to the tall wrought iron fence, peering between its bars at the structure.

"This is crazy." Chelsea squeezes my hand. "If only we could phone him, or something."

Then we discover there are public tours of the palace. "Should we do it?" Chelsea asks.

"I don't know. We're not going to see Griff. I'm sure the royal family isn't anywhere near where the public is allowed in."

"I have visions of us distracting the tour guide, hiding in a nook behind a suit of armor, and then sneaking off to try to find Griff."

"You've been watching too many movies."

"It could work."

"It could get us arrested."

"*That* would get Griff's attention."

I burst out laughing and pull her against me in a hug. "True."

We find a nice place for dinner and return to the hotel for an early night, both of us jet-lagged, then after breakfast we arrive at the palace to buy tickets for the morning tour. We're in a group of about twenty people, mostly older than us, including some American ladies all together who seem to be having a great time.

We learn some Erian history and the story of the castle, originally constructed in the eleventh century, but added to and remodeled numerous times since then. Griff has talked about his country and his family, but this brings it to life—seeing portraits of Griff's ancestors hanging on the walls, antique furniture, and artifacts with historical significance. We study the suits of armor in a round tower room, and oil paintings in a large gallery.

"Where does the royal family live?" asks one of the American ladies.

"They have residences in different wings," the tour guide answers. "Unfortunately, we can't tour those areas."

"Oh." The woman's face falls. "We want to see where Prince Griffin lives."

The guide chuckles. "As do many."

Chelsea and I exchange knowing glances.

"From time to time we do catch a glimpse of family members going about their day," the guide continues, leading us down a massive corridor with marble floors and gilt everywhere. "Queen Mari enjoys spending time in the gardens."

Nobody seems excited by this news. They want to see Griff.

"Great. We're Griff groupies, now. Get me out of here," I whisper to Chelsea.

She giggles. "Not a chance."

We tag along with the crowd, absorbing Erian history. The guide leads out outside onto a terrace overlooking the grounds. Chelsea sighs with delight at the trees, shrubs, and manicured lawns. Huge stone planters overflow with flowers and vines.

"Some day I'd like a garden," she says to me.

"You want me to move to the burbs?"

She grins. "Is that terrible?"

"I can't afford a house like your dad's."

"Phhht. You mean *we* can't afford it. And I don't need a house like that."

We can't afford it. Yeah. We're a "we" now. I fucking love that.

After how I grew up—the chaos, the lack of safety, the feeling that I didn't deserve anyone's protection, never mind their love and acceptance—to have that safety and security, that love and acceptance with Chelsea is like a miracle. It's something I never thought I would have and I'm so fucking grateful and honored.

"Prince Griffin!"

Both our heads jerk around. One of the ladies in our tour group has just squealed Griff's name.

The other ladies all point and shriek as well and, following their gaze, we see Griff.

My heart fucking stops. I'm not breathing, either. Just...petrified.

"Oh my god." Chelsea grabs my hand.

Griff looks across the lawn from the distant terrace he walked out onto. From here, we can see his smile, and he waves.

Tugging Chelsea's hand, I move apart from the group and closer to the stone railing around the terrace. I'm staring at Griff so hard it's a wonder he doesn't burst into flames.

The ladies are all in a tizzy at seeing Griff, flapping their hands at him.

I know the instant he lays eyes on us. His posture changes. His head tilts. He goes very still.

"He sees us," Chelsea murmurs.

"Yeah."

She releases my hand to press both hers together beneath her chin in a gesture of supplication. "Please, Griff," she whispers.

He's gone in a flash, back into the castle. Murmurs of disappointment surround us, and the tour guide directs us back inside. We walk back through St. Cyllan Hall as the guide directs our attention to the paintings on the walls. As we move toward the Grand Vestibule, I see movement in a doorway.

Griff.

I catch Chelsea's hand and jerk my head toward Griff. She lets out a small gasp, and without speaking, the two of us fall behind the troop of tourists, watching Griff.

Christ. He's a prince, standing in an arched stone doorway, surrounded by gilt and velvet and crystal. He's wearing all black—narrow pants, a fitted shirt, his body lean and strong, his posture regal.

I remember the first time I saw him, his clothing so different than today—camo pants and a T-shirt—his gait cocky and confident, his smile hinting at a smirk, his eyes dancing with humor. I remember how affected I was, like I'd just seen beauty in the midst of horror.

I feel the same today.

Every cell in my body reacts, every nerve ending on alert, like a shot of adrenaline, like a flood of happiness dousing me.

While the others pass into the vestibule, Griff strides up to us. "What. The. Fuck."

He looks angry. And incredulous. And...beautiful.

Color stains his high cheekbones, his eyes flash, and his sculpted mouth thins into a straight line. "What are you doing here?" he grates out.

My heart slamming in my chest, I smile slowly. "We came to see you."

CHAPTER

THIRTY-TWO

Griff

I cannot fucking believe this. Ford and Chelsea are here? In the palace? Just appearing out of nowhere? Did I accidentally drop acid last night?

No. I've had the odd edible, but nothing like that.

I rub my eyes. "What is happening?"

"Griff." Chelsea lays a hand on his arm. "Can we talk somewhere?"

I give her a long look. "Chels," I choke. "Why are you here?"

"That's what we want to talk about."

The tour guide appears in a door opening. She sees us standing close to Griff. Her eyes pop open and she emits a small squawk. "Should I call security, your highness?"

"No. It's fine. They're coming with me."

She frowns and hesitates. "Yes, your highness."

"Your highness," Chelsea whispers with a wicked little glint in her eyes.

I narrow my eyes at her. "Don't start." I sigh. "Come with me."

I lead the way through a corridor, a locked door, up a set of stairs, down a hall, and into my apartment.

Chelsea gazes around. "This is where you live?"

"Yes."

"It doesn't look like the rest of the palace."

"That's the idea. Can I get you something? Tea? Coffee? Whiskey?"

"Whiskey would be good," Ford says. "Bring the bottle."

I almost smile.

I turn and walk over to the bar cart and fill three rocks glasses with Eria's finest triple distilled single malt aged in oak bourbon casks. I'm with Ford; I could drink from the bottle right about now.

Like a good host, I hand them glasses and gesture at the couch and chairs arranged in front of the fireplace. They sit side by side on the couch and I take a chair. Apart from them. Where I belong.

I wait.

Ford chugs back some whiskey and says, "You're not next in line to the throne anymore."

"I am not," I agree. "You heard that."

"Yes. But only last week. Apparently it happened *two months ago*."

I incline my head.

"You didn't think to tell us?" Chelsea says in a hushed tone. "Something that important? We have questions. What happened?"

"What does it matter to you?"

She flinches and I see the hurt in her pretty eyes.

Ford gives me a hard look laced with rebuke, and shame twists inside me.

"We care about you," he says. "You should know that."

"You're getting married." The words erupt unbidden from my mouth.

They both stare at me.

The silence expands and thickens.

Chelsea closes her eyes. "Oh, Griff."

"Don't fucking pity me," I grind out with a tight jaw.

She drops her head back to huff out a sigh toward the ceiling. "Oh my god."

Ford swipes a hand across his brow. "I'm not sure I know what's happening here."

"How did you hear we're engaged?" Chelsea asks.

"Certainly not from you."

"Oh, fuck off with that," Ford shouts. "I tried to call you. You changed your number."

More guilt heats my gut.

Chelsea arches an eyebrow at me.

I almost smile. Look at her, sitting there so confident, so in control, reading me and my emotions and taking charge. Challenging me. What a woman she has become. I love her so goddamn much. "I saw it on Instagram," I finally say.

She nods. "Okay, here it is. You were gone." She leans forward, her drink clasped in both hands. "Forever. We love each other. We want to commit to each other." Her eyes warm and soften. "But we both feel like there's something missing in our relationship. There always will be." She pauses. "It's you."

Christ. My nose stings and my throat thickens. I want to cry. For a moment I can't speak, and I drop my gaze to the amber liquid in my glass. "I still don't know why you're here."

"We want to know if you're happy," Chelsea says. "That's the main thing. If you're happy and satisfied with your life, that's what matters."

I stare at her. Fuck. Her sweetness and generosity make me feel like a fucking maggot.

"Are you?" she asks.

I lift my chin. "I'm happy about the change in the law. I didn't want to be king and now I likely never will be."

She nods, Ford studying me carefully.

"Then I'm happy for you," she says softly. "We also want to know..." She pauses, apparently gathering her courage. "If it makes a difference. If you no longer being in line to be king means you can come back to Chicago. If you can...come back to us."

My chest squeezes almost unbearably. I look to Ford, to see if he's in agreement with what she's saying, or if he's freaking out.

He's watching me. Steadily. Patiently. His green eyes are cool and calm.

What do I say?

I gulp down my whiskey and jump to my feet to get a refill. I busy myself pouring. My hands rattle the bottle against the edge of the glass. "Anyone else?" I hold up the bottle.

Ford beckons in a "bring it here" gesture. My lips twitch.

I hand him the bottle and he sloshes a generous amount into his glass. Chelsea's still sipping hers.

I sprawl back in my chair.

"You haven't answered," she reminds me.

"Right. Well." I move my foot over the carpet, tracing the abstract design with the toe of my shoe. "I thought it might make a differ-ence." I clear my throat.

"And...?" Chelsea says.

My brain is a shambles. "I found out you are engaged." I wet my lips. "It was...I was happy for you. Truly. When I left, I knew it was for the best. I thought you would be able have a normal life. A normal relationship. All your dreams and hopes and goals. And when I saw that you were having that...I knew that no matter what has happened here, no matter that the law has changed and Catrin will be queen, I couldn't go back." I draw air into my lungs, imagining I'm wearing a suit of armor like the ones that stand in Centre Tower.

"Oh," Chelsea breathes.

"Fuck," Ford mutters. "I thought we talked about this! When you were trying to leave last fall. We told you—*we* get to decide what our best interests are."

My eyes burn and I don't look at them. Right. He did say that. I ignored him.

Also, I now know how it feels when someone else acts based on your best interests...and fucks things up. Like Rhys did to me.

"But you thought about it," Chelsea says.

"No!"

"Yes, you did." To my horror, she rises and walks toward me, dropping to her knees in front of me. "Look at me, Griff."

I can't. But I can't *not* look at her. I lift my gaze to her beautiful brown eyes. I'm addicted to her sweetness, to her optimism, to her trust. Her willingness to risk everything for a chance at happiness. Her faith in me when I don't deserve it.

She takes my hands in hers. "Were you going to come back to us?"

My throat is so tight I can't speak. After a moment, I say, "I thought about it, yes."

"And you didn't come because you found out we're getting married."

The word is ripped out of me. "Yes."

She lays her cheek on my knee. "Griff."

She's disarming me, piece by piece. Each gauntlet. The poleyns that cover my knees. The pauldrons. The cuirass that protects...my heart.

Ford appears next to her, both of them kneeling before me. He covers her hands on mine.

"It hurt," I whisper. I'm vulnerable now. I may as well be honest. "It fucking hurt. But I truly was happy for you, that you're moving on. That you have each other."

"We need you," Ford growls. "Fuck, Griff."

"It can't be."

"Why not?" Chelsea asks, lifting her head. "Why not?"

"What about your lives? Your political ambitions," I say to Ford. "What about that?"

"We've talked about it," Ford says confidently. "I think we all feel the same. All we want is to make a difference. You don't have to be king to do that. I don't have to be United States president to do that."

"Chelsea." I free a hand to stroke her soft cheek. "Your father. Your career. You're doing amazing things."

Her lips tighten and she blinks. "I can still do amazing things. Our life is nobody's business."

"That's incredibly naïve," I say bluntly but softly.

"I remember a time when you told me you admire that about me."

Christ. *Stab me in the heart, why don't you?* "I do admire that." And I still have that overwhelming urge to protect her even though I've learned she can take on anything.

"We talked about hope. How important it is."

"How hurtful it is when you're disappointed."

"But hope reminds us that things can always change. It gives us a path forward." She pauses. "I haven't given up hope. I won't give up that hope. That we can do this."

I have felt hopeless. I hate that feeling. It's helpless and she's right. We need hope. But I'm afraid to let myself feel it.

One corner of her mouth lifts. "I know it may be naïve. But I've learned a lot about myself, and I can handle it. I *can*, Griff."

"And who knows?" Ford asks. "The world is changing. If I try to run for office and it becomes an issue, we reevaluate and change plans."

"I don't think you two know what you'd be getting into."

"Maybe not," Chelsea agrees. "But maybe we want to try."

"Not *maybe*," Ford says. "If there's any possibility that you can come home with us and give this a shot...without ruining your life... without doing harm to your country...we want to try."

"Christ." Still going to fucking cry. This man. This warrior who wants justice and fairness. Who's going to fight for him?

I want to be the man who does that. I want that so goddamn

much.

"Come home with us. It's nobody's business but ours. We don't owe anyone explanations."

"I don't think it's that simple," I choke out, desperately, painfully wanting to believe that.

"I love you, Griff." Chelsea gazes up at me. "We both do. I think the three of us together can be amazing. I think we can do amazing things. It might just be different. We may not be working for applause...but we'll be working for a cause."

She's really going for the jugular.

I look between them, both of them clear-eyed and sure of themselves. The love shining in their eyes reaches deep inside me, grabs me, and squeezes tight. I lose my breath. "I love you, too," I choke out. "Both of you." I set down my drink and lift my hands to touch their faces. "I can't believe this."

Chelsea lays her hand over mine. "Will you come home with us?"

It's all I want. But would I be a selfish arsehole to agree to that? Would I be ruining their lives? I want to be honorable and generous like they are. I'll sacrifice what I want so they can be happy, even if I'm miserable.

"It's what we want," Ford says. "I want you and Chelsea to be happy. I'll work hard to make that happen."

Emotion shoves at the walls of my chest. I'm going to burst from it. "All right. I'll come."

Chelsea's face glows, touching that soft, vulnerable place inside me. Something I've almost forgotten exists, and the genuine pleasure on her face thaws that frozen part of my soul.

Ford smiles. "Excellent."

Chelsea rises and leaps onto my lap, throwing her arms around me, smothering me with kisses. "Griff. Oh, Griff. We'll *all* work hard to make this happen. Because it might not be easy."

"But it'll be worth it," Ford adds.

I grip his hand and kiss Chelsea. "So worth it."

THIRTY-THREE

Chelsea

Griff presses against my back. His hands fondle my butt.

I've discovered I like to have my ass played with. I'm so sensitive back there, and I love it...but we haven't done this before.

"This is a first for all of us," Ford says roughly.

I breathe through my jitters.

"We'll be gentle," Griff whispers from behind me.

"So gentle," Ford agrees.

We're in Griff's bed, in his bedroom, the door securely locked.

Griff's fingers continue to play, caressing my cheeks, trailing over the crease between my butt and thighs, smoothing down the backs of my legs. Sensations shiver down my legs and up my spine, and I wriggle against Ford.

"Like that?" Griff's murmur grazes over me.

"Yes."

He strokes back up and trails a finger between my cheeks. At the same time, Ford lifts my chin and kisses me--delicious, warm, hungry—and I sink into delight, sensation sizzling across my flesh, heating me.

Griff moves behind me and then his stubbly jaw rasps over the sensitive flesh of my ass. Hands on my hips, he kisses me there, first softly, wetly, then with a nip. An electric jolt flashes through me.

"Easy," he whispers, a hand stroking my back. "I want your ass."

Another bolt of electricity shocks through my body at his bold words. We've done a lot of things together, but we haven't done this. Apprehension tightens my muscles, but their gentle caresses and worshipful touches soothe my nerves.

Ford covers one breast with his hand and plays there, toying with my nipple, kissing my mouth, while Griff uses hands and lips and tongue to caress my butt. I ache with emptiness, pulsing and throbbing, my entire body a hot flush of burning need. My mind spins away from me and I give myself over to it, pleasure sweeping through me.

"You can do this," Ford whispers, shifting so I'm atop him, my legs parted on either side of his hips. Draped across his chest, I pant as cooler sensations tickle the flesh of my rear, Griff drizzling lube over me. With slick hands he massages my cheeks in a sensuous rhythm, fingers dipping lower and lower into the crease between. White hot pleasure cascades through me and I groan.

"So pretty here," he murmurs, his thumb circling my entrance.

Ford slides a hand between us, and I lift myself on trembling arms so he can grasp his cock. Griff's hands grip my hips to poise me above Ford's thick erection, then lower my pussy onto it. He fills me gloriously, hot and pulsing, and I clench around him, letting my breath out in a slow hiss. Ford groans and holds my hips.

Griff's fingers continue their magical tour of my backside, sliding deeper between my cheeks, down to where Ford's body joins mine, and even lower, playing with Ford's balls. Ford gives another ragged moan and thrusts up into me.

"Fuck," Ford says, his voice low and thick. "You feel so good, Chelsea. So hot and tight."

We don't use condoms anymore and Griff has shared that he hasn't been with anyone else, so they're both bare.

Griff groans. "Unreal." His fingers return to me, slippery and hard, and he probes at the tiny, tight entrance. I tense—I can't help it. His hand on my lower back strokes softly. Reassuringly. "Relax," he murmurs. The tip of his finger breaches me then.

I stiffen and arch my spine, throwing my head back. "Aaaaah."

With Ford already inside me, the sensation is indescribable. Ford fills his hands with my breasts as Griff fingers my ass, probing in delicate strokes that send flames licking over my body.

He plays like that a long time, forever it seems, while my body spirals into tightly coiled need, heat whipping through my veins like fire. And then I feel Griff rise to his knees behind me, and I quiver in anticipation. He moves against me, lean and hard.

"Relax," he whispers again, and Ford lifts a hand to my chin, cups it and raises it so I'm looking at him. The emotion blazing in his green eyes reaches out to me. His lips part and he watches me intently, with warm tenderness and erotic hunger. A flush darkens his cheekbones.

My arms quiver as Griff's fingers probe and retreat in a wicked rhythm. I tip my head back, still holding Ford's heated gaze as the blunt head of Griff's cock meets my backside. He pauses, hand on my back warm and strong...and then he invades me. Flames lick around my stretched rear, and a cry falls from my lips. Ford's fingers tighten on me, Griff's hands grip my waist. He bends over my back and I feel the dampness of the perspiration clinging to him.

"Okay, love?" he whispers in my ear.

I give a jerky nod, my body burning with pleasure, a sense of rapturous fullness consuming me. "Can you feel him, too?" I ask Ford in a choked voice.

"Yeah. Christ, yeah. It's incredible."

"Brilliant," Griff chokes out.

They begin to move, and I push back against Griff's invading flesh, Ford lifting his hips. Griff meets my thrusts, withdrawing and easing back in slow, thick slides, careful at first, until he and Ford find a matching rhythm.

"Chelsea." Griff's voice caresses me from behind. "Your ass is so tight. So sweet. So hot."

I clench at his words, drawing a long rough sound from him.

"Fuck," Ford groans. "It feels like I'm fucking both of you."

"Yeah." Griff drops a hand from my waist to brush across Ford's abdomen, taut and rippling as he bucks his hips, fucking up into me while Griff fucks my ass.

Overwhelming sensation slams into me, surrounding me, the thick flesh pressing into me, filling me, scorching me, every nerve ending burning with carnal flames.

This is the wildest, wickedest thing I've ever experienced, but what astonishes me is the intimacy of it, the way all three of us come together at that one point, our bodies joined so closely, so completely, both of them inside me like they belong there, an intimacy I've never known before.

I want to see Griff, so I shift sideways, taking my weight on one arm and reaching behind me with the other for him, finding his hip. I look over my shoulder at him, taking in the absorbed expression of fierce pleasure on his face, his jaw tight, his lips drawn back. He opens his eyes and catches my gaze. Adoration blazes on his face and I feel it like sunshine, feel it soaking into my skin.

"Yeah," he grinds out. "Beautiful. So precious."

The pace of their thrusts picks up. My womb tightens and my body strains toward release. Ford cups one breast, the soft flesh surging into his palm with each pounding drive into me. I can't stop the small cries and whimpers that tear from my throat, the flames burning in my core flaring higher, hotter, pleasure streaking through me.

An orgasm like I've never experienced explodes inside me, my body clenching around the two spears of flesh filling me, crammed into me, hitting ultrasensitive nerve endings inside me I didn't know were there. My cries sound distant and shattered in my own ears, my vision dark, my world centered on the excruciating pleasure wracking my body.

"Ah, Christ!" Ford bites out the words as he drives up into me and holds there, and the hot pulses of his release flood me. Griff drives faster into me, taking me in hard, ruthless possession, hands so tight on my hips he's leaving bruises, but I don't care. And then he comes, too.

"Fuck." The word tears from him in a tortured roar. "Fuuuck." He pulls out and his hot semen lands on my lower back and bum, his body tight against mine.

I'm destroyed. I tumble to the bed, pressed between hot, sweaty male bodies, all of us shuddering and gasping.

"Warrior," Griff pants.

Eyes closed, Ford smiles. "Prince."

Griff's hand squeezes my hip. "And our queen."

A fierce rush of emotion swirls inside me. This is messy and chaotic and filthy. It's pain and pleasure and bliss. And...it's beauty. Serenity. Unity. It's perfect.

Gratitude and appreciation swell inside me, adding an additional layer to the love I feel right now.

I can do this. I can love two men. I can be loved by them. It won't be easy. But I'm stronger than I knew.

"Your Royal Highness." I bend one knee slightly in a curtsy, although apparently I don't have to as I'm not a citizen of Eria.

Griff wants his parents to meet me and Ford. I'm freaking out inside. It's weird enough that we have this unusual relationship, but his parents are the King and Queen of Eria. And we're having dinner in the royal palace. Jesus.

Ford greets them as well. Queen Mari is lovely, with a warm smile. King Tomos is more aloof, studying us with a sober expression.

"It's lovely to meet you," Queen Mari says. "Please have a seat."

I wait until she's seated, as I learned in my quick decorum lesson from Griff, then take a chair.

"What would you like to drink?" Griff asks his mother.

"Gin and tonic would be lovely, Griff, thank you."

He takes care of his parents, then Ford and me. I accept a glass of white wine. I'll drink it very slowly.

Queen Mari asks questions about our trip and what we've seen so far, which isn't much. She and Griff mention a few places we should visit, including a national museum, a nearby national park, another castle, and a large shopping arcade.

"We have some lovely shops," Queen Mari says. "We're a small country, but we enjoy fashion and style."

I meet her eyes and smile. "Thank you. I love history, but shopping is fun, too."

We make small talk and, remembering some of my reading just before our trip, I ask about a recent recommendation to enact a Criminal Code in Eria. "It surprised me that you don't have one," I say. "I understand that many criminal offences are common law offences rather than being specified in legislation."

This earns me a look of surprise from the king. "Yes," he says slowly. "Attempts to pass a Code have been made and never succeeded, but I think the time is right."

"Chelsea has an interest in crime and crime prevention," Griff says, and the note of pride in his voice spreads warmth through my chest. "Her work involves getting people to vote and have a voice in the policymaking process."

A spark of interest flares in King Tomos's eyes. He starts asking me questions and at times Ford comments too, and Griff tells him about Ford's career. The conversation flows more easily after that and continues through dinner.

Later, back in Griff's apartment, he bestows a royal grin on us. "You two were absolutely brilliant," he says. "You completely won over the king."

"Yay." I smile, too. "I wasn't trying to do that, but I'm glad."

"Of course you weren't trying. You were just being you. And you are lovely." He kisses my forehead. "And Ford, you are incredibly clever."

"They're still going to flip out when you tell them you're leaving," Ford says dryly.

"Probably so." Griff nods. "But maybe they'll understand better why I am."

"We should get back to the hotel," Ford says to me. "It's been a long day."

Griff nods. "I'd invite you to stay here, but it would take some time to get security clearances and such."

"We understand. But...we'll see you tomorrow?" I look at Griff.

"I'll take you on a sightseeing tour, like you did for me in Chicago. I owe you."

I laugh. "Right. You do."

Having successfully met Griff's parents without a messy confrontation fills me with even more hope for our future together, more confidence that I can take this on. There are still questions and problems for us to overcome, including my own father, but I choose to believe we can deal with them.

The look on Dad's face is almost laughable.

I bite my lip and glance at Ford, then Griff.

"I don't want to know the details," Dad says.

"That's fine," I say. "Some things are personal."

He closes his eyes and shakes his head, then runs a hand over his bald head. He looks terrified that we're going to discuss our sex life with him. Also confused. And sort of…defeated.

"Chelsea." He looks at me. I see all the questions in his eyes. The things he doesn't want to say. The things he doesn't know how to say.

"It's love, Dad," I say quietly. "Love is hard to explain, but it's the most important thing in the world. I know you love me, and you want me to be happy, and I'm sorry I've chosen a path that's not, er, traditional. But love is never wrong."

"I worry about what your life will be like. What kind of…I don't want you to be hurt."

"I know." One corner of my mouth lifts. "The guys tell me I'm naïve, and maybe I am, but I want to think that most people won't care. We're living our lives honestly. Being true to ourselves. And all of us together are strong enough to handle anything."

He shakes his head. "Yeah, that's naïve. There are horrible people in this world, honey. There are people who hate. They won't understand this."

I swallow. "I know."

"You've chosen a difficult path."

"Maybe so. But I feel like I don't have a choice. I love Griff and Ford and we need to be together. I believe in hope. And love." I pause. "And I believe in myself."

Dad's eyes crinkle up, though his smile has a hint of sadness. "I believe in you, too." He looks at Griff and Ford. "And this isn't easy for me, but I believe in you as well. I've seen Chelsea flourish and grow since you've both been in her life. I want you to promise me that you'll look after her. Always."

"Absolutely, sir," Griff says.

"You have our word," Ford adds.

At one time his request would have annoyed me. But I remember him telling me that they want to protect me because I'm important. And my heart swells with love and happiness.

Then Dad shocks me by looking back at me and saying, "And you'll look after them?"

I smile slowly, my heart expanding. "Always."

~

We're having dinner at a nice restaurant on North Lasalle—Griff, Ford, and me.

Griff doesn't have bodyguards anymore; because he's so far down the line of succession the palace doesn't pay for that. We're always cautious when we go out, but over the months that he's been back, the media attention has died down. Not completely, but enough that we can go out occasionally.

Tonight we're having dinner with another "throuple." I met Kassidy a while back when we were doing work at the high school her daughter attends. She and her two guys are open about their polyamorous relationship, and I was super curious, of course. She offered to get together to talk about it any time and I've taken her up on it.

She, Chris, and Dag sit opposite us at the table for six. We're sharing a couple of bottles of wine and laughing a lot. They're all great people—it sounds terrible, but they're all very normal. They're also totally cool about meeting a prince, for which I'm grateful. They tease each other and argue, but the love they share is obvious.

"When we told Chris's parents, they didn't have a good reaction," Kassidy says.

Chris snorts. "It was terrible. I didn't know how homophobic they were. Okay, yeah, maybe I did." He grimaces. "And on top of that, they didn't believe that I could love two people. I told them there isn't a finite amount of love. Love is endless. You *can* love two people at the same time."

This I already know.

"They gradually came around, especially after Trinity was born," Kassidy adds.

"Grandchildren will do that." I smile.

"One thing to remember is that although the three of you have a relationship, there are actually three other relationships," Kassidy says. "Between Chelsea and Ford, Chelsea and Griff, and Ford and Griff."

"That's true," I say slowly, glancing at the men on either side of me.

"And each of those relationships is just as important as the others. You need to work to make sure that *all* those relationships get a chance to grow."

"We went for some counselling," Dag says. "I don't know if the same counsellor is still around, but Kassidy can probably put you in touch with someone. Just to talk about things and how you'll deal with them."

"You all are amazing," I say.

"Our lives aren't perfect." Dag's lips quirk in a sexy bad-boy smile. "We fight and don't communicate properly and have differences of opinion about child rearing and finances and—"

"Home décor," Kassidy puts in with a mischievous smile.

"Yeah." Dag smiles at her. "So many scented candles."

"I love scented candles, too," I say with a grin.

"Finances." Ford rubs his face. "That was one of our first hurdles."

"We just bought a house," I tell Chris, Kassidy, and Dag. "In Lincoln Park."

"Oh, nice!" Kassidy's eyes light up. "Have you moved in?"

"Yes, a few weeks ago. We love it. It's a new build on a double lot, so we have a nice garden." Pleasure fills me at the thought of my shady retreat where I can learn to grow flowers. I catch Ford's eye; he knew that was important to me. "But Griff has a little more money than Ford or I do. And by a little, I mean a lot."

"A fuck of a lot," Ford mutters.

"It's *our* house," Griff says. "I wanted to do that for us."

"We insisted on having a legal agreement done up," I say. "And that caused a lot of tension."

"Understandable," Kassidy says.

"Then he treated us to a trip to Paris." Another warm slide of pleasure fills me. Luckily the good memories have replaced the memories of arguments over money on the trip.

"Oh, that's so nice." Kassidy smiles. "Communication is the key. But it is with every relationship, right?"

"Absolutely."

"There are still people who can't accept our relationship. It's sad, but we can't worry about them," Chris says. "And we've been through some rough times. But every time we've found our way back to each other."

"Because we love each other," Kassidy says. "And the alternative to not being together is just...unacceptable."

"Yeah." I nod, my heart warm, recognizing this. "That's how we felt, too. Even knowing how our lives could change and be different than we hoped or expected."

Not being together would be unacceptable.

EPILOGUE

Ford

"Chelsea, usually we're talking to you about things like democracy and voting rights and racial discrimination in voting. But tonight, we're talking about something more personal to you. Thanks for coming on to speak to this."

Griff and I are sitting in our new living room in our Lincoln Park home, watching Chelsea on television, being interviewed by Bethany Yang. It's not the first time we've watched Chelsea on TV, and it won't be the last, the way her career is taking off. But tonight's a little different.

"Thanks for having me, Bethany." Her smile glows.

"There's been a lot of gossip about you in recent months," Bethany says. "I'm sure you've seen or heard it."

"I try not to pay much attention to that," Chelsea replies, smiling. "I have more important things to worry about. But yes, I'm aware of it. Which is why I'm here."

"Let's go back in time a bit. You were the subject of a lot of scrutiny when you started dating Prince Griffin of Eria. Obviously, he has a reputation as a playboy, but he's reformed that image after serving in his country's military, fighting in Afghanistan, and then starting a non-profit organization to help veterans." They pause their conversation for a video clip they've put together about Griff.

He covers his eyes with his hand and shakes his head. "Jesus."

I grin. "Sure, they make it all about you, your highness. By the way, you look hot in that helicopter."

"Nonetheless," Bethany continues, "he's considered one of the world's most eligible bachelors. How did you two meet?"

"We met at a charity gala." Chelsea relates the true story of how she and Griff started dating.

"Then he left to return to Eria. That must have been devastating for you."

"It was difficult, yes. I'd come to care for him a great deal. But I'd always known that he had a duty to his country and that he would leave at some point."

"Then you started a relationship with another man, Ford Sullivan, who works as an Assistant U.S. Attorney in the Special Litigation Bureau."

"There you go." Griff nudges me with his shoulder.

"I don't get a whole video montage."

He laughs.

"And Ford is running for city alderman in next month's election," Bethany adds.

Griff gives me a thumbs up.

"That's right. I'm so proud of him. He'll be a great alderman. Ford and I have been friends for a long time. We're very close. We were friends first, and then our relationship became more than friendship."

"And he proposed marriage to you. You two are engaged."

"Yes." I watch Chelsea's chest lift as she pulls in a fortifying breath. "We won't be getting married now, but we are still in a relationship."

"So the engagement is off?"

"Well, we're not engaged to be married. But we're still committed to each other."

"And can you confirm the rumors that Prince Griffin is part of that relationship? He's now back in the United States and is no longer next in line to the throne after some legislative changes in Eria."

"Yes." She keeps her eyes and voice steady. "I can confirm that the three of us are in a relationship. I'm in love with two men, and lucky me, I don't have to choose between them."

I almost cringe, because we're heard some of the stupid, sleazy comments people have made about Chelsea having two men. But we know Bethany well enough to trust that she won't do that. She and Chelsea planned this interview and Bethany assured us she'd take it seriously.

"And what about them?" she asks kindly. "What is their relationship?"

"We all love each other," Chelsea says, with another smile. "And that's all I'm going to say about that. Some things about our relationship are private."

"Of course. Now, polamory isn't unheard of. It's a real thing."

"It *is* a real thing. It's basically a form of ethical non-monogamy that involves committed relationships between two or more people. It's different for everyone, but the most important thing is that everyone is in agreement with the boundaries of the relationship. It's totally possible to have a polyamorous relationship that's happy and fulfilling, depending on the people."

"There must be challenges," Bethany says.

"Of course. There are with all relationships. The hardest thing for us is a lack of acceptance by the community. We've been very lucky to have the support of our families, and our friends, and even our employers, but there's a stigma attached to non-monogamy. We're all careful to not internalize negative messages about our relationship and we hope that by being open and honest about our relationship, we can open people's minds."

After a little more innocuous chatting, they end the short segment and go to commercial break. |

Griff and I turn to each other.

"She did fantastic," he says.

"Amazing. I can't believe she took this on. She's the one going out there and addressing it. She's a fucking queen."

"She is. Our queen."

We say that a lot.

Griff and I aren't going to lie or hide our relationship, but Chelsea's right—some things are private. We can share some details in the hopes of stopping rumors and educating people and maybe helping to knock down barriers, but some parts of our lives are ours alone.

We're adjusting and learning and falling more and more in love. Together, we'll be strong enough to deal with whatever happens. We have faith in us. We have hope. We have love.

Thank you so much for reading Royally Indecent! Would you like a bonus scene?

Sign up for my newsletter for exclusive access to it!

Have you read Kassidy, Chris, and Dag's stories? They have their own epic ménage romance in **Rule of Three**.

If you follow the rules, you miss all the fun...

One-click Rule of Three now!

And read on for an excerpt!

AUTHOR NOTE

I haven't written a ménage à trois romance for years, even though I love to write them. I had this idea in my head and the characters came to life, but for a long time they took a back seat to hockey romance. I hope that readers who have loved my earlier ménage stories will find this one, and I hope I've lived up to my past successes. (That is terrifying, to be honest! Kassidy, Chris, and Dag are a tough act to follow!)

I have so many people to thank for helping me get this story finished (finally!) and out in the world. I started this story in May, 2019, so I was working on it for literally three years. In between other books, of course. I kept coming back to it, but truthfully, I was intimidated by this story. I wanted it to be worthy of these amazing characters and it scared me. Finally, Heather Roberts, my amazing publicist at Elle Woods PR, gave me a little boot in the butt, and I sat said butt down in the chair and finished 25,000 words in a week. Thank you, Heather!

Special thanks to Joy Rist and Michelle Fortune for reading the chapters set in Afghanistan because I have zero knowledge of the American military. Any mistakes are mine!

Also, thank you to Kat Mizera, for beta reading this book and giving me such great feedback. You really helped pull it all together!

Thank you to PG Forte as always, who listened to me babble about this story and titles and covers. You are such a good friend.

Thanks to editor Sasha Knight! We haven't worked together before, and your developmental suggestions were absolutely perfect. I am so grateful that you could fit me into your schedule!

Also thank you to Carolan Ivey, who I have forgotten to thank so many times! You are the Blurb Wizard for sure, thank you for nailing my blurbs every time!

To cover artist Dar Albert—you are so patient with my pickiness! I always love what you come up with, thank you for the beautiful cover on this book and many others.

Also as always, thank you to my assistant Stacey Price who patiently deals with all my random requests, mistakes, and things I forgot. You are amazing!

And always, always thanks to *you*. I love my readers. Thank you for buying my books, reading them, and sharing the love. I appreciate you so much!

EXCERPT: RULE OF THREE

After a while, Dag said, "Come dance with me, Kassidy." He set down his drink and rose to his feet. He held out a hand, and she looked at Chris, who smiled and nodded. She took Dag's hand and followed him back to the dance floor, feeling a little like she were being led down a dark downtown alley at midnight, nerves fluttering in her tummy and her pulse leaping.

They moved to the music, a throbbing Latin drumbeat. Dag was a good dancer—of course—nothing flamboyant, but he knew how to move his body with an athletic grace. She let herself absorb the music, let it move her body, never taking her eyes off his face. When the rhythm slowed and merged into a slower song, he slid his hands over her waist, hips, around almost onto her ass. His heat enveloped her, the scent of his sultry aftershave filled her head as she slid her arms over his shoulders. Their hips moved together to the beat of the music.

Sex.

It felt like sex. Liquid heat slid through her body and pooled between her legs.

She bit her lip and looked over to where Chris sat. He'd crossed one ankle over the other knee, one arm stretched out along the back of the couch, looking so big and handsome and watching them.

Watching you with anyone would be a turn-on.

He lifted his chin in acknowledgement of Kassidy's glance. She was almost afraid to tear her gaze away from him and return it to the dangerous man she was dancing with.

"Chris is watching," Dag said.

"Yes."

"He likes to watch."

Dag knew that about him?

Their gazes locked. His hands slid lower on her hips, to just below the curve of her ass and his fingers moved. Dear god, he was pulling up her skirt. And it was short enough to begin with. Her pussy pulsed.

The silky fabric slid higher, bunching a little beneath Dag's fingers. "What are you doing?" she asked him through tight lips.

"Giving your boyfriend a show," he said with a wicked glint in his eye.

"And everyone else in the bar."

But she didn't stop him.

"Nobody else is paying any attention to us. They're all watching those girls."

The female couple was now dancing even dirtier, grinding their bodies together. They were so beautiful and sexy it was hard to take her eyes off them.

"Hot," Dag said. They watched. The girls turned to face each other again, and then they kissed. A long, lingering kiss on the mouth, hands buried in each other's long hair.

Dag and Kassidy looked at each other. The air sizzled around them. They were both aroused and maybe that was why she let him continue to ease the skirt of her dress up, his hands on her hips sliding the fabric higher. She looked back at Chris, now with both feet on the floor, leaning forward with elbows on his knees, still watching them, his gaze scorching her with erotic intensity.

And maybe that's why she still didn't stop Dag. She was pretty sure the cheeks of her butt were showing now—she was wearing a pair of cheeky panties, but they didn't cover much.

Then Chris was striding toward them, joining them on the dance floor. He pressed against her back, his erection hard against her, and nuzzled her neck. The three of them danced together, hard bodies pressed against her front and back.

Chris pulled her hair aside to mutter in her ear. "That was so fucking sexy." She pressed her ass back against him, tightened her fingers on Dag's shoulders.

"Your girlfriend is hot, Chris," Dag said.

"I know."

The music picked up pace again and they continued dancing, still close, just changing the tempo. Heat sizzled up and down Kassidy's spine and she felt hypnotized by the beat of the music, the hot desire of two men, lost in the utter sensuality of it. She lifted one arm above her head and hooked it around Chris's neck, four hands on her body. Her breasts swelled and her nipples tingled. She ached to be touched there.

By the time they decided to leave the dance floor, every nerve ending in her body was on fire, sizzling and snapping with sexual tension.

The three of them sat on the couch side by side again, damp with perspiration and a little breathless. Some of their friends had already left, others had disappeared, perhaps into the crowd on the dance floor, and they were alone. Chris set his hand on her bare thigh and picked up his drink with his other hand.

"I should get going." Dag set down his empty glass. "I'll come by for my car tomorrow."

"Why don't you just stay at our place again?" Chris said. "Saves you a trip tomorrow."

Kassidy's blood surged in her veins, hot and scary, as she waited for Dag's response. A response that seemed…significant. Weighty. A response that took forever.

"Okay," Dag finally said.

Her chest tightened.

"I'm ready to go too," Chris added. "Kassidy?"

"Sure." She licked her lips.

A couple of yellow cabs waited on Oak Street when they emerged from the alley where the club was and Dag lifted a hand. One pulled up and all three of them climbed into the back. The night air had cooled her heated skin, but now inside the taxi the air was heavy, pulsing with thick arousal. There was enough sexual energy in that vehicle to power the small hybrid car for many miles. Her heart pounded all the way home, and she stared at her bare knees, once again in the middle of the two men. It was only a short ride back to their place, and when she unlocked the door and let them into the condo, her heart sped up even more. She could hardly breathe, the sense of anticipation tightening her lungs.

They walked into the condo, Chris leading the way and flicking on a lamp. He turned and the three of them stood there, snared in a net of erotic tension.

Chris held out a hand to Kassidy and she drifted across the living room to take it without a word. He slid his hand into her hair, cupped the back of her head and kissed her. She melted into him, already a semi-liquid puddle of arousal.

"Watching you dance with Dag was fucking hot," he whispered against the corner of her mouth.

Questions backed up in her brain but none of them came out of her mouth. Then Chris did the same thing Dag had done, started sliding up the skirt of her dress, baring the back of her thighs to Dag.

This was a dangerous game they were playing. She was so turned on, so fevered with hunger, it made her afraid of what she might do.

They were just fooling around, making each other—all three of them—hot and bothered. How far would they go?

"What panties are you wearing?" Chris murmured.

Her throat was so tight she could barely speak.

"Show us," he urged.

She couldn't move, her body locked into place, her heart racing.

"She's not going to show us her panties," Dag said. "Kassidy's a good girl. Isn't that what your sister said?"

His words mocked her, the words her sister had used, her sister who always made fun of her and made her feel like a straight-laced prude, even though she wasn't. She was different from Hailey, sure, but it wasn't like she was totally naïve.

She didn't want to be a good girl. And she wanted Dag to know that. The sexual tension that had been building inside her for the last week, so much that fast, hard sex with Chris in the shower and even up against the bedroom door had still not quite satisfied her, was leading her into doing naughty things. A heavy ache pulsed in her pelvis.

She took a step back, lifting up her dress. She glanced at Dag, who stood there watching them with scorching intensity, his mouth a tight line of self-control.

"Nice," Chris said. "Don't you think, Dag?"

"Very nice."

Her panties were a band of pink lace around her hips. She bit her bottom lip, knowing how wet they were. Dag smiled at her. Her fingers trembled, clutching the fabric of her dress.

"You haven't told her, have you?" Dag looked at Chris.

Chris's eyes met Dag's.

Kassidy's gaze darted back and forth between them. "Told me what?"

"No," Chris said.

"Are you afraid Kassidy will be shocked?" Dag continued. "Because she *is* a good girl."

"Told me what?"

Chris's eyes narrowed and his body tensed next to her. Dag's eyes gleamed and his wicked smile made her body pulse again.

"Told you..." Dag's gaze moved over her face. "About the three-somes we used to have."

Her mouth did drop open a little. Okay, she wasn't naïve, but the idea that Chris and Dag had done that...gave her a jolt. She turned to Chris.

He gave her a sheepish little smile. "It was a long time ago."

Wow.

She wasn't jealous. She knew Chris had had girlfriends before her. She even knew some of them. They were all done and gone before she came along.

"Does that disgust you, Kassidy?" Dag asked.

"No." She had to close her eyes against the wave of heated arousal that shimmered through her body, a sharp, forbidden thrill.

"Or does it turn you on?"

How could she admit that to Dag...to Chris!

She met Chris's gaze. "It turns me on."

"Oh sweetie." Chris's voice was a groan.

They were just talking about it. It wasn't like they were going to do it.

"Who did you do it with?" The words slid out of her mouth.

They exchanged a glance then Chris said, "It doesn't matter who, sweetheart. Like I said, it was a long time ago. Before you."

Curiosity scorched her. She wanted to know what happened—who did what to whom. The idea of two men making love to her at the same time seemed incredibly hot. Her skin tingled and tightened with electric pulses of heat and longing.

Their eyes met once again, exchanging some kind of wordless communication. She wanted to know what they were thinking. What if they wanted to do it? What if they wanted to share her, like they apparently had shared girls before?

A moan leaked out of her. Her breasts swelled and ached, her nipples tingled and her pussy clenched hard at the idea of being with two men.

Chris was such a conservative guy, she could hardly believe what they were telling her. His earlier revelation that he wanted to watch her with someone else had been a prelude to this shocker. But then he looked into her eyes and sparkles shot through her body at the question she saw on his face.

It wasn't because of her sister. She had nothing to prove to Hailey. Kassidy was her own person and comfortable with how she lived her life. But at that moment, she wanted to be the bad girl. She wanted excitement. She wanted that adrenaline rush that Dag got from taking risks, making dangerous business deals, jumping out of airplanes. And she wanted Dag.

She licked her lips and turned her attention to Dag. He watched her with hot, predatory eyes, his beautifully shaped mouth smiling slightly, and she knew he wanted her too. She'd known it all along.

She would never cheat on Chris. Never. She'd never been tempted, not even once. If he wanted this, it wouldn't be cheating. But it was the baddest thing she'd ever contemplated doing in her entire, careful life.

Once again she met her boyfriend's eyes. "Do you want to?" he finally asked out loud.

She couldn't do it. She wanted to. How could she do something like that? Arousal swelled and burned inside her, and she countered, "Do *you* want to?"

Other Books by Kelly Jamieson

Heller Brothers Hockey

Breakaway

Faceoff

One Man Advantage

Hat Trick

Offside

Power Series

Power Struggle

Taming Tara

Power Shift

Rule of Three Series

Rule of Three

Rhythm of Three

Reward of Three

San Amaro Singles

With Strings Attached

How to Love

Slammed

Windy City Kink

Sweet Obsession

All Messed Up

Playing Dirty

Brew Crew

Limited Time Offer

No Obligation Required

Aces Hockey

Major Misconduct

Off Limits

Icing

Top Shelf

Back Check

Slap Shot

Playing Hurt

Big Stick

Game On

Last Shot

Body Shot

Hot Shot

Long Shot

Bayard Hockey

Shut Out

Cross Check

Wynn Hockey

Play to Win

In It To Win It

Win Big

For the Win

Game Changer

Bears Hockey

Must Love Dogs...and Hockey

You Had Me at Hockey

Talk Hockey to Me

Bears Hockey II

The O Zone

Good Hands

Scoring Big

Stand Alone

Three of Hearts

Loving Maddie from A to Z

Dancing in the Rain

Love Me

Love Me More

Friends with Benefits

2 Hot 2 Handle

Lost and Found

One Wicked Night

Sweet Deal

Hot Ride

Crazy Ever After

All I Want for Christmas

Sexpresso Night

Irish Sex Fairy

Conference Call

Rigger

You Really Got Me

How Sweet It Is

Screwed

Firecracker

Royally Indecent

About the Author

Kelly Jamieson is a best-selling author of over forty romance novels and novellas. Her writing has been described as "emotionally complex", "sweet and satisfying" and "blisteringly sexy." She likes coffee (black), wine (mostly white), shoes (high heels) and hockey!

Subscribe to her newsletter for updates about her new books and what's coming up.

Find out what's new...
www.kellyjamieson.com

Contact Kelly
info@kellyjamieson.com